THE VISION

The vision formed. Bavmorda approached the crucible. It had filled with milky fluid, and in it shone the face of Fin Raziel as she had been those many years ago, still beautiful, still radiant. Out of the bowl came the ghostly echo of Fin Raziel's voice: "You may defeat me but you will not defeat the child, Bavmorda. The mystery of the child is larger than you, and in that mystery your reign will end. Here is the sign, Bavmorda ... "

Fin Raziel's face faded, and the milky fluid formed into a shimmering circle that Bavmorda knew too well.

Eyes blazing, the queen leaned close to that hateful mark.

Lightning and fireballs crackled off Bavmorda's fingers and slammed into the bowl, ricocheting in all directions. The opaque fluid swirled into foul steam. When the bowl had been seared clean, the mistress of Nockmaar raised her arms and uttered a sound even more terrible than her laughter — a long wail of hollow triumph. She knew, and all who heard her knew, that no matter how often she might blast that vision it could always be conjured again, for its essence lay beyond her power.

By Wayland Drew
Published by Ballantine Books:

THE ERTHRING CYCLE
   The Memoirs of Alcheringia
   The Gaian Expedient
   The Master of Norriya

DRAGONSLAYER

WILLOW

WILLOW

A novel by
Wayland Drew

Based on a screenplay by
Bob Dolman

From a story by
George Lucas

A Del Rey Book

BALLANTINE BOOKS • NEW YORK

Library of Congress Catalog Card Number: 87-91656

ISBN 0-345-35195-9

Manufactured in the United States of America

First Ballantine Books Edition: February 1988

Forget all you know or think you know;
Abandon power and enforced decree.
Inward, where the deepest rivers flow,
Find the currents of eternity. . . .

The Book of Fin Raziel

CONTENTS

NOCKMAAR

How beautiful were the Death Dogs! How powerful their shoulders and how elegant the curves of their hairless tails! How gracefully they moved beside their handlers through the drifting mists and smoke of Nockmaar.

From the high balcony of the conjuring room, each man and dog looked to the queen like a single creature, *her* creature—the man in his leather armor, black as the beast's skin; the dog tensed for command, its shoulder touching the man's thigh. Bavmorda smiled down upon them. She drew her cloak tight against the chill of morning. She waited.

They were practicing the kill. A few prisoners had been brought up from the dungeons and they huddled together behind a buttress where the dogs could

1

not see them. Across the courtyard, a sally port swung open and a footbridge dropped over the moat. Through that gate, the prisoners could see the slate hills of Nockmaar Valley; they could imagine the freedom beyond.

The captain of the guard looked up and saluted. Bavmorda nodded. Each prisoner was told to run. One by one, with whatever energy and hope remained, they dashed for that gate, for those hills. One by one, the Death Dogs slipped their leashes, streaked through the courtyard, and leaped at the prisoners' throats.

No one reached the gate.

Bavmorda smiled. When the spectacle was over she swept away, striding around the balcony on the morning inspection of her domain. All the mountains to the west were hers, far beyond the valley of Tir Asleen. To the north, the billowing volcano of Nockmaar lay under her command. To the east, she controlled even the sun itself, for had she not moments ago uttered an invocation in the conjuring room, and was not the sun rising obediently? Only the south lay beyond her control.

Only the south.

Bavmorda scowled, thrusting her arms into her sleeves. There it lay, that soft land, stretching a hundred leagues under its mocking coverlet of mist. And there at that moment came a bitter reminder of what Bavmorda feared most. A score of carts, guarded by Death Dogs and mounted troops, wound out of the southern hills and approached the walls of Nockmaar. The monthly Gathering was coming in.

Bavmorda nodded in sour satisfaction. Kael was punctual, as always. On the first night of the waning moon the Gathering began. Kael's troops and Kael's Death Dogs fanned out from Nockmaar Castle to seize all women pregnant beyond the sixth month. From all the southern fiefdoms they brought them— from the seafolk to the east; from the fen people where the vast marshes drained through labyrinthine creeks into the tributaries of the River Troon. From the mountains south of Tir Asleen they brought them, and from the farmlands of Galladoorn, and sometimes even from the wild reaches across the River Freen. Occasionally Kael's troops brought even little Nelwyn women to the birthing rooms to vent their small groans and bear their small offspring. Not often, however; Nelwyn women usually perished on the journey.

"Baugh!" Bavmorda flung her arm in sudden disgust at the little column. Five bolts of lightning stabbed low above the wagons, leaving five smoking craters in the slate hills. Terrified horses bolted, spilling the pathetic human contents of the carts. Death Dogs snarled and circled. Women screamed. Troopers cursed and lashed out to cover their sudden fear.

Bavmorda whirled away, pulling her gown close around her. How sick and tired she was of birth, birth, birth! Death was so much cleaner, so much

more predictable, *controllable*! How she hated these
heavy women with their dumb animal *love*—love of
husbands, of infants, of life itself! They were like a
sea, an endless breathing body rising from the south
and threatening to engulf her. And somewhere,
somewhere in that body was the seed of the child
whose birth caused a needle of dread to pierce Bavmorda's heart.

How she hated that child!

Gown sweeping, she stalked back into her conjuring chamber. She glanced at the night herons,
hunched ready to do her bidding. She glowered at the
trolls and serving minions, who bowed away and busied themselves with pointless tasks. She scowled at
the three druid priests, who tugged their gray beards,
and bobbed their gray heads, and rubbed their
gnarled hands, murmuring placations. She stared in
all directions through the slits of the tower, out over
the bleak crags of Nockmaar.

"Why?" she demanded, flinging out her hands.
Ten fireballs slammed against the walls. The druids
ducked. One bolt streaked through a window slit
straight at the full moon in the west, as if to strike it
from the sky. One grazed the leg of a cowering
server, and the others hastily dragged him down the
stairs, so the queen would not be troubled by his
shrieks. Cleaner-trolls scrubbed up behind them,
grunting. Two other bolts spawned mutant horrors—
an albino toad, eyeless and legless, wriggling through
shredding skin; a sac of eyes rolling in milky fluid.

"Why?" Bavmorda turned on the three pale druids in their priestly robes.

They knew well what she was asking. She was asking why she, Bavmorda, Sovereign of Nockmaar, Sorceress Magnific, Primal Priestess of Cults and Covens, should be subject to such a niggling, uncertain, human thing as fear. In particular, why should she be humiliated by the *fear of a child?*

The priests knew many answers. They could have reminded the queen that she was mortal and therefore the victim of uncertainties. They could have said that not even Bavmorda's sorcery was more powerful than the laughter of a child. Or they could have observed that her will had long ago been bent by cruelty and greed into an evil thing.

All of these were true.

But they could not speak the truth or any part of it. To have done so when Bavmorda was bristling with rage would have condemned them as they had seen other truth-tellers condemned. Truth-tellers got torn apart on the spot, even while they were speaking. Death Dogs ate their livers. Muttering trolls mopped up their remains.

These priests were not truth-tellers; they were survivors. The first spread soothing arms and smiled. "Your Majesty, it is only because the world is jealous of your power. Soon our rites will wipe away that jealousy, and Your Majesty shall have peace thereafter."

The second nodded agreement. "With respect,

Your Majesty, no great work was ever quickly accomplished."

"Quite so, Your Majesty." The third bowed deeply. "Also, so long as some wildness remains, there," he gestured to the south, "beyond Your Majesty's enlightened reign, some minor, temporary irregularities are inevitable. Soon, General Kael will certainly give you control of Galladoorn and all that land." He straightened up, radiating confidence from his outstretched arms.

Bavmorda gazed balefully at the three of them. The moment of greatest danger had passed. They would not be ripped apart by fireballs. They would not be shredded by bodiless teeth. Their bones would not be mashed by invisible jaws. They had survived again. For now.

"Also," the third priest said unctuously, "we share the certainty that Your Majesty has the mother even now within her power, and that her labor will deliver this child into Your Majesty's hands."

Bavmorda laughed. "Yes! I feel it *here*!" She clutched her belly. Her laughter was a terrible thing, like a frenzied bird. Loosed, it filled the chamber, shrieking and tearing at the walls. The night herons hunkered on their perches and gazed at the flagstones, longing to be far away, where ghostly fishes moved through the cool fens of the Troon.

Pale as ash, the three druids showed their teeth. "We are certain, Your Majesty. Our tests confirm that the woman in the birthing room. . . ."

"Again the vision! Conjure it!"

They bobbed obediently. Counterclockwise around a great stone crucible in the room's center they began a shuffling dance, kicking aside bones and fleshy refuse. Bavmorda watched with her cloak folded tightly about her, like a cocoon. In unison they uttered their Chant for the Unfolding, adding those codicils for the vision the queen required. Their voices quavered. All other conjurings predicted Bavmorda triumphant, omnipotent, immortal. Only this, which they had chanced upon by accident, through a flawed chant, foresaw her doom. In it Fin Raziel appeared—Fin Raziel, Bavmorda's old enemy, who had thwarted so many of the queen's early schemes. She appeared as if alive in this vision, as if Bavmorda had not long since vanquished her.

The vision formed. The druids fell back. Bavmorda approached the crucible. It had filled with milky fluid, and in it shone the face of Fin Raziel as she had been those many years ago, still beautiful, still radiant. Out of the bowl came the ghostly echo of Fin Raziel's voice: "You may defeat me but you will not defeat the child, Bavmorda. The mystery of the child is larger than you, and in that mystery your reign will end. Here is the sign, Bavmorda. . . ."

Fin Raziel's face faded, and the milky fluid formed into a shimmering circle that Bavmorda knew too well.

Eyes blazing, the queen leaned close to that hateful mark. Her cloak parted. Her bony arms emerged.

Priests, night herons, and trolls all scrambled for cover. They fled onto the balcony, down the spiral stairs, behind the pillars of the chamber. Lightning and fireballs crackled off Bavmorda's fingers and slammed into the bowl, ricocheting in all directions. The opaque fluid swirled into foul steam. When the bowl had been seared clean, the mistress of Nockmaar raised her arms and uttered a sound even more terrible than her laughter—a long wail of hollow triumph. She knew, and all who heard her knew, that no matter how often she might blast that vision it could always be conjured again, for its essence lay beyond her power.

A wet snuffling came from the top of the stairs. "Your Majesty . . ."

Bavmorda whirled, pointing long nails. "You dare intrude!"

"Mercy, Your Majesty! Don't burn! Don't kill! The Princess Sorsha commands me!" A dungeon-troll groveled there, half on the floor, half on the top steps. Rank hair covered his scalp to the eyebrows. He was noseless. He slobbered through swollen orange lips. Long toes and fingers slapped wetly on the flagstones. His eyes flickered, shifted malignantly. He bore with him the stench of the dungeons and of death.

"Speak!"

"Sorsha, Your Majesty." He pointed down the steps. "She bids you come."

"Out of the way!" Her lips curled in disgust, the

hem of her gown raised high, Bavmorda swept past him and descended.

Behind her, two tower-trolls seized the interloper by the ankles and dragged him downstairs. Two others wiped up the puddle of slime he had deposited.

The priests held a whispered conference.

"If it *is* the child," the first said, his eyes sharp with fear, "you know what powers protect it!"

"We should flee," the second hissed. "We should escape!"

"Fools!" the third said. "Where will you hide? Do as you've been told! Begin the Ritual!"

Moments earlier, a child had been born in one of Nockmaar's birthing rooms. These were grim dungeons—dark, cold, and wet. Dim light filtered through shafts from the courtyard far above, and with it the sounds of raucous soldiery and Death Dogs at their work. A few small candles guttered in wall sconces. Two trolls squatted in a corner, pulling at shredding skin.

Nothing announced the birth of this child. She had no time to be named, no time to be properly bathed and swaddled. No physicians attended the mother, only an exhausted midwife.

"Ethna!" the mother whispered, gripping the midwife's wrist. "You mustn't let her die."

The woman smiled wanly, fearfully. She glanced at

the trolls. "Go," she said, and one of them scampered out.

The mother's grip tightened. "You know, don't you, Ethna? *You know!*"

Ethna looked away from that desperate gaze, clouded with the pain of giving birth. She attended to her work. She nodded.

The troll she had dispatched hurried on his errand down a corridor, past cages filled with pregnant women. He climbed a spiraling flight of stairs, scampered down another drier corridor, and then up a second staircase to the western tower, and the door of the princess's chamber. He slapped with slack fingers. "Sorsha, Your Highness, pardon. A birth . . ."

Inside the room, a young woman awoke and was on her feet in an instant, her dagger in her hand. She shook her head when she saw where she was, and drew a deep breath. "Very well," she called through the door. "Go back. I'll be down at once." She pulled on a woolen tunic and trousers, found her boots, and belted her dagger around her waist. A moment later she was following the troll downstairs, wishing she were elsewhere.

Sorsha had been dreaming of a boar hunt.

It was a happy dream. In it she rode Rak, a stallion so black he glistened. They skirted the edge of a woods along the bank of a broad river. The boar charged from a thicket without warning, giving Sorsha no time to draw an arrow. Dust spurted from his hooves. Red eyes fixed her. Gleaming tusks hurtled at Rak's belly. They had no room to maneuver. Rak leaped clean over the beast, galloped a few lengths down the riverbank, then wheeled and charged, ears flat and teeth bared in fury. The boar was slower in turning, and they were on him while his shoulder was still exposed. Sorsha's lance went clean through him, pinning him to the ground. He squealed, thrashing helplessly while his life gushed away. His stout legs pumped to the last. His eyes blazed hatred until their light went out.

That was the kind of hunt Sorsha loved, the kind of dream she loved. . . .

And then something struck her door, and the death shrieks of the boar became the craven whining of the troll: "Your Highness, a birth . . ."

Sorsha loathed this duty to which her mother had assigned her, this routine watching of hapless women giving birth. She hated the inspection of the newborn, searching for the Sign. She had grown numb to birth, silently vowing never to become a mother.

She preferred the hunt and the battle. She preferred storming some far-off stronghold with a band of Kael's raiders. She preferred the windswept company of soldiers to these lurking trolls, these harassed midwives, these imprisoned mothers who sullenly turned their faces from the sight of her. She longed to be in the field, away from Nockmaar. Out there, under the tutelage of guardians handpicked by Bavmorda and General Kael, she had spent the last five

years, flourishing happily, challanging all, learning
well the arts of defense, the tactics of assault. She
had grown strong, and quick, and wily.

She was eighteen now, handsome with the aloof
and watchful confidence of women who live out-of-
doors. Her arms and face, and the V at her throat
where the tunic opened, were slightly tanned. She
did not freckle in the sun, despite her pale skin and
her inheritance of her father's red hair.

That hair had been the curse of her childhood. For
as long as she could remember her mother had cast
spells to turn it black, blonde, brown, anything but
red. Bavmorda hated it. She hated all memories of
her husband. Sorsha's hair maddened her, especially
since none of her spells to change its shade worked
permanently. Always it had grown back—red.

When Sorsha had returned from the field three
months before, and Bavmorda had seen her abundant red tresses, the queen's fingers twitched toward
it. A spell began to form on her lips. But Sorsha was
no longer a child. "No!" she had said simply. "It is
not my father's hair. It is mine. Please leave it alone."

Sorsha supposed she hated her father, but she
wasn't sure. When she thought of him he was just . . .
distant. He was just another man, no better and no
worse than the rest.

All men were distant for Sorsha.

She strode down the last staircase and into the
dungeon corridor, looking neither right nor left at the
pathetic women in their cages. Some groveled,

stretching their arms through the bars and pleading for water, for food, for any attention. Others had taken themselves out of the dungeons, out of their bodies. These sat rocking on their straw pallets, smiling, whispering, singing softly. Still others stood defiantly, glaring their hatred.

Sorsha ignored them all. She entered the birthing room, knowing exactly what she would see. The walls glistened with seepage. Trolls crouched in the shadows. The exhausted mother lay on her filthy straw pallet, staring terrified at her.

Ethna cradled a small bundle, and her gaze, too, was full of dread.

"Well?"

The widwife swallowed hard. Mouth grim, she folded back the blanket to reveal the child.

Sorsha stopped.

The child had red hair, she was looking directly at Sorsha with steady eyes, and she was laughing.

To some of the women who heard it, that laughter sounded like the tinkling of crystal once made by the elfin glasssmiths far south of Nelwyn Valley, but to most it was the sound of water—water free in a green world.

It turned all sounds to silence in that grim place. Murmuring women hushed. Even the trolls stopped their guttural chatter and turned large ears toward the sound, astonished.

Sorsha stepped forward then. Her hand closed over Ethna's wrist, and her dispassionate eyes held the midwife's, for Ethna had recovered the child too quickly. "Wait! The inspection."

Ethna's chin rose defiantly. "Your Highness, this child . . ."

"The inspection," Sorsha said again.

She unfolded the blanket.

Naked before them lay the laughing child, perfect in every way except that on the soft flesh inside the left elbow she bore a faint brown mark—the Sign.

Sorsha knew it well. When she had been assigned this task, Bavmorda had scratched the Sign on the wall of the banquet hall. "That!" she had cried. "*That* is what you look for!" And then she had obliterated it with white-hot jets of flame, leaving the wall scoured clean. And Sorsha had seen it often since. Sometimes Bavmorda would sear it into the oaken hearts of trees before she had them hacked to kindling. Sometimes she would carve it into the backs of screaming prisoners before they were loosed for the sport of Death Dogs.

Now, when she saw it on the arm of this laughing infant, Sorsha felt only relief, nothing more—relief that her onerous duty had ended. Relief that she could go back to the field. "I must get Mother," she said. Then, remembering that it was dawn and that her mother would be chanting an invocation to the sun, high in the conjuring room where only priests were permitted, she pointed to the nearest troll squatting beside the door. "You. Come with me.

Ethna, prepare the child. You know what must be done!"

As soon a Sorsha had gone, the mother struggled up. *"Ethna!"* She grasped the midwife's shirt. She was trembling and weak, but her grip held like a vice. "Ethna," she whispered hoarsely, "you must save her! You know you must!"

Tears brimmed in Ethna's eyes. She bit her lip and shook her head, glancing at two trolls, who were creeping close now, muttering.

"You must!" The woman clasped her with both hands. "Listen to me! The child is larger than we are, Ethna, larger than anything! Don't think! Feel! Do what you feel! Save her!"

"Here!" One of the trolls said, kicking Ethna's leg. "Get away from her!"

"Back!" said the other, elbowing her in the stomach. "Back! Back!"

Ethna swallowed. She brushed away the tears. She took a deep breath, then moved. Clutching the child close, she kicked hard into the face of first one troll then the other. They fell back shrieking, and Ethna dashed past them, through the door and down the corridor, past the arms of women reaching to touch her as she ran, and to touch the child.

Seconds later, Bavmorda arrived with Sorsha close behind. When she heard the howls of the trolls she knew what had happened. "Guards! Where are you!"

She swept into the birthing room and bore down on the mother, snatching away the pathetic bundle of rags the woman had hastily gathered. *"Where is that child?"*

The mother smiled. She lay back and closed her eyes.

"Kill her!" Bavmorda snarled, and vengeful trolls leaped to do her bidding.

"Find that baby, Sorsha! Use dogs! Bring her to me alive, do you hear me? *Alive!"*

The queen swooped back through the door just as the commander of the dungeon guards hurried up with two men. He was trembling. His face was ashen under the black helmet.

"You! How could you let this happen?"

"Your Majesty, I . . ."

"Listen!" The sound Bavmorda heard lifted her beyond rage into blind fury.

Laughter.

Throughout the dungeon, in all their loathsome cells, women were laughing. Laughing at her.

"Kill the lot!" Bavmorda flung out her hand.

White flames seared the corridor.

Ethna did what the mother had told her. She did not think, she felt. And her instincts served her well.

She went to earth like a threatened animal, into the network of tunnels beneath Nockmaar. Over the years she had discovered their secret entrances and used them when she could. She preferred that dark labyrinth to the horrors of the castle. She was safe there from the drunken advances of the guards, from the horrid gropings of the trolls. She could escape in those tunnels from the cold efficiency of Princess Sorsha. She could think there, and remember, and dream. Sometimes, safe and alone in the deep silence, she slept. But the greatest comfort her secret gave her was the knowledge that someday she might escape through that tangle of passageways. She might flee. Someday, when she had summoned her courage, she might take her chances with the Death Dogs and the troopers and, perhaps, reach Galladoorn again. Now she followed her first impulse, pausing only long enough to snatch up a little sugar and a gourd of milk for the child. Deep in those passages she waited, shivering, holding the child close, listening to the rumble of alarm drums far above.

Go to water: that was her second impulse. She knew better than to attempt that immediately. The hills of Nockmaar were high and barren, and the nearest south-flowing stream was Eastern Brook, two leagues distant. In that terrain among the crags, the dogs would have her in no time. For a day and a night she waited, until the hue and cry died down.

At midnight on the second day, she crept out of a brush-covered opening among the crags. Behind her, Nockmaar volcano smoked and growled on one side and the castle loomed on the other. Ahead lay the headwaters of Eastern Brook, flowing away south into the great fens of Galladoorn.

It was an ideal night. Clouds hid the waning moon, and a restless wind covered the sounds of her passage. Furthermore, she would have the perfect companion. She had taken only a few soft steps before a white goat waiting among the outcrops lifted its head. The animal stared placidly and rose at Ethna's approach. The goat's udder was full, so Ethna was able to feed the child well, diluting the rich milk with water trickling from the rocks. When she had finished she climbed with her precious burden onto the goat's back, and the sturdy little animal set off east away from Nockmaar, taking the highest path.

Ethna's plan was to follow Eastern Brook all the way down to Galladoorn. Then she would swing west and cross the River Troon under cover of darkness. After that, she would work her way northwest again until she reached the safety of the fabled kingdom of Tir Asleen. It would mean a journey of many months.

She had guessed that Bavmorda and General Kael would send troops and dogs fanning to the west, assuming she had fled that way in panic, and she was right. No one anticipated her cunning. The land between Nockmaar and Eastern Brook was only lightly patrolled. Just twice that night the goat paused, and Ethna heard the distant howling of Death Dogs and the clatter of hooves in the valleys below. Each time she muffled the laughter of the child against her bosom until the dread sounds faded.

At dawn they reached the brook and bade farewell to the goat, who pushed up its muzzle for the child to touch. Ethna waded into the cold water and turned south. For many nights she persevered, taking shelter by day, accepting the succor of shy animals who came to the need of the child, and in time the brook deepened into the river and the river broadened into the fens. Bog people found her drifting half-dead, clinging to a floating log. They took her into their huts, and warmed her, and nursed her back to strength.

Even here in the depths of the marshes, where fogs hung like drapes and the swamp gasses sometimes gleamed like spectral lanterns, the oarlocks of Kael's boats creaked in the darkness. Death Dogs clambered into stilted huts. Women shrieked. Men cursed and died, throats gone.

Cautiously, always by night, the bog people moved Ethna and the child south into the safety of their small fortress. Thence, cavalry escorted her west across the River Troon and a few leagues beyond. Alone in the wild, their food exhausted, Ethna and the child once more relied on the kindness of animals, who succored them and guided them along secret paths. At last, when they reached the headwaters of the River Freen, Ethna rejoiced for she knew that only a few leagues beyond, high in its lush mountains, stood their destination—the sanctuary of Galladoorn.

But here the brave midwife's good luck ran out. Here roaming Death Dogs chanced upon her scent and bore down upon her fast, long frustrated and eager for blood.

She had only a little warning, only time enough to bind together a makeshift boat of driftwood, using vines and strips of her clothing. She had time enough to spread a little cradle of soft reeds inside, and to wrap the child in her shawl and lay her in. She had time enough to kiss her, and just time enough to launch the frail little craft into the waiting arms of the current.

Then the first dogs were on her.

Bavmorda swept into the conjuring room at Nockmaar that dawn to find her three priests ecstatic. Robes high, they were prancing skinny-legged around the vision-bowl. Caught up in their mirth, even the tower-trolls were chortling and swatting themselves.

"Oh, Your Majesty," the chief priest greeted her, "what a vision we have for you! What a *vision!*"

"Look!" said the second, stepping back.

"Behold!" said the third.

Staring suspiciously, pulling her cloak tight, Bavmorda drew close.

Milky fluid cleared in the crucible. Bavmorda saw a thinly wooded riverbank. A knot of Death Dogs ripped and tore at a corpse, while several more raced to join them. A squad of Kael's cavalrymen followed, with a few wiry dog-trainers loping beside them, clinging to their stirrups. When they reached the corpse, one of these trainers ordered the dogs back, and with a few lance jabs at the torn throat, severed the head from the body. He lifted it by the hair, high enough for the troopers to recognize Ethna. The troopers uttered a ragged cheer, fists raised. The man dropped the head back onto the bloody corpse, and the dogs swarmed in.

Bavmorda grunted in brief satisfaction. "And the child?"

"The child," said the first priest, clearing his throat. "Yes. The child."

"The child." The second priest turned to the third. "Did *you* notice what happened to the child?"

The third priest sighed. "The fact is, Your Majesty, we don't know. But now that they've found the midwife . . ."

"Fools!" Bavmorda murmured. But she did not fly into a rage. She kept gazing into the bowl, beguiled by what she saw.

Even feeding, how magnificent were the Death Dogs!

UFGOOD REACH

From the mountains of the two High Kingdoms, the River Freen flowed southward a hundred leagues to the sea. At first its course was swift, plunging down the steep descents of the foothills, but then it slowed as it approached the Lake of Fin Raziel and eddied there, coursing through the deep caverns at the lake's south end until it surged out in a spectacular cascade, as if from the spout of a great pitcher, dropping twenty fathoms to the pool below. Then it crossed the Middle Plains in slow meanders and wound through the Hills of Cherlindrea, ever south, and broadened down the whole length of Nelwyn Valley, and then narrowed once more and hurried on for three-score leagues until it touched the sea with five salty fingers, thirty leagues south of the Troon.

Once, the people of those lands called the rivers
the Two Sisters, for legends said that before Bavmorda tightened her grip on the High Kingdoms,
they had been alike as twins. The Troon had flowed
as pure and fresh as the Freen, the legends said, and
salmon had once swum up it to spawn, as far as the
ford of the Western Road. Herons had once poised
along its marshes, and great bears had taught their
cubs to scoop fish from its falls. So clear had the
Troon been in its still pools, the legends said, that
elves journeyed to them to read prophecies in the
magic sand-tracery of clams, five fathoms down, and
to preserve those patterns forever in their crystal
chalices. Once, the legends said, like its sister, the
Troon had been a river of life.

No longer. Now, thickened by death, it flowed
brown and sluggish. Banks once verdant were mud-
caked and slimy, strewn with deadfalls and unearthly
offal. Every day, the Troon bore its burden of bloated
corpses to the sea. Every night, trolls crept from their
lairs to the shores of that river, lured by the stench of
carrion. Some eagerly followed it north, seeking the
very evil at its source. The Troon had turned loathsome down its length, a running sore on the land, an
infection in the sea.

But the Freen was still pure. In its high tributaries,
where the child began her journey, the waters of the
Freen sang in their fords and rapids; they swirled like
stately dancers in their pools.

Swiftly from the place of Ethna's death, the currents of the Freen bore away the strange little boat. So exultant were Kael's troops over the slaying of the midwife that they failed to realize until too late what she had done. By then, the little craft was far to the south, bobbing through the rapids of the first canyons. Eagles swooped down, stretching their talons to snatch the child from danger, but their help was not required. The boat rode high, and the child laughed in the spray. Later, however, other creatures did assist. When the boat snagged in a quiet backwater, a brown bear shouldered through the undergrowth to nudge it free, and an otter dislodged it from a sandbar at the north end of the Lake of Fin Raziel.

The child began her voyage down that lake at night, helped by a northern breeze. She kept silent. Something immense moved around her in those waters, searching back and forth, swelling up the surface over a round back, whipping up whirlpools with an enormous tail. Safely through this turbulence went the little boat, and safely past the island in the center of the lake, where the child turned her head in the darkness to hear sorrowing melodies and the chants of invisible choirs. Safely on—down the length of the lake and over the falls, where the little craft was taken into hundreds of tiny hands and borne down through the spray on a cloud of shimmering wings to the quiet pools below. She laughed as she drifted down, and small voices—very, very small voices— joined her in that laughter.

At dawn, she moved into the quiet meanders of the Middle Plains. All that day fish swam out from overhanging banks to hasten the little craft downstream. Their dorsal fins surrounding it like protecting sails, they brought it to the ford where the Freen crossed the Western Road. The child made this last passage at dusk, escaping by only seconds a troop of cavalry picking their way across the stones. The child heard the clatter of hooves. She heard coarse laughter. She heard the clink of harness and arms. Then she was past; the water deepened and the currents bore her on.

Before midnight she came to the conical Nelwyn Hills, and through the rest of that calm night the boat passed down Nelwyn Valley, through and around villages where small people laughed, and ate, and slept beside their hearths in round houses. It passed the entrances of the copper mines and the flourishing gardens of the marshes. It passed many isolated farmsteads nestled among their hedgerows, until at last it rounded a broad bend and came to the tree-lined bank of Ufgood Reach.

Here, just before sunrise, the boat slowed, turned gently in the current, and slipped in among the reeds under the trees on the north side. The child listened, wide-eyed. She heard reed stalks rubbing on the hull. She heard cattle lowing from the little farm nestled nearby. She heard blackbirds waking and muskrats creeping along the bank to gaze at her, their whiskers quivering.

All of this the child heard, but still she waited. Then, close at hand, she heard the happy voice of a young girl, calling. Raising her arms, the child in the boat laughed in answer.

Sun gathered on the hilltops, flowed down the slopes, filled the long bowl of Nelwyn Valley.

The hawk, having circled all night above the driftwood boat, now rose in the new sun, spiraling slowly up and up until the whole valley lay beneath him, with the silver Freen winding down its center. Far to the north it saw the domes of the fisher-Nelwyns nestled among their marshes and their conical hills. It saw Nelwyn boats with arching prows and sterns winding through the channels to join others already fishing in the Freen. It saw nets cast, silver fish gathered up.

To the south, the cabins of Nelwyn hunters and woodcutters dotted the hillsides and clustered beside streams that tumbled to the Freen. Farther south, where the farms began, the hawk watched cattle rising in their pastures and small sleepy men stretching in the sun. Far to the south, where the river left Nelwyn Valley and deepened and began its long run through the Low Kingdoms to the coast, the hawk saw a doughty little trading ship being loaded for a voyage.

Directly below lay Nelwyn Village, and outside it, the homestead of Ufgood Reach. It was small, even by Nelwyn standards—two thatched and white-washed domes joined by a short porch. Wattle fences enclosed a few pens. A patchwork of small fields stretched down to weeping willows on the bank.

The hawk's keen eye saw the child's boat come safely to rest beneath those trees. It saw a Nelwyn girl pause in her game of hide-and-seek, part the bushes, and discover the child. It heard her call excitedly to her brother.

And then the hawk soared higher and higher still until it vanished, turning north, following the river home.

It was going to be a hot day, an irksome day, a day when nothing good would happen.

Willow Ufgood knew it.

All the signs were bad.

For one thing, he had dreamed of his father, and that was always ominous. This dream was especially foreboding, because in it Willow was exposed as a trickster, a mere magician, and not the grand sorcerer he longed to become. People laughed at his magic, mocked him, threw pulpy, foul-smelling objects at him, while Shnorr Ufgood stood as if alive, shaking his head and saying, "Willow, Willow, more magical it would be if you plowed a field, mended a fence, thatched a roof!" He swept his cane out over the slope toward the river. "Look at the farm! Going to wrack and ruin while you play tricks, talk gibberish!"

In his dream, Willow had shuffled from one foot to the other, as if he were thirteen, saying, "But, Father, maybe someday. . ."

"Dreams! Crazy dreams!" the old man had said, waving his stick and wandering off toward the river. "Can't eat dreams! Can't eat thistles, either!"

Willow woke. He sat up and looked through the window. His father was gone. Only the unrepaired fences and unplowed fields of Ufgood Reach sloped down to the banks of the Freen.

The second bad sign was that Kiaya, up before him as usual and already baking bread, had let Mims and Ranon go to the river. Willow fretted constantly about the children. He imagined hundreds of dreadful fates that might befall them, many associated with the river. After all, when you were as small as a Nelwyn, even a pike spelled trouble, even a trout! "What if . . ." Willow would say, rubbing his hands and pacing the kitchen, "but what if . . ." And Kiaya would reply, "Oh for goodness sake, Willow, let them *be*! Let them *live*! If they don't *try* things, how will they ever learn? Here, stir the soup!" Or perhaps she would just kiss him, and laugh, and hug him until he stopped his fretting.

The third bad sign was that Bets was ornery. The moment he entered the pen and saw the sow's pink eye fixed on him, the pink ears pointed at him, he knew that plowing was going to be difficult. He was right. Bets balked at the harness, then stomped twice on his toe. And when he bent over to pick up his seed-sling, the sow lifted him with its snout and sent him somersaulting into the haystack. So when at last he got to work in his field and saw Mims and Ranon running toward him from the riverbank, waving their arms excitedly, he knew they were bringing more bad news.

"Dada! Dada!" Ranon called. "We found something in the river!"

"Come see!" little Mims shouted, stumbling along behind her brother. "Oh please, Dada, come quick!"

Willow dropped Bets's reins and struggled out of the heavy seed-sling. The pig found itself hitched to a plow with no plowman on the handles. It tugged. The plow lurched and toppled, anchoring the pig where it stood. Bets grunted and glared evilly at Willow.

He dropped to his knees and embraced his children as they came running up. "What's *happened*? Are you all right?"

"We're fine," Ranon said.

"But you have to come and *see*!"

They each took a hand and hurried him down across the field and through the trees to the water's edge. "See?"

There, caught in a tangle of arrowleaf and wild iris, Willow saw the little boat, and inside, the child. She was smiling, reaching toward him.

"A baby! A new baby!" Mims shouted, clasping

Willow's hand with both of hers and jumping up and down.

Ranon had pulled off his boots and was wading out.

"No!" Willow shouted. "Don't go near!"

"But Father . . ."

"Look at it! Have you ever seen wood like that? Tied with . . . *cloth*! It's from far away, Ranon. North of the crossroads, even! Who *knows* where it's been?"

"But a *baby*, Father . . ."

"It could be diseased. Could be in a spell! Could be a disguised sorceress! It could be . . ."

"Silly Dada!" Mims said decisively, shaking Willow's arm. "It's not! It's *none* of those things. It's just a little baby, and it needs help."

"Not so little," Ranon said, edging closer to the boat. "It's a lot bigger than you, Mims, when you were born."

"Exactly!" Willow said. "It's a Daikini. Keep back!"

Mims wrinkled her nose. "What are Daikinis?"

"Giants," Willow said. "From up north. They're terrible! Greedy! Vicious! You can't trust them, Mims." Willow hurried along the bank as he spoke and returned with a long driftwood pole, which he pushed out toward the boat.

"What are you *doing*, Dada?"

"We'll send it downstream. There're people who'll look after it. We can't afford . . ."

"No," the child said quietly. "You won't, Dada. You won't."

And she was right. Even while he intended to push the little boat back out into the current, Willow was drawing it closer, through the waterplants.

Mims smiled.

"That's what you tell *us* to do, isn't it, Dada?" Ranon said.

"What?"

"Trust your feelings."

"Well," Willow said, gathering the child into his arms, "perhaps we should get her dry. Perhaps we ought to feed her."

The child gurgled and grasped his finger.

Willow smiled.

At that moment a shout came from the fields above the bank. "Ufgood! Where are you, man! Get up here!" It was a coarse voice, as if Bets the sow were calling him in her grunty way.

Willow's eyes widened. "Burglekutt!" he whispered. "Oh no!" He passed the child to Ranon. "Keep her quiet, for goodness sake! If Burglekutt finds out we've got a Daikini here we'll *really* be in trouble! Do something. *Play* with her!"

He scrambled up the bank and through the screen of trees to the field. Kiaya was bustling down from the house with her skirts hiked up and her long hair flowing. "My husband hasn't stolen *anything*!" she was shouting. "Get away from those seeds!"

Bending over beside Bets, with his fat hand

plunged into Willow's seed-sling, was Burglekutt.
Burglekutt the Prefect. Burglekutt the Beadle and
Bailiff. Burglekutt the stingiest, meanest money-
lender in all of Nelwyn Valley. He was short, even for
a Nelwyn, but he was enormously broad. When he
wore any of his robes of office with pointed hats, he
looked like a small pyramid. High-living had turned
his thick jowls warty, and years of greedy cunning
had beaded his eyes so that, beside Bets the sow, he
looked like a pig himself, a pig rearing up on his hind
legs and grunting, "Ufgood, where'd you get these
seeds?"

The likeness was so striking that Willow laughed.

"Funny, is it?"

"No, Mr. Burglekutt, the question isn't funny. It's
just that . . ."

"Maybe you'll be amused when you miss another
mortgage payment and I *own* this land!"

"No, sir. Oh no."

"Well then, answer civilly, Ufgood. Where did you
get seeds to sow this year?"

Kiaya stood with her fists on her hips, feet planted
firmly apart, breathing heavily.

"Speak up! Where'd you get 'em?"

Willow hesitated. The truth was that, knowing his
need, his neighbors had given him seed from their
own granaries. But lest Burglekutt might take re-
venge on them, Willow did not dare to tell the truth.
Instead, he lifted his chin defiantly. "Maybe I used
my magic."

"Magic! Ha!"

Willow winced.

"You're no sorcerer, Ufgood! Everyone knows that! You're an imposter, a charlatan, a clown! Now tell the truth! *I* sell the seeds around here and I didn't sell any to *you*. You stole them from my granary!"

"He did *not*!" Kiaya stamped her foot. "We may be poor but we're honest, and it's none of your business *where* we got them! Maybe Willow *did* conjure them. Maybe he has more magic than you know. Or maybe we gathered them from the roadsides. Or maybe they just drifted down the river—a gift! Aha! We'll never tell, will we Willow?"

Willow shook his head.

"But I'll tell you *this*!" Kiaya took a fist off her hip and pointed at Burglekutt's pudgy nose. "These are not *your* seeds, and this is not your land."

"It will be." Burglekutt flung his arm over Ufgood Reach. "One more bad year and it's mine. There'll be a great barn! An inn! A countinghouse!"

"Well not *yet*! It's still ours, and we'll thank you to get off it, won't we, Willow?"

Willow nodded.

Burglekutt gulped in outrage. He held his breath so long he began to turn purple. His eyes bulged. "Magic, eh? So that's what he has! Well, it'll take more than magic to keep this land if you miss another payment. *One more*! I'll have you off in no time! Off! Off!" Flinging his arm out again, Burglekutt whirled around with his nose in the air, tripped over Bets, and fell flat on his face in hog dung.

Squealing wickedly, Bets lunged to her feet and rooted him in the rear end as he struggled to get up.

Kiaya laughed. "Serves you right! You want our land so much, go ahead! Eat it up!"

Spluttering and gagging, Burglekutt heaved himself to his feet. "You'll pay!" he croaked. "Mark my words!" And he lumbered off to the road.

"You shouldn't be mean to him," Willow said when he had gone.

"Oh, I can't *help* it!" Kiaya stamped her foot again. "The man is such a *toad*!" She leaned over and patted Bets, who was grunting happily. "Good Bets! Good pig!"

Mims and Ranon appeared then at the top of the riverbank. They had managed to drag the little boat all the way up to the edge of the field. "Mama! Come see!"

"What's that, Willow? What do they have?"

"A baby."

"A what?"

"A baby, Kiaya. A girl. She came drifting down the river in that little boat, and it landed here. We're going to send her on. We're not going to keep her. Kiaya. Kiaya, did you hear what I . . ."

But she was already running across the field toward Ranon and Mims and the small object on the ground between them. Willow hurried after her.

"Don't fall in love with her! Nobody fall in love with her!"

But it was too late. Mims and Ranon were already laughing with the child, and when Kiaya saw her she clasped her hands and gasped. "Oh, poor thing," she said, bending down and gathering the child to her breast. "Poor little thing! She's cold and wet, Willow. And hungry, too. But look how *good* she is! Not crying at all!"

"Kiaya, please put her back. Do you know what'll happen if Burglekutt finds out?"

"Oh poof! Burglekutt!"

"Well he *is* the Prefect. And you know what's happened whenever Daikinis . . ."

"Babies don't count."

"Of course they count!"

"No they don't! Babies don't make wars. They don't have enemies. Come on, children. We'll feed her and give her a nice bath. Send the boat on, Willow. She won't be needing it."

"Come up soon, Dada." Mims smiled. "You can help, too."

Willow watched his family head toward the house, the children dancing beside their mother, jumping up to peek at the infant. He carried the little boat back down to the river's edge and was about to launch it when he noticed a curious thing. None of the strips of cloth binding it together was tied. They looked as if they had been wrapped up in haste, and left loose. But they were not loose now. Willow tugged at one and found it stiff as iron. The same was true of all the other lashings; no knots, yet they could not be freed. Some power that Willow could not see had secured them there. Magic!

Willow glanced around. No one else was on the river or the bank. He rolled up his sleeves. He spit on his hands. If magic had fixed those strips of cloth in place, then magic—*his* magic—could loosen them. He closed his eyes. He spread his hands over the boat. He prepared the only spell he knew for the loosening of things—the spell that might be used to hasten a late spring, or to free a pig's leg if it got jammed between large stones: *"Yawn tamath efforcut frume!"*

It was a dangerous venture, sorcery! Sometimes, if charms didn't work, they recoiled. Sometimes the re-action was like laying your hands on a hot stove, and sometimes like being struck by lightning. You never knew. Still, if you wanted to be good, you had to take the risk. You had to practice.

"Yawn tamath efforcut frume!" Willow declared again.

No lightning, no explosion hurled him back against the bank. Had it worked? Cautiously, he opened one eye.

Yes! But not quite as he had intended. The cloth lashings were still firmly in place; it was not they that had been loosened, but the boat itself. The little craft was moving across the mudbank and through the weeds toward the middle of the river where the swift currents flowed.

Delighted not to have been struck by yet another failed charm, Willow laughed and followed it, running along the shore and then up the bank where he could see it better. Gracefully it swept along until it had reached the exact center of Ufgood Reach, the spot where Willow and his family would sometimes come to watch bluebirds play on summer evenings.

There, the boat vanished.

One instant it was sailing on; the next, gone. Perhaps, Willow thought, walking back to Bets, perhaps it had just sunk, sucked down in some freak vortex. Or perhaps his charm had worked belatedly and the bindings had loosened after all, allowing the little craft to fall into its parts—driftwood and reeds—parts too small to be noticed in the swirling currents.

Dumping Burglekutt into the mud seemed to have restored Bets's good humor. For the rest of that morning the sow contentedly hauled the plow, often uttering explosive little strings of grunts, like laughter, and by noon Willow had plowed and seeded more than half the field. They took a break together, sitting in the shade of a chestnut tree, watching the flowing river. "A long way," Willow said, nodding.

Bets turned an eye on him, and cocked a pink ear.

"She didn't come just from the ford at the crossroads. She came from farther than that." Willow nodded again. "Much farther."

Bets grunted and turned back to gaze at the current.

"And you know what? I think she must have had a lot of help to make that trip. That's what I think, Bets. This baby has *friends*." Willow stared at the current, too, chewing reflectively on a sweet stalk of grass. The river coursed on, seaming and smoothing its surface in an ever-changing enigma. *Think what you like*, it seemed to say. *Then do what you must*.

All afternoon Willow thought and worried. What *should* he do? The child certainly did not look evil, but he well knew that Evil had many faces. What if he and Kiaya and the children had been fooled by a disguise? What if they had taken in something that would destroy their little family? Destroy the village? Destroy, perhaps, even all of Nelwyn Valley? Willow shivered. He glanced anxiously at his small house sitting on its rise at the highest point of Ufgood Reach. Whenever his plowing took him close, he could hear laughter there, the laughter of his family and the wonderful, contagious laughter of the child given by the river.

No, no. It was impossible that she could be an instrument of Evil. No disguise could be *that* complete. But—Willow looked behind—what if she were the *target* of Evil? What if she were hunted? What if her pursuers raged into Nelwyn Valley, burning and killing and destroying? Willow shuddered. How awful to be so small, to be so torn by fears and premonitions! How awful to know deep down that you were a sor-

cerer, yet to be powerless to ward off Evil! Still—
Willow smiled—he had loosed the boat with his
spell. *He* had done that.

Late that afternoon, when Willow and Bets had
finished their plowing and come in from the fields,
Willow found his little house full of color and happiness, as usual. No matter how tired he was, or how
worried, his heart always lifted as he reached the
porch and raised the door latch. Some of the color in
the house came from costumes and props—part of
his magician's paraphernalia. Part of it came from
Kiaya's bright rugs and beaded tapestries, but most
of it radiated from the wonderful paintings that Mims
and Ranon made each day. They gathered and
ground their own dyes, smoothed their own wooden
panels with river sand, trimmed their own little
brushes from dried stalks and, talking quietly as they
worked, painted vivid depictions of imaginary worlds
and monsters, sometimes funny, sometimes frightening. Sometimes it seemed to Willow that they were
peopling another world. Once, when he interrupted
her to ask what she was doing, Mims had laughed
and answered, "We're doing *our* magic, Dada."

"But what's that?" Willow had asked, indicating a
sinuous, two-headed creature near the top of her
painting.

"Mmmm . . . a dragon! An Eborsisk dragon!"

"Good heavens! What's it doing?"

"Waiting."

"Not for me, I hope!"

The little girl reached for Willow's hand. "Oh, Dada, I hope not too!"

Every day there were new paintings, new creatures. Every day as he came up the path, Willow would pretend not to see Mims' small face in the kitchen window or to hear her shouting, "Here he comes!" But he never had to pretend when he opened the door. Always, his surprise and delight were real.

So it was that afternoon. "Surprise! Surprise!" they shouted as the door swung back.

His family had given their whole day to the child. Ranon had fashioned a cradle for her, and Mims had decorated it with strings of beads. Kiaya had knitted a little woolen blanket to lay inside. They had all gathered flowers from the woods and fields and spread them around the child, like tributes. Mims and Kiaya even wore some in their hair.

All of them, even the child in her new cradle, spread their arms wide in greeting. She had been bathed in the stone tub and fed. She had had a good sleep. Now she was wide awake and laughing.

Willow laughed, too, despite his fatigue and worry. She was so beautiful! And his family were so much in love with her already. He bent over and picked her up. "Well, little lady, it looks as if you've made yourself at home."

The child gurgled and reached up for his nose, and Willow saw the Sign inside her elbow. He held her gently, peering close. "Kiaya . . ."

"Shh." She laid a hand on his arm. "Go get washed," she said to Mims and Ranon. "Supper in a few minutes."

"Kiaya," Willow said when they were alone, "what *is* this?"

"A birthmark."

"But, have *you* ever seen such a birthmark?"

She shook her head.

"So *strange* . . . Look, it's as if it were painted with a tiny brush—a fairy brush!"

Kiaya nodded again. She was still holding her husband's arm, and she was biting her lower lip. "I know. And Willow, there's something else. It's her eyes. Look at her eyes, Willow. Look close."

Willow did. They were not the eyes of an ordinary infant. This child's eyes were like deep, still pools of time. As he gazed into them, Willow felt that he had begun a long journey, a long, spiraling journey that would end where he began and yet not where he began. "No, please!" he said. "Not me!"

The child laughed.

"You see? Willow, what should we do? Should we take her to the Village Council?"

"Uh-unh." Willow glanced fearfully at his wife. "No!"

"But Willow, she's not *ordinary*! You can see that."

"That's just it, Kiaya! You know what the Council will think if we take her to them. They'll see right away that she's a Daikini, and they'll take one look at that mark on her arm, and they'll think that she's a bad omen, or part of a charm or something. You know how they are, Kiaya. The first sign of a flood or a drought in the valley and they'll blame me for it. Somebody'll say, 'Ufgood did it! Ufgood brought around that Daikini child, that strange one! And Burglekutt'll say, 'Yaaaz, that's right, and he's a sloppy farmer, too! Let's *get* him!' And that'll be the end of the farm."

"Oh Willow, you fret too much. Calm down. The High Aldwin would never let..."

"The High Aldwin! Exactly! Another good reason for not saying anything. Tomorrow the High Aldwin's going to choose me as his apprentice!"

Kiaya sighed and shook her head. "Don't get your hopes up about that. The High Aldwin hasn't chosen an apprentice for six years. And besides..."

"Besides what?"

"Well, your magic's still a little, hmm, off."

"*Off!* My magic? Why, do you know what I did this morning down the river? I cast a spell that..."

The child cried out sharply, and what Willow was about to say vanished as abruptly as the little boat had vanished into the river. At the same moment, Mims and Ranon came running back.

"Oh Dada," Mims said, "she likes you, doesn't she? She likes you very much."

And indeed the child was gurgling joyfully, gripping Willow's collar.

"She looks as if she's going to lift you right up!"

"We're not going to let her go, are we, Father?" Ranon asked.

Willow worked the small hand free. "Looks more as if she's not going to let *us* go!"

"May we take her with us to the fair tomorrow?"

"Certainly not! There'll be crowds. Animals. Besides, it's going to be hot. Quite hot."

"But what will we do? We all want to go. Who'll stay and look after her if we don't take her?"

"I will," Kiaya said, setting supper on the table.

"But Mother, the prize for bread! The prize for weaving!"

"They can wait another year. Come for supper, now."

"But Mother . . ."

"I've decided, Ranon. We won't talk about it anymore. Come now. Your supper's getting cold."

Willow laid the child in the cradle and wrapped around her the beautiful newly knitted blanket. She was looking intently at him, and again Willow was drawn into her gaze. Again he felt himself beginning a long and fearful journey. He stepped back and held up both hands, palms out, and again the child laughed.

She kept gurgling as the Ufgoods ate their supper, until at last she fell asleep.

"Doesn't she cry?" Willow asked. "Most babies cry."

"Maybe she doesn't know how," Ranon suggested.

Mims shrugged, finishing her cake. "Oh," she said, "she knows how. She just won't do it."

Kiaya smiled. "Why not, Mims?"

"Because she doesn't need to right now. And besides, it would only be for herself."

Kiaya and Willow looked at each other. They looked at the sleeping child. They looked long and thoughtfully at their own small daughter.

A light rain began to fall and continued all night, conspiring softly with the river at Ufgood Reach, germinating Willow Ugfood's freshly sown fields, whispering promises into the thatched roof of the little home.

NELWYN FAIR

Everyone loved the fair. Everybody came. They came in their boats from the north end of the valley, and from the Copper Hills, and from the broads in the south. Some traveled half the night in order to be present for the ceremonies at sunrise, and some, like Willow and his children, had less than an hour's walk.

The fair was held in the meadows on the outskirts of Nelwyn Village, near the ruins of the first settlement. There the ancestral Nelwyns, escaping down the Freen from persecution in the north, had landed and settled and begun to build. The ruins of their old brochs and wheelhouses still stood in the meadow, and in preparation for each fair these ancient walls were garlanded with flowers and blessed by friars. In the fields around, the ceremonies were held, the

45

competitions judged, the races run. Children gamboled, old friends met and gossiped, and young lovers strolled off together to quiet places on the riverbank. It was a time for much merriment, the fair, and a time also to reaffirm the vigor of the Nelwyn people and the health of the great Freen and the valley which it nurtured.

The symbol of that health was the Wickerman, a majestic woven statue to which each Nelwyn contributed a festive decoration—a ribbon or a garland or bouquet or a beaded necklace. When it was raised in the center of the common, all musicians played, all Nelwyns cheered, and the Wickerman presided over the fair and the community, a large and bountiful emblem of Nelwyn spirit.

By noon the fair was in full swing. The sun shone in a cloudless sky, the dancers whirled to sprightly Nelwyn reels, the honey wine flowed abundantly, and laughing children raced in all directions. Old friends embraced, clapping each other on the back. Farmers traded livestock. Merchants spread their wares on the long deal tables before their tents. Even Vohnkar, stern chief of the Nelwyn warriors, strolled through the crowds and smiled. It was a scene of great high spirits and conviviality.

No one had any hint of terror approaching. No one except Mims. Twice during the morning, the little girl had stopped running with her friends. She paused to listen, her eyes suddenly apprehensive, her head turning back and forth across the breeze from the north. No one noticed her. Each time she herself decided she had imagined something, and was soon back shouting happily among her friends.

At noon, Willow's turn came on the magicians' stage. All candidates for Apprentice to the High Aldwin had drawn lots to perform, and Willow was last. By that time, the crowd had thinned considerably. The acts had not been very good, there were many other distractions, and wonderful fragrances were luring people to the dining tents. Besides, the tug-of-war combat between miners and farmers had just begun in the adjoining field. Willow's name, when it was announced, was drowned out by the roars of loyalists urging on their teams.

But Willow had his own cheering-section, and they were so enthusiastic that they even drew some curious spectators away from the tug-of-war. Willow's boyhood friend, Meegosh, stood solidly in his leather miner's apron, one arm around Ranon and the other around Mims. All three wildly applauded every trick, even the old pull-the-feathers-out-of-nowhere maneuver, which Willow actually did quite well. Meegosh slapped his apron and yelled, "Bravo! Bravo!" so lustily that he attracted the attention of Burglekutt. The Prefect watched disdainfully from across the fairgrounds, pudgy hands spread on his stomach.

"And for my final amazing feat," Willow shouted, "I will make an entire . . . pig . . . *disappear*!"

"Bravo!"

"Hurray!" Ranon and Mims shouted.

"Humph!" Burglekutt grunted.

Ranon and Mims lugged a wriggling piglet onto the stage, and Willow held it with one hand while spreading his cloak with the other. The piglet nipped him on the hand and twisted free, scurrying around the stage, much to Burglekutt's delight.

Meegosh covered his face.

Willow scampered after it. *"Whuppity bairn! Whuppity bairn!"* he chanted, spreading his cloak so that he looked like a small bat. *"Deru! Deru!"*

The pig vanished.

The crowd gasped.

Willow lifted his arms calmly and triumphantly. But the cloak thrashed and churned. Muffled squealing issued from it, and a second later the pig thumped back onto the stage and scrambled away. Burglekutt roared. The crowd hissed and booed. In the field beside the stage, a mighty cheer arose as the miners triumphed in the tug-of-war, pulling the farmers face-first into the dirt.

"Never mind, Dada." Ranon reached up to put his arm around his father's waist. "It wasn't your fault."

Mims nodded. "Next year we'll get a better pig."

"Good show!" Meegosh said, clapping his friend on the back as Willow came off the stage. "Much better than last year. Just needs a little . . . refining. Come on, Willow, cheer up!"

"Quite a spectacle!" Burglekutt snorted. "Made a fool of yourself again, eh, Ufgood? Disappearing pig!

The only thing you'll see disappear is your farm!"
Laughing, he headed for the food tent.

"Round the bend!" Meegosh grinned, poking Willow.

"Meegosh, I don't feel like that just now. And besides, we're getting too old for . . ."

"Round the bend!"

"All right. Round the bend!"

"Fat rear end!" Meegosh shouted after Burglekutt, cupping his hands.

"He's a donkey . . ."

"And I'm your friend!"

The two old friends chuckled at their own childishness, and Willow immediately felt better. The children laughed with them, although Mims suddenly paused and lifted her head as if she had heard a faint sound from far away. The men moved off, not noticing her distraction, and soon she ran after them.

"Never mind Burglekutt," Meegosh was saying. "When the High Aldwin picks you as his apprentice this afternoon, you won't have to worry about Burglekutt anymore, ever again."

"I hope you're right."

"Of course, I'm right. Wait and see."

They shared a good meal and enjoyed the rest of the fair until the shadow of the Wickerman, with all its wreaths and drifting streamers, touched the High Aldwin's throne. Since noon, people had been gathering in a big circle around it, and when the two friends arrived with Ranon and Mims, Meegosh had to stand on the remnants of a crumbled wall and lift the children on his shoulders to see their father honored by the High Aldwin.

Like a strange bird, the shadow of the Wickerman fluttered across the throne. The crowd hushed.

The High Aldwin appeared.

He came out of the ground, out of the ruins, out of the shadow. One moment, there was an empty throne; the next moment, the High Aldwin was sitting in it. "Good afternoon," he said.

"Good afternoon, High Aldwin," the crowd chanted in unison. Burglekutt and the other councillors bowed deeply.

He was very small, very old. His face was almost lost in white locks and braids, bushy beard and eyebrows. Out of this mass shone two blue eyes. His embroidered cap glowed eerily in the shadow of the Wickerman, and small lights twinkled in his starry cape. In his right hand he clasped a staff surmounted by an owl's skull, and by frail wings of leafy gold.

"Are we ready? Are we ready?" He seemed a bit befuddled, as he always did on first appearance. Some said it was because he had just wakened; others, because he had been swept so fast through infinite space.

"Yes, High Aldwin," the Council said.

"Then let us begin. Bring forth the candidates."

This year there were only three.

"Ufgood?" Burglekutt said, spreading his arms in astonishment and turning to the rest of the Council.

"*Ufgood* was chosen to be among the candidates? Is this a joke?" He laughed mirthlessly, but no one joined in, and the High Aldwin silenced him with a baleful glance.

The crowd grew still. The shadow of the Wicker-man passed, and the High Aldwin stood in the sun. "The Great Mystery," he began, looking hard at the would-be apprentices, "is the bloodstream of the universe, and sorcery is the way to its energy. Sorcery is not magic. It is not skill. It is not thought or knowledge." He leaned close, and his blue gaze embraced the three of them. Willow felt enshrouded, closed off from his children and Meegosh. He felt alone. The High Aldwin's voice deepened, grew more resonant. "Forget all you know or think you know. You will need only your intuition, your own deep feeling for what is right and good. Answer now!" He raised four fingers. "Which finger contains the power to enter the bloodstream of the universe?"

Hesitating, the first candidate chose the index finger.

The High Aldwin shook his head. "Next!"

The second, wavering, finally selected the little finger.

Again the High Aldwin shook his head. "Next!" He turned to Willow.

So intimidating was his manner, so piercing that gaze from his sky blue eyes, that Willow lost all confidence. He trembled. "That one," he said, pointing to a middle finger.

Sadly, the High Aldwin shook his head. The failed apprentices heard him speak, although his lips did not move. *You have forgotten what I told you. You have forgotten the simplest, most important thing of all.*

Still shaking his head, he stood up. The candidates drew back. "No apprentice this year!" Smoke curled from the place where his staff struck the ground.

The crowd released a long and disappointed sigh and began to disperse. Only Burglekutt spoke. "Just as I expected! Well, begone, the lot of you. It's over for this year. Clear off, there, Ufgood! Don't pester the High Aldwin!"

Willow had lingered behind and approached the throne. "Sir, forgive me but I have to talk to you. It's a matter of great importance. I have something . . ."

The Aldwin's gaze turned to him, but it was not, this time, the enfolding stare that Willow had felt earlier. It was cool and dispassionate, even a bit amused.

"Sir, I have a child . . ."

Mims screamed.

It was the high, piercing, sustained scream of a child who has seen something so terrible that she wants to blot it out completely, wants to remove it from the Earth and from all memory. "Look out! Look out! Look out!"

Meegosh had just taken her off his shoulder. She was standing on the ruin of an old wall, pointing north. Her eyes were shut tight.

"What is it?" the crowd asked, seeing nothing.

"What's wrong with that child? Is she having a fit? Is she . . ."

Vohnkar's shout of warning joined Mims's scream —too late!

A Death Dog rounded the bend at full speed and was among the revellers before they knew it. The brute was one of the largest and strongest of Bavmorda's creatures, bigger than any Nelwyn. For several days it had run hard on the faintest scent, pausing only to lap water from the Freen and to rip apart an occasional fawn or rabbit. Its pace quickened as the scent grew stronger, leading it down at last into Nelwyn Valley. Its eyes blazed as it charged. White froth had formed a crust across its chest and shoulders. Great muscles and sinews rippled under its hairless skin.

Willow seized the High Aldwin's arm. "*Do* something!"

The old man looked at him in surprise. "*I* do something? *I*, Willow Ufgood?"

The beast ripped through the village, straight for Mims. The scent was so strong it was crazed by it. It snapped and tore at random. The Wickerman toppled at a blow from its shoulder. A heavy cradle from which a screaming mother barely had time to snatch her baby crumpled like twigs in its fearsome claws. People scattered in all directions from the mayhem.

Only Mims held her ground. As the dog bore down on her, the child standing on the mound of ancient stones grew calm. She stopped her screaming.

She ceased jumping up and down. As Willow shouted her name and ran toward her, Mims opened her
eyes. Wide. She looked at the dog.

The creature was only three bounds away, its
blood-flecked jaws open to strike. But in that instant
it faltered. Its left forepaw folded and its knee hit
hard on the flinty path. It snarled in fury and was up
again at once, but the instant was all that Vohnkar
and his men required. Willow reached Mims and
swept her aside just as two stout arrows slammed into
the dog, the first narrowly missing its heart, the second slicing up through its throat and into its jaw.
Howling, it reared on its hind legs, clawing air.
Vohnkar moved in, struck once, twice with his sword,
dancing under the lashing talons. All Vohnkar's band
were shouting now, the ululating war cries of Nelwyn
warriors that had struck terror into the hearts of bigger men. Moving like lightning, another warrior
leaped up and slashed the dog across the head and
Vohnkar came in again to deliver the coup de grace
with a lance through the creature's heart. Dead but
still snarling, still slavering, the dog yet stayed on its
feet until a swarm of ordinary Nelwyns hacked it
down with spades and sickles.

Throughout, Mims surveyed the tumult as if she
had seen it all before, seeming quite calm in Willow's
arms. "Mommy," she said. "The baby."

"Beware!" Vohnkar shouted above the chaos.
"Watch out for more! Look to your children!"

"Ranon! Come on!" Willow looked wildly for

Meegosh, but he was busy on the other side of the common, tending to wounded. Carrying Mims and clutching Ranon's hand, Willow ran for home, a dozen horrid images in his mind. But when they burst in, Kiaya was peacefully rocking beside the window, feeding the baby.

"Thank goodness!" Willow exclaimed, embracing her. "Thank goodness you're all right!"

"Why? Willow, what *happened*!"

"A dog," Ranon said. "*This* big. It attacked the fair. Killed people."

"No!"

Willow nodded, biting his lower lip. "I knew it! I knew something awful would happen!"

Kiaya held the baby close. "You think it's *her* fault? It's *not*!"

"Of course it's not her fault, but it happened because she's here. I know it! We have to take her to the Council, now. Everyone must know. Besides, the High Aldwin will tell us what to do."

Kiaya held the baby close. "I'm afraid, Willow."

He nodded, embracing them. "Oh Kiaya, so am I. But we can't just be *afraid*. We have to fight back. We have to *act*! Right, Mims?"

"Right, Dada."

"Ranon?"

The boy nodded. "We have to look after her," he said. "And everyone must know."

"Let's go, then."

Kiaya found her shawl, and the little family went up their path toward the village, huddling together.

"When you come back, Dada," Mims said. "I'll have lots of pictures for you."

"Don't be silly." Willow laughed and laid his hand on the child's head. "I'm not going anywhere. We're just taking the baby to the High Aldwin, so he can tell us what to do."

"Lots of pictures," Mims said quietly. "I'll make one for you every day..."

The commons was a shambles. A few people were hurrying through it, avoiding the corpse of the Death Dog, but most were already inside the meeting hall. This was the largest and oldest building in the village, and for special occasions and debates, everyone gathered in its shelter. By the time the Ufgoods arrived, the High Aldwin's chair had already been carried inside and the old man was sitting with his eyes half-shut, listening to Burglekutt speak.

Alone among the councillors, Burglekutt had found time to change into official robes, and he stood in his pointed hat and flared gown, a small pyramid. Bits of what he was saying drifted back to Willow: "...sighted...hills to the south. Who knows how many more? I say...find what they're hunting for! Give it to them!...Nelwyns lost their lives!"

Many in the crowd murmured agreement.

A second councillor rose. "The dogs are just a sign. A sign of worse to come. Maybe drought. Maybe plague. Who knows? I agree with Prefect

Burglekutt. We must find what they want and give it
to them. Furthermore, we should throw whoever's
responsible into the pit!"

More murmurs of assent. At the back of the
crowd, Willow cringed, and Kiaya gripped his arm
with both hands.

The High Aldwin rose then and the crowd fell silent. "Willow Ufgood!"

Willow gulped and raised his hand. "Here!"

"Come forward!"

The crowd shuffled, opening a path, and Willow
walked through them, carrying the child. Meegosh
moved over and joined Kiaya and the children.

"Earlier," the High Aldwin said, "you tried to tell
me something. What was it, Willow?"

Willow bowed his head. "My children, sir . . . My
family . . . We found this baby on the river."

The crowd murmured again, and the High Aldwin
raised a hand and silenced them. When he brought it
down it came to rest on the head of the child, who
was smiling at him. "This is a Daikini child," he said
softly. "But there's something . . ." His eyes closed.

"You hear that?" Burglekutt lunged to his feet. "A
Daikini! Here in Nelwyn Valley. *That's* what the
beasts want! Let's give it back to them!"

"But you can't!" Willow exclaimed. "They'll kill
her!"

Burglekutt's small eyes gleamed. "You hear that?"
he asked the crowd. "Hear this fellow tell us what to
do? We have our *own* children to protect, that's what

I say! What's a Daikini child more or less? She's not one of us!"

"Life is life!" Meegosh shouted above the grumbling of the crowd. "Life is precious!"

"Burglekutt, don't talk nonsense!" Vohnkar spoke clearly, his eyes level. His hand rested on the sword which had spilled the guts of the Death Dog.

But many were frightened enough to support Burglekutt's suggestion. A few, nodding grim agreement, shook their fists.

The High Aldwin had entered a trance. One hand still rested on the head of the child, and the other gently folded back her arm to reveal the Sign inside her elbow. He gaped. His eyes rolled back into his head. For a moment it seemed that he might vanish. In fact, he even went a bit transparent; Willow could see right through him. But then he collected himself. Firmly in place, he raised both gowned arms and spread them wide. The crowd fell silent.

"This child is no ordinary child. I cannot tell you everything about her because I do not know all. I cannot see the end of her long journey." He turned sternly toward Burglekutt. "But we shall have no more talk of giving this child, or any child, to dogs to tear apart!"

There was a long silence, broken only by the soft laughter of the little girl in Willow's arms.

"Someone," the High Aldwin continued, "must take this child north, along the shore of the great river, beyond the northern limits of our valley, to the Daikini crossroads!"

The crowd gasped. The thought was so astonishing, so terrifying, that they were stricken dumb. For any Nelwyn, the prospect of leaving the valley to the north was frightening enough, but to go as far as the Daikini crossroads was impossible. Only maniacs, only witless, wandering fools had ever reached the Daikini crossroads, and what happened to them became the stuff of fables with which Nelwyn mothers warned their children. In fact, many people who heard the High Aldwin that day half believed that the Daikini crossroads was a fabulous place that did not exist at all.

"*The Daikini crossroads,*" the High Aldwin repeated somberly, as if to impress its dread reality upon them.

"But . . . but who'll *do* that?" someone asked at last.

"Ufgood!" Burglekutt said, pointing. "I nominate Willow Ufgood. After all, it's only fair that the man who interrupted the journey of this Daikini baby, here, in our community, should be the one to take it on its way. Ufgood, you're it!"

Many in the crowd nodded agreement, grunting. "Right, right . . . only fitting . . . only fair . . . what comes from meddling . . . his duty. . . . " A few applauded.

"But I have a family! I have a farm!"

"You should have thought of that before you interfered." Burglekutt folded his fat arms. "Too late now."

The High Aldwin sighed deeply. He held out a hand, palm up. "The bones," he said. One of the councillors scurried off to the vault for the divination bones, returning moments later.

Ceremoniously, the High Aldwin shook the little leather pouch of bones to the east, the south, the west, and the north, and then he bent and scattered them. Slowly, he knelt and considered the significance of their alignment. Slowly, he nodded. At last he looked up and beckoned Willow close. "The bones tell me nothing at all," he whispered. "You must help me, Willow Ufgood. Do you have any love for this child?"

Willow hesitated. He looked at Kiaya, then at the baby who gazed sweetly into his eyes. "Yes," Willow said, "of course I do."

The High Aldwin sprang to his feet. "The bones have spoken! Willow will take the child. The safety of Nelwyn Valley is in his hands."

"Praise the bones!" Burglekutt shouted.

"Hurray!" shouted the crowd. "Praise the bones! Hail Willow Ufgood!"

"But . . ." Willow said.

"But you will need help. You will need protection. The outer world is a corrupt and perilous place. The journey to the crossroads is long, and the child is hunted by beasts. I now ask all of you: Who will journey with Willow and protect him?"

"I'll go," Vohnkar said quietly. He looked from the High Aldwin to Willow. He nodded.

Two stalwart warriors stepped up beside him.

"I'll go."

"And I."

"Vohnkar!" the crowd shouted. "Vohnkar will go!"

"Not Vohnkar!" Burglekutt waved fat arms in consternation. "No, no, no! Vohnkar's our best warrior. What if more beasts come? We need him here! He should protect *us*."

"Not Vohnkar!" the crowd shouted. "Vohnkar won't go!"

"Step back, Vohnkar." Burglekutt waved his hands. "Back. Back."

"Well," the High Aldwin asked, "if not Vohnkar, *who*?"

The crowd fell silent. Men shuffled their feet and rubbed their noses. Holding the child, Willow looked inquiringly at friends and neighbors, but they avoided his gaze.

"I'll go," Meegosh said.

"Good!" Burglekutt declared. "Excellent! Praise the bones! Hail Meegosh!"

"Yes." The High Aldwin looked sourly at Burglekutt. "We have two brave men. And now, this expedition needs a leader. According to the bones, Prefect Burglekutt, that leader is *you*."

Burglekutt slapped his chest and staggered back.

His hat tipped over his forehead. He went pale. "Me?"

The High Aldwin nodded. "You."

"Praise the bones!" the crowd shouted.

"Vohnkar!" Burglekutt pointed. "You and your warriors! Pack your things!"

It took two days for the expedition to organize and pack the supplies for the long journey. They were a tense two days in Nelwyn Valley. No one could forget the ferocity of the Death Dog in its charge. The memory was too vivid, the graves too fresh, for any-one to feel secure. Vohnkar and his men rigged trip-lines across all tracks and paths, and patrolled the perimeters of the village until the time came to leave.

By dawn on the third day, all was ready. They gathered as the mist was rising at the burial ground of the old settlement, where megaliths and dolmens loomed out of the long grass. Willow and his family arrived to find Meegosh and his mother already there. The old woman wrung her hands and wept in-consolably, convinced that she would never see her son again. The Ufgoods huddled together, looking down to the place where the road curved and entered the forest like the mouth of a dark tunnel.

"Are you frightened, Dada?" Ranon asked.

"No," Willow said. "Yes."

"I don't blame you," Mims said. "I would be too, if I didn't have *me* along. Without me, the fairies in the woodland might cast a charm on you and put you to sleep for a hundred years!"

"And without me," Ranon said, "the brownies could catch you and tie you down and tickle you to death!"

"Trolls!" Mims said, wide-eyed. "Trolls might skin you alive if I wasn't there to stop them. They might take your face and . . ."

"Mims, please. I hate trolls. You know I hate trolls."

"I could guard you against them. I could carry your spear."

Willow laughed and embraced his children. "What a lucky father I am! I wish I could take you both with me, but I have Vohnkar to protect me. And besides, who'd look after your mother if we all went?"

Ranon shrugged and nodded.

"That's true," Mims said. "I'd better stay."

Vohnkar and his two warriors had appeared out of the mist and were waiting down the path. Lances and bows rose over their packs like slender horns.

Kiaya had woven a papoose-basket and lined it with fur, designing it so the child could be tucked snugly inside, in her blanket. "I miss you already," she said as she helped Willow fit on the shoulder straps of this basket. "I love you." Tears brimmed over. She brushed them away with the back of her hand.

Willow took her into his arms. "I love you, Kiaya.

Keep well. Don't find any more baby-boats in the river."

She kept weeping.

"That was a joke."

"I know." She sobbed against his chest. "Remember to keep her warm and feed her properly. And take this. It will bring you luck." She handed him a braid of her hair.

"Kiaya, you cut your hair?"

"Keep it here," she said, tucking it into Willow's jacket above his heart.

Burglekutt was approaching. They could hear him grumbling in the mist. Mims scowled and pointed at the sound.

"Urglekutt, Schmurglekutt,
Fat Burglekutt,
Pain in the forehead,
Pain in the *butt*!"

"Ouch! A bee!"

"Mims! Stop that!"

Burglekutt appeared, rubbing his bottom. "What I don't understand," he said, "is exactly what we're supposed to *do*. Journey to the Daikini crossroads and nothing else? Wait for a sign? Leave the child there and come home again? Who knows?"

"*I* know!" The voice echoed among the runestones and dolmens in the ancient burial place beside the path. Mist moved through the long grass like fingers through hair. At first they saw nothing. Then the closest runestone moved, changed shape. As they watched in astonishment, arms grew out of its sides and rubbed themselves together. A cowled head appeared on top. Strands of mist formed a long white beard. The stone became the High Aldwin. "Very cold here! Very bleak!" A hand vanished into the folds of his cloak and reappeared holding a small flask. "Mead, anyone? No? Well then..." He took a swig, tapped the stopper back in, and smacked his lips. "That's better. Now draw close, draw close. Here's what you should do."

The six adventurers gathered in front of him.

"You are going into the outer world, and that's no place for a Nelwyn, no place at all. Stay as short a time as possible. When you get to the Daikini crossroads, give the baby to the first Daikini that you see, then hurry home."

"That's all?" Willow asked.

"That's all."

"But," Meegosh said, "a lot of Daikinis are mad."

"And a lot of them are bad," Willow said.

"And a lot of them are mad *and* bad," Vohnkar said, touching the shaft of his curved sword.

"They're also big!" Burglekutt added. "Very, *very* big!"

"So," Willow asked, "how do we know when we find a good one?"

The High Aldwin closed his eyes and shook his

head. "That doesn't matter. Just give the child to the *first* one and get home as fast as you can."

"But . . ." Willow began, hearing the soft laughter of the child in the basket on his back, "but what if . . ."

The High Aldwin's blue eyes fixed him. "What's the matter, Willow? Don't you trust me? Need a sign? Very well then." He stooped and picked up a fist-sized stone. "Follow the bird. Go where the bird goes. *Tuatha! Lokwathrak! Tuatha!*"

He hurled the stone upward, and it soared far above the mists. When the first rays of the rising sun touched it, it unfolded into a dazzling white dove which continued to rise, spiraling, until at last it headed south.

Burglekutt had been backing up, shading his eyes. "Good! It's going back to the village. Home."

"What?"

"That way!"

The High Aldwin seemed momentarily flustered. He took another quick nip from the flask. "Wrong charm! Too early in the morning. Too cold. Ignore the bird, follow the river. Trust me. All will be well. But I warn you: Don't go beyond the crossroads!"

As Willow turned to go the High Aldwin plucked at his sleeve and beckoned him in among the rune-stones and dolmens, letting the others go ahead. "What's the *matter* with you?" the old man whispered when they were alone. "What *is* the matter with you, Ufgood?"

"Sir? I don't . . ."

"Yesterday, when I asked you which finger contained the power to enter the bloodstream of the universe, what was your first response?"

Willow laughed. "Sir, it was so silly. . ."

The High Aldwin cuffed him lightly on the ear. "Just tell me what it was!"

"Well, it was to choose my own finger."

"Exactly! Exactly, you idiot!" He swatted Willow several times, his blows as light as birds' wings. "Oh Willow, Willow, if only you could have faith in your*self*, in what you *feel*! More than anyone else, you have the power to be a great sorcerer, but you must *trust* that power! Listen to your own heart." He fumbled in the folds of his robe and drew out three round objects. "Here. I'd go with you if I could, but I'm bound to this valley. Take these. You'll need them."

"Acorns?"

"Magical! Anything you hurl them at will turn to stone. But remember, there're only three."

"I'd like to throw one at Burglekutt!"

"No, no. If you use sorcery for evil, you will become Evil. You have much to learn, Willow. Learn well. Farewell!" The High Aldwin lifted his arms and vanished. Where he had been the mist swirled away from the sun.

Willow tucked the acorns safely into his pocket beside the braid of Kiaya's hair. When he got to the path, the rest of the expedition had gone ahead except for Meegosh, who waited to help carry the baggage pole. For the last time, Willow Ufgood embraced his wife and children. He settled his end of the pole on his shoulder. And then, in the sun of the new day, he and Meegosh set off through the meadow, to the place where the forest opened like the mouth of a dark tunnel.

From the slopes behind them the Nelwyns called good-bye—a long, sorrowful sigh.

Many wept.

So began the long journey of Willow Ufgood, a journey destined to end even more strangely than it began.

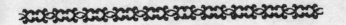

DAIKINI CROSSROADS

For several leagues northward through Nelwyn Valley the road was broad and level. It led straight through the forest along the old flood plain on the east bank of the river, where the trees grew tall and open. Through them, the travelers could see the Freen and often the forest creatures that went down to the bank to drink.

Vohnkar sent his two men to scout ahead while he led the little procession, lance at the ready. Burglekutt followed next, carrying only his staff of office and his heavy self, sweating copiously and complaining at every inconvenience—a muddy quagmire, a toe stubbed on a projecting root, a horsefly nipping his fat neck. Behind him struggled Meegosh and Willow, bearing the baggage of the expedition slung on the sagging pole between them.

As it approached the northern end of the valley, the road curved away from the river and narrowed, becoming a cart track, and then a trail, and finally a footpath so overgrown that even Vohnkar sometimes lost it.

Burglekutt kept falling back so that Meegosh frequently trod on his heels. He was frightened by every sound—even the squawk of a raven, even the sudden scolding of a squirrel—and his cries were so loud that they often brought Vohnkar gliding back, hissing for silence.

They were entering a region where few Nelwyns ever ventured. Only hunters in close pursuit of game dared come this far north, and they never lingered, for beyond the end of the valley the Daikini world began. Vohnkar moved slowly here, taking all precautions, often scouting far ahead before he beckoned them on.

On the second night they camped in a small cave at the very end of Nelwyn Valley, a considerable distance away from the path. It was a secure campsite. They built a small fire and ate well, and Burglekutt was soon asleep and snoring. The warriors took turns keeping watch, and there came a time late in the evening when Meegosh and Willow were alone with Vohnkar beside the fire.

They were old friends. They had known each other well when they were boys, but their ways had parted years earlier. Vohnkar had left the valley for a time, while Willow and Meegosh had taken on the jobs and homes of their fathers. They had seen little of each other since.

Now they sat together as they had when they were boys, beside the river, or among the boughs of a great oak, or in some cave like this one.

"It's a good place, Vohnkar."

The warrior nodded. "The last. Beyond here we'll be in the open. Many nights."

Meegosh leaned forward. "Have you . . . have you *been* to the Daikini crossroads, Vohnkar?"

"Oh yes."

"And beyond?"

Vohnkar nodded. "Once." He looked at them through the smoke. He looked into the watching eyes of the child in Willow's arms. "When I began my quest."

"A quest? What for?"

"Tir Asleen."

"Tir Asleen! But that's just . . ."

"Just a legend? Just a myth?" Vohnkar peered at Meegosh, his eyes narrowing in the drifting smoke.

"Well . . . yes. Isn't it?"

Vohnkar smiled.

"But it *is* just a myth, isn't it, Vohnkar? You didn't *find* Tir Asleen."

"No."

"Then your quest failed."

"Oh no!" Vohnkar laughed softly, shaking his

head. "If my quest had failed, my friends, we would
not be here now."

Then, looking often at the child, he told them a
strange story.

Vohnkar's Tale

Legends say that in the olden times all the land
was open, all the land was free. They say that in
those days, the broad road led north out of Nelwyn
Valley all the way to the Far Mountains and the High
Kingdom of Tir Asleen. They say that all Daikinis
once lived in harmony under the good king, and
there was little to fear on that highway through his
domains. Some brigands prowled, of course, so that a
prudent man would carry a good blade, and from
time to time marauding bands of trolls would swarm
out of the swamps in such numbers that they would
have to be beaten back by Asleen cavalry. But such
events were rare.

In those days, many travelers passed along the
road. Messengers and administrators used it to reach
all the domains. Merchants used it to peddle their
wares from the backs of horses and from lumbering
caravans. Strolling players, minstrels, and acrobats
used it to make festive the many fairs and carnivals.
Adventurers used it to travel to strange lands. And,
because there were two splendid festivals a year at

Tir Asleen, ordinary folk used it to journey to that great castle each spring and fall.

Like all Nelwyn lads, Vohnkar had heard these fables. Unlike most, however, he longed to see the world beyond the valley. Perhaps because he was an orphan who had grown used to long solitudes while hunting in the hills, it was easier for him to leave. Early one morning he put his few belongings into a sack and set off northward to find the fabled castle of Tir Asleen. He traveled out of the valley northward, finding his way without much difficulty until he reached a woods beyond the Daikini crossroads. There he lost the road and never found it again. Far afield he wandered, and farther still. For three years he journeyed in strange lands. He reached the Western Sea and voyaged with men whose dragon-vessels slid through drifting fields of ice. He went north to the lands of the white bear and saw herds of strange deer so vast that their antlers shimmered in his dreams like a moving forest. He journeyed east, welcomed among the tents of nomads who urged him to stay forever, for the coming of a small man had been foretold by their seers, and Vohnkar's courage in the hunt fulfilled all their prophecies. Long he lingered there . . . But still he was restless, still the castle of Tir Asleen glimmered like a jewel in his memory, drawing him onward in his quest. Regretfully at last he turned west again, taking with him a ruby earring and a golden necklace, mementos from a lady of those silken tents. . . .

Many months he journeyed westward, home. He had much time to think about Tir Asleen, to imagine how it must appear, and it grew ever more fabulous in his imagination. He had time to consider the strange way in which he had been led around it in his adventures, until he had encircled the place where it was said to be. He had time to muse on how he had been changed since his departure from Nelwyn Valley, for he had learned the skills of the field from all the peoples among whom he had lived. In those years he had served an apprenticeship. Now, he was a warrior.

At last, famished and exhausted, he found his way back to the lands north of Nelwyn Valley. There in the mountains, in the midst of a fierce blizzard, he huddled alone in a cave and prepared for death. There was no warmth left in his small body. Cold had turned his feet clumsy and his fingers stiff. He embraced his weapons and curled into a ball, so that he might be found like a warrior, like those northern swordsmen he had seen frozen so perfectly that it seemed they must spring magically to life at a touch.

So, he lost consciousness.

Elves found him before he died. They bore him down into their deep caverns, warmed him, and fed him well until his strength returned. He told them of his long quest for Tir Asleen, and when he asked them if the castle really existed, they stroked their beards, and nodded, and looked away. But when he asked if they would take him there, they sadly shook their heads. That was beyond their power, they told him. Not even they, with all their craft and stealth, with all their caves and passages through the mountains, could go to Tir Asleen.

A hundred questions flooded out of Vohnkar, but the elves would say no more. Steadfastly they closed their wise eyes and bowed their small and bearded heads. However, they told him, because of his devotion to Tir Asleen, he should wear forever this gift, this silver elfin ring, cunningly crafted and engraved. Then they wrapped him well in furs, and took him through their passages and high passes to a place where, far in the distance, he could see the looming mass—not of Tir Asleen—of Nockmaar.

When he saw that dark and smoking castle, when he heard for the first time the distant howls of Death Dogs and felt the dread of Bavmorda's power in his stomach, Vohnkar knew that his adventure had ended and his duty had begun. He understood why he had become a warrior in the long years of that circling quest. He must give up his own freedom for the safety of Nelwyn Valley. He must dedicate his skill to his people and, with all his heart and strength, fight to protect them from the savagery of Nockmaar.

And that is what Vohnkar did. . . .

The fire had burned low. The baby had fallen asleep, smiling, during Vohnkar's tale. "And now, my friends," the warrior said as he rose, "I believe there was another reason for that quest, although I do not understand it, or know what Fate we are moving in, Willow Ufgood, you and I."

Vohnkar gently unbent the child's arm to reveal the Sign on the inside of her elbow. Beside it he held the mark engraved on his silver elf-ring.

They were the same.

As they traveled the next day, Willow often felt traces of the old road under his feet—the earth packed firm by generations of boots or hooves and trundling wheels. Occasionally there was even a stretch of cobblestones. Where the Freen meandered, the abutments of old bridges still lay among the rushes at the fords.

North of Nelwyn Valley, however, they left the last vestiges of the road behind, and they began to encounter many difficulties. The path wound away from the river into thick forest. Uprooted trees and jumbled rocks had fallen across it, and the travelers often had to make long and exhausting detours. Several times they stumbled on the sites of ancient battles or ambuscades, where rusting weapons and armor poked out of the roots and where yellowing bones lay strewn like sticks. Once Burglekutt kicked aside what he thought was a boulder and shrieked when a helmeted skull rolled face-up, leering at him. Once in the wind they heard a strange creaking, and came upon thirteen skeletons swaying in a macabre dance on rope so rotten that even as they watched one of the gibbets broke, dropping its grisly load clattering to the ground. Farther on, Vohnkar pointed grimly at a place where a horse and rider had died together against a tree, and creepers had bound their bones together. Many times they came upon the corpses of trolls, sitting or lying, years dead, their skin dried tough as oak, their agate eyes still blazing hatefully.

Evil and death, death and Evil; the two mingled as palpable as smoke in that foul forest, and they were glad to leave it behind.

The region they entered, however, was even more terrible. Some blight had stunted all vegetation there. The forest grew in its usual profusion and variety, but to only a fraction of its height. Oak trees that should have risen a hundred feet and cast a huge umbrella were now only a little taller than the Nelwyns. Birch groves were even shorter. There was no friendly cover in that region, and on the slopes on the far side, they could see dark horsemen passing.

"We'll wait for night," Vohnkar grunted.

They made a little camp at the edge of the woods and rested and ate. Frightened, hot, pestered by flies, the baby had begun to fret. Willow had trouble keeping her quiet. Several times Burglekutt had cursed at him, and once he even threatened to strike the child. "Don't you dare!" Willow said, clenching his fist.

Now, Burglekutt ordered silence again.

"There's no point shouting at her," Willow sighed,

78 WAYLAND DREW

lifting the baby out of her basket. "Besides, she's sick."

"She's *not* sick," Burglekutt said. "Give her to me!" He grabbed her roughly and began to shake her, holding her at eye level, saying, "Now see here, young lady..."

The child threw up violently.

A splat of thick vomit hit Burglekutt between the eyes.

"I told you," Willow said, taking her back. "She's really sick."

"Is she going to *die*?" Meegosh asked.

"No." Willow cleaned the child with moss and sweet water. "She's just hot and tired and upset by all of this. She'll be fine when she gets some proper rest and food."

Burglekutt washed, sputtering, while the warriors sat cross-legged, smiling at him. "Those horsemen," he said, "they were Daikinis. We should light a fire so they can see us. We should give her to them."

Vohnkar shook his head, eyes narrowed. "Daikini, yes. But also Nockmaar."

"Nockmaar?" Meegosh's eyes widened. "How do you know?"

"My friend tells me." Vohnkar smiled slightly, stroking his sword. "She is whispering the news. Nockmaar blood has made her happy, other times."

"Do you think they're looking for us?" Willow asked.

"Yes."

"W-will they have th-those d-d-dogs?"

"Yes, Burglekutt. But if you keep shaking like that you'll get so thin they won't want you."

The three warriors laughed quietly. Vohnkar checked on the horsemen's progress. They were headed east, away from the blighted area, off on some false scent. Later, in the still dusk, the Nelwyns heard the Death Dogs howling far away. All of them shuddered, even Vohnkar. "Only a fool is not afraid," he said when he saw Willow looking at him. "How is the little one?"

"Better, Vohnkar."

"Let me carry her across this place. We shall have a quiet journey tonight, and you have enough to bear."

They did have a quiet passage. They moved through that stunted region in a cool night, by the light of stars. Vohnkar cradled the child in one arm, smiling at her often. Several times, secretly, he touched the enigmatic birthmark on her arm. Several times he whispered strange words that none of the other Nelwyns would have understood, even if they had heard.

For a time, a brown bear traveled with them. He had crossed to meet them from the other side. He regarded the little procession solemnly as they passed, then turned and ambled beside them, a few paces off. Burglekutt began to hiss and fling his arms to shoo the bear away, but Vohnkar silenced him.

"Fool! Do you not see what he is doing. Do you not see that he is our friend?"

And he showed them how the bear was keeping downwind between them and the dogs, so that the scent of his body would cover theirs.

At dawn the bear was gone. They were among hills again, and traveling on a track wider than any they had seen for several days. Not only that, but it showed signs of recent use—heavy use—so much, in fact, that Vohnkar motioned them off into the forest. The walking was much more difficult there, and Burglekutt whined so insistently that an exasperated Vohnkar finally booted him in the rump and sent him sprawling.

Seconds later, they were all on their bellies. Willow pressed his hand on the child's mouth and whispered frantically for silence.

A troop of Nockmaar cavalry had rounded the bend ahead.

Wide-eyed in the bushes, Willow knew for the first time what it meant to be paralyzed by terror. He could not even have reached the stirrup on one of those black horses! A blow from a hoof would have crushed him! He could have been skewered on any of those iron horns sticking out of the beasts' faceplates!

Even more terrible than their mounts were the massed troopers, the first Daikinis Willow had seen. They were enormous. Armor clanked as they rode. Leather tunics wrinkled like heavy skin, and capes swelled behind like bats' wings. Helmets slung from their saddles grinned like monstrous skulls. Most hideous were their weapons. Quivers of iron-tipped arrows rattled on their backs, and great bows of horn and sinew curved across their shoulders. Maces and spiked chains swung from their saddles. All carried swords hooked at the end, for gutting.

When they halted beside him, Willow crushed his face into the earth.

"The throats!" Vohnkar whispered to his warriors. *"And the eyes!"*

Galloping from the south, a messenger had met the troop at that moment. "Nelwyns!" he shouted, reining in his lathered mount. "Nelwyns have the baby. One of the dogs tracked her to their valley, but she's gone. We think they've brought her north."

"This far?" the lieutenant asked.

"Probably not. It's too soon." The scout twisted in his saddle. "Fan out across the plain and keep close watch. They'll try to cross at night. I must report to Sorsha and General Kael. How far is their camp?"

"Twelve leagues. They're laying siege to Galladoorn."

"Galladoorn! Ha! The last jewel in Bavmorda's crown! Except for the Nelwyns, and the Nelwyns count for little except sport." The two men laughed harshly. "Good hunting to you, my friends! May you kill a score of the little pigs before nightfall and feed your dogs with them."

"Aaargh!" Burglekutt murmured, burrowing deep into the damp moss.

"*And may you encounter a little pig like me, my friend*," Vohnkar whispered, eying the scout's bared throat. "*Were I not charged with the safety of the child, those would be your last words!*"

Still laughing, the troopers and the scout rode off in opposite directions, leaving the road empty once again.

The Nelwyns huddled in council.

"We should go back," Willow said, shuddering with fear for Kiaya and his children. "If they go to the village . . ."

"We can take the baby with us," Meegosh said. "We'll outwit them!"

"Think!" Vohnkar's level eyes steadied them all. "Do you want to lead them back to the valley again? No! Fulfill the mission. Come! Keep to the woods!"

They pressed on. The next day they reached a causeway across a vast and steamy swamp. Creatures from another age bellowed in the distance, their howls swirling in the mists so that they seemed to loom over them. Twice, when leathery birds swept past on creaking wings, Burglekutt covered his head and scampered in little circles, squeaking like a doomed rat.

Past the marsh, the road wound through a range of flat-topped hills and at last reached a broad plateau. Here in the evening of the following day, they came to the Daikini crossroads.

There could be no mistaking it. The road continued north, but a much broader highway crossed here, leading west and east as far as they could see. This was a highway for Daikinis, men much larger than the Nelwyns, and for their mounts and carriages. Even if the crossroads had not found such a grim place in Nelwyn lore, Willow would have known where they were.

The place of death, the legends called it.

The place of the end of dreams.

Many battles had been fought there. Many men had died. So steeped was the place in horror that Willow could *feel* it, even while he stood on the last slope looking down. He could feel the ground shake with the charge and clash of cavalry. He could hear the terrible song of arrow volleys, the hiss and smack of swords on leather armor, and the shrieks of slaughtered horses and mangled men. He could hear merciless laughter and screams as captive throats were slashed and torturers set to their grisly work. He could smell blood, and flayed flesh, and the stench of burning meat. Even from where he stood he could see the gibbets, the mounded graves, the scattered bones—all evidence of what Daikinis had done to each other at this place. One glance told Willow why his ancestors had fled south, away from the hosts of large men, to find peace in the glens of Nelwyn Valley.

He shut his eyes and turned away, hugging the

child close. "I don't want to go there, Vohnkar," he whispered. "I can't. I can't."

The warrior laid a firm hand on his shoulder. "You must," he said. "You have a duty."

Down they went together. With Burglekutt keeping to the rear, they descended the last slope and approached the Daikini crossroads.

The sun had just set. Reflecting off low clouds, the afterglow drenched the place in red. Close up, it was even more horrible than it had been from the hilltop. The contorted remains of horses and men lay everywhere, some mere skeletons, some dried black, some fresh and putrefying. Corpses on gibbet ropes swayed as if still caught in the currents of violence that had swept that place. Carrion birds circled, stretching scrawny necks.

"I don't like it," Burglekutt said. "I want to go home."

"Quiet!" Vohnkar muttered, his narrow eyes sweeping the crossroads and the hills. "We all want to go home. We're staying until we've done what we came to do."

"Well, can we at least get away from *them*?" Burglekutt pointed toward a high wooden scaffolding directly across the road. Two iron cages hung there from stout chains. A grinning skeleton sat in the closer, draped in rotted rags. One hand gripped the bars and the other dangled through, a finger pointing at them. As the cage swung, the finger swept over them, and back.

One of the warriors cursed softly.

"Poor devil!" Vohnkar said. "I wonder what *his* crime was."

"M-maybe just being here?" Willow suggested.

Vohnkar shook his head. "Not even Daikinis do that to ordinary folk," he said. "Only to the really bad ones."

Willow squinted at the other cage, but it hung farther back in the gloom, and he could see nothing but a pile of rags in the bottom.

"Let's move away from them," Meegosh said in a small voice. "For once I agree with Burglekutt. Those things make me shiver!"

Vohnkar beckoned. They moved across the road to a little thicket that had somehow escaped ravaging. Here, in the last of the light, they stood in a huddle, looking up and down the highway. The baby began to whimper, and Willow took her out of the basket. "She's cold," he said. "We should have a fire."

"Fool! Idiot!" Burglekutt hissed. "You want to bring all Nockmaar down on us?"

Vohnkar shrugged. "Not much danger. Fires are common along here. People stop for the night, camp. Look, there's one now, down to the east, at the base of that hill. There's another. Besides, it's a quiet night and a flat road. We can hear anyone coming from miles away. Willow's right. The child needs warmth and rest." He looked around. "Willow, Meegosh, Burglekutt, gather up some firewood before it gets too dark. We'll keep watch." He took the child from Willow.

While the three warriors took up positions, the others spread out and began to gather sticks.

"Not too far," Vohnkar called after them. "Keep close enough so we can hear you call. Hurry!"

"No wood. No wood," Burglekutt complained, trotting behind Willow.

"Of course there's no wood! I've picked it all up! Go over there. See? There's lots there."

"It's dark over there!"

"No darker than here, Burglekutt! Go on!"

So exasperated was Willow, so preoccupied with hurrying to gather enough fuel, that he did not notice he was going under the low-sweeping arms of the scaffolding where the iron cages hung. He saw only a sudden richness of good hardwood—wood that would burn down to warm embers. He did not realize when he passed beneath the first of the cages, the one with the leering skeleton. He did not know that he was under the second cage until a puff of wind moved it and rusty iron squeaked.

Then he knew.

Perhaps he would have escaped if he had dropped flat on his belly and wriggled away snakelike. He made the mistake of straightening up slowly, horrified, seeing the shadows closing him off from Vohnkar.

Creaking, the cage swung directly overhead.

Willow took one step toward safety.

With a clang and a rattle and a terrible hoarse cry, the mound of rags in the cage exploded into human shape. Or almost human shape. A claw on the end of a cadaverous arm dropped through the bars and snatched Willow up by the scruff of the neck. Wood went flying.

"Gotcha!"

Willow hung, strangling.

"Water, Peck! Tell your friends I want water, or I'll strip the meat from your scrawny bones!" The voice rasped like a dry hinge.

Helpless, Willow swung. Through bulging eyes, he saw a small human pyramid appear below him. "Ufgood? Is that *you*?"

"Water!" The claw shook Willow like a sock.

Willow fumbled at his collar. He gasped. "Burglekutt! Get Vohnkar!"

MADMARTIGAN

"A Daikini!" Burglekutt shouted, waving his arms and scampering back toward the warriors. "Ufgood's found a Daikini! Now we can go home!"

Vohnkar sprang up. He had been comforting the child and starting a small fire from the sticks close at hand. "Where is he?"

"There." Burglekutt pointed toward the scaffold. "He's, uh, talking to him. Actually, there's a bit of a problem. You'd better come."

Vohnkar beckoned his men. "Bring torches!" And in a moment they had all gathered below the arms of the scaffold.

Torchlight glimmered on a weird scene. In the one cage, the skeleton leered and pointed, revolving uncannily, always facing them, no matter where they

moved. In the other cage, a scarecrow figure dangled
the hapless Willow from one long arm.

"You *are* a Daikini, aren't you?" Burglekutt
asked.

The man's parched, cracked lips parted in a kind
of smile. Teeth gleamed. He wiped the filthy back of
his free hand across his mouth. "Water, little Pecks,
or your friend's crows' meat!"

He was a frightening specter. His eyes glinted in
the torchlight out of a tangled mass of long black
hair. Stubble covered his chin and cheeks. His clothes
were such filthy rags that it was hard to tell what they
might once have been—perhaps a cotton shirt, a
leather vest and high boots, a neckerchief, a sash.

"Water!"

His big hand tightened on the scruff of Willow's
neck.

Willow's tongue stuck out. He nodded frantically.

Vohnkar was still cradling the baby in one arm. He
took a firmer grip on his lance and motioned his men
around the cage.

"Burglekutt," Meegosh said, "give him water."

"*My* water?" Burglekutt clutched the leather flask
slung around his neck.

"It's not your water! It's everybody's. And there's
lots more where that came from. Give the Daikini
some!"

Grumbling, Burglekutt crept close and tossed the
flask up through the bars. The prisoner dropped Willow and grabbed it with both hands, almost letting it

fall in his eagerness to uncork it. Water splashed over his head and face. He drank and drank, smacking parched lips and uttering groans of pleasure. Little by little, he revived. "Thank you, Burglekutt," he croaked, winking. "You're a good little Peck, I can see that. Now hack off this chain and we'll be friends for life." He rattled the lock on the cage.

"Don't do it!" Meegosh had run in and dragged the half-conscious Willow back to the edge of the torchlight. "Keep back till we've decided what to do!"

"Do?" Groaning, the man in the cage struggled to his knees. "Do? Why, you're going to let old Madmartigan out of this rat trap, aren't you, little friends? You're going to set him free so he can thank you with all his heart and walk away." He splashed more water on his face and beard. He squinted against the glare of the torches. His teeth gleamed in an innocent smile. "After all, didn't I let your friend go?"

"A Daikini! Definitely a Daikini!" Burglekutt exclaimed. "He's all we need. We can leave the child with him."

"What? Child? Of *course*, you can leave the child with me! I *love* children!" He eyed the lances of Vohnkar and his men. "But you have to let me out first. How else can I look after him?"

"Her!" Willow croaked, rubbing his throat.

"Her. Of course. Hello there, my dear! Hello!" A long arm waved out of the cage.

Vohnkar handed the child to Willow and shifted his lance into his left hand. "How do we know..."

"Look!" Meegosh shouted.

Torches suddenly appeared a short distance down the road. They heard the clatter of hooves and the rumble of wheels coming fast, accompanied by raucous singing and laughter.

"Take cover!" Vohnkar hissed.

"They're Pohas!" the caged man shouted as the Nelwyns scurried into the bushes. "Don't leave me here! They're a bunch of scurvy Pohas! They'll roast me alive!"

A mud-caked wagon clattered up at full gallop, scattering dust and sparks from several torches. The driver hauled the sweating horses to a halt and four half-naked drunks tumbled out, carrying torches. All were bald. All wore sleeveless jerkins. All were wildly tattooed with bizarre signs and creatures. They lumbered around the crossroads, scavenging debris, looting fresh bodies. One of them soon discovered the cage, and his shouts brought the others. Roaring and hooting, they smashed the skeleton apart and played a reeling game of football with the skull.

The man in the second cage had vanished under the heap of rags, but the Pohas discovered him, prodded him out with torches, and set him and his cage on fire. Lurching and roaring in glee, they left him wreathed in smoke and piled back into their wagon, galloping off to other places, other random brutalities.

When they had gone, the Nelwyns scrambled out of hiding and flung dirt on the flames. The Daikini was prancing on the hot rags, yelping, beating at his smoldering clothes. Even Willow felt sorry for him. "What'd you *do*?" he asked, cradling the baby while the others beat out the last embers. "Why are you in there?"

"Why? *Why*?" The Daikini rubbed his singed arms and spat out dirt. "Who knows? Who has to *do* anything? Might as well ask why those Pohas came just now. Argh! How I hate them! Give me one good sword and I'd tattoo them right through their fat bellies!"

"That settles it!" Burglekutt said, peering down the road where the Pohas's torches had dwindled to a dot. "We're not staying here! We'll let him out and give him the baby."

"Bravo, Burglekutt! Good fellow! Open this door!"

Willow backed up, holding the child close. "No. I don't trust him. He nearly strangled me."

Burglekutt tapped his chest. "I'm the leader of this expedition. I say we follow orders. The High Aldwin told us to bring the child here and give her to the first Daikini." He pointed to the cage. "He's it!"

"Follow orders!" Meegosh said disgustedly. "Now there's *real* leadership!"

Vohnkar smiled. "Still, Burglekutt's right. Those *were* the High Aldwin's orders. We should follow them."

"Absolutely!" said the Daikini, who had been listening closely. "The High Aldwin knows what's best. Don't delay!" He rattled his cage.

Vohnkar came close and looked steadily into Willow's eyes. "Is that not enough, Willow? Do you want to know *why*, also?"

"Oh no, I don't expect to know everything, Vohnkar, but the High Aldwin told me to trust *myself*. And I don't feel right about this. The man is a scoundrel! A ruffian! *Look* at him!"

"Hurry up, Vohnkar!" Burglekutt called from the edge of the road. "We're going back. As far as I'm concerned, the job's done."

Vohnkar sighed. He shouldered his lance. "I must look after him. We'll go slowly at first. You'll have time to catch up. How about you, Meegosh?"

Meegosh swallowed. "I'll stay with Willow."

Vohnkar pointed to the grinning skull, lying where the Pohas had kicked it. "Think carefully, my friends. This is no place for Nelwyns. For the last time, are you sure?"

They nodded together.

"Very well, then. Farewell." And he raised his hand in salute.

"Farewell," the other warriors called, also saluting. "Until we meet again." Then they turned and followed Vohnkar into the darkness.

The man in the cage watched them all depart. He shrugged skeptically. "I don't know, Peck. If I were you I'd just follow orders too. Don't even think about it. Just let me out and head home."

"Don't call me Peck. My name's Willow."

"Believe me, Peck, I'll look after that darling child. Just hand her over."

"I don't trust you."

"Don't *trust* me! *Me?* Don't judge by my present unhappy circumstances, little friend. Didn't you hear Burglekutt say I was chosen? After all, I'm the first Daikini you've met."

"Burglekutt's troll dung!"

"He *does* look a little like troll dung. Well, what are you going to do?"

"I'm going to think," Willow said. "We'll stay here tonight. In the morning I'll decide. All right with you, Meegosh?"

Meegosh nodded and went for their baggage.

Willow spent a long, bad night. He fed the child and cradled her as she slept, huddling close to their little fire. He was afraid of every sound in that awful place—the creaking of the cages in the wind, the grumbling of enormous frogs in the swamp beyond the crossroads, the howling of wolves or dogs far away. All night the Daikini shifted restlessly in his charred cage, muttering snatches of obscene soldiers' songs, chuckling at strange happenings in his dreams.

Willow shivered to hear him. He could not bear to give him the child. He felt as much love for that sleeping infant as he felt for Mims or Ranon. He held her close. He rocked her. He hummed the little Nel-

wyn lullabies that he had heard from his mother and
from Kiaya beside the fire at home. He leaned forward to drop twigs into the fire. And at last, unde-
cided still, he dozed.

He dreamed.

In his dream, a white bird lifted him far above that
place of death and carried him back to Nelwyn Valley. The sun rose as they flew, bathing the country-
side in warmth and light. People stood in doorways,
waving as they passed. There were no Death Dogs,
no battles, no tattooed Pohas. When they arrived at
Ufgood Reach, the bird descended gently until Willow stood in his own garden, and Kiaya and his children were running toward him in the slowness of
dreams, their arms stretched in welcome. Then the
bird was leaving, rising, and when he turned to give
thanks, the bird became the child. . . . .

Hoofbeats woke him, coming fast along the road
in the first light. A single horseman raced past before
Willow had time to take cover. It didn't matter; the
man was dying. He stared at Willow dully, clasping
the reins and the pommel of his saddle with one hand
while the other arm swung limp, a slack doll's
arm. He wore no helmet, bore no weapons. Blood
streamed from a terrible gash on his head. Wild-eyed
and squealing, gleaming with sweat and blood, his
horse had taken the bit in her foaming teeth.

Willow stared in horror. In no time the man had
cantered past and vanished in dust and distance.

"Wha-what was that?" Meegosh asked.

The cage creaked. "Fugitive. Messenger, maybe. Galladoorn. Smells like trouble. Let me out, Pecks."

No sooner had he spoken than another horseman came tearing toward them. Meegosh ran down to the road. "Hey!" he shouted. "Stop! What's going on? What's wrong?"

This rider bent low over his mount's neck, lashing the creature hard. He kept looking back as if winged devils were after him, and he did not notice Meegosh until his horse shied at full gallop, lurching sideways so violently that they almost fell. The man cursed and swiped at Meegosh with his whip, narrowly missing him. "Off the road, wretch! Out of my way!"

Shaking, Meegosh hurried back. "Willow, this is terrible! We have to get away from here."

"I agree," the man in the cage said grimly. "We should *all* get away. There's a battle coming. I can smell it."

"You're a warrior?"

"Best swordsman that ever lived!"

"Willow! A swordsman! He could help us. He could protect . . ."

"Don't listen to him, Meegosh."

"Help you? Of *course* I could help you. Let me out and you'll see. In times like these, honest men need all the help they can get, and I can tell you're both honest men. Woodcutters, right?"

"I'm a miner. And my friend's a farmer."

"I knew it! Miners, farmers: victims of a rotten

world, just like me!" He shook his head dolefully. "Depraved. Corrupt."

"Drink?" Meegosh asked, handing up a cup of water.

"Thank you, my friend."

"Shh," Willow said. "Listen."

A distant rumbling came, like thunder. It grew louder, drew closer.

"What's *that*?"

"An army." The caged man drank. "A few thousand fools on their way to death."

"Friends of yours?"

"Maybe. Maybe not. We'll see." He peered through the bars at the banners of the approaching vanguard.

"If they are, they'll need you," Willow said. "They'll let you out."

The man grunted. "We'll see."

The column snaked down toward the crossroads. It was an impressive sight. A mounted troop rode ahead under drifting pennants. They were as large and purposeful as the Nockmaar troopers Willow had seen earlier, but far less sinister. They seemed more like hunters than warriors, lightly armed and clad in the skins of the forest, and there was a wild freedom in the grace with which they rode.

The man in the cage laughed quietly. "Airk's men!" he said.

"Wh-who are they?"

"Galladoorn scouts. Best horsemen in the world."

"Will they hurt us?"

"Not unless you're from Nockmaar, Peck. Then..." He made a rattling sound and drew his thumb across his throat.

Behind the cavalry came ranks of foot soldiers, keeping pace to the tap of drums. They, too, were lightly armed. Although more disciplined than the cavalry, and obviously weary from a long march, they were talking and laughing jovially. One of them struck up a song, the drummers picked up the rhythm, and a moment later the whole column was singing.

Officers rode on the flanks, and as they approached the crossroads, several of them broke off and galloped forward to confer.

"They look like good Daikinis to me, Willow. As good as you can expect."

"Better than *him*, that's true." Willow nodded. "The High Aldwin must have been thinking of them."

They crept out together. "Sir," Meegosh said. "Excuse me..."

The officers glanced at them and turned back to their maps.

"Sir?" Willow tugged at a stirrup and a horse shied. The rider cursed and flung his foot out, brushing Willow's head. "Get back, Peck! This is no place for Nelwyns! Off to the woods with you!"

Willow scampered back, choking in dust.

"Well, well! What do you have there, my little friend?"

He whirled around. Another officer had come up beside them, unnoticed in the noise and confusion. He rode a handsome bay mare. Mauve plumage shimmered on his helmet, and his armor glinted in the new sun. Behind him on a smaller horse, a standard-bearer carried the leather pennant of the commander in chief.

"A . . . a baby, sir. A Daikini baby. Will you take her, please? Will you look after her?"

The big man leaned down and gently touched the child on the forehead. He smiled bitterly through his red beard and shook his head. "We're going into battle, little ones. That's no place for her. Find a woman to look after her. And look after yourselves as well. If I were you, I'd put some distance between myself and this place." He reined his horse smartly, and was about to gallop back to the column.

"Airk! Airk Thaughbaer!"

"What? Who's there?" The officer peered into the shadows of the scaffolding, where the shout had come from, and then trotted his mount in under the overhanging structure. Willow and Meegosh followed. "Madmartigan! So! Well, I knew that you'd end up in a squirrel's cage, sooner or later."

"What are you doing this far north, Airk? Where are you leading these poor fools?"

"To the river," Airk Thaughbaer growled. "Nockmaar has destroyed Galladoorn."

"The *castle*?"

Airk nodded, walking his horse around the cage. "Burned it to the ground. Bavmorda's on a rampage. Her troops are headed south, killing everything. We're going to try to stop them at the River Troon."

"Let me out of here! Give me a good sword and I'll fight for you!"

"Ha!" Airk smiled bitterly and shook his head. "After that stunt at Land's End? That was the last straw, Madmartigan."

"But this is different! Galladoorn! Bavmorda *really* destroyed it?"

"To the ground. And killed everyone."

"Let me out, Airk! Give me a sword!"

The big man laughed sourly, wheeling his horse away. "You'll get out, Madmartigan, one way or another. I know you. As for giving you a sword, I've done that once too often. No, I need good men now. Men like those. Men I can rely on."

"You can rely on me, Airk. If . . ."

"To save your own skin, oh yes! You can always be relied upon for that, but for nothing more. Goodbye, Madmartigan. I don't think we'll meet again."

"Airk . . ." But the commander was gone, galloping with his standard-bearer back up to the head of the column.

When the last of the baggage wagons had rumbled past, and the rearguard cavalry had trotted out of sight, when the noise had faded and the dust had begun to settle, Willow asked, "Is that *true*, Madmartigan? What he said about you? That you look after only yourself?"

"What? Certainly not! For one thing, I love children. That little girl, for instance. Why, I . . ."

"I don't think you know the first thing about babies."

Madmartigan leered. He dangled a long arm through the cage, waving Willow closer. "The truth is," he said as the Nelwyn edged toward him, careful to stay out of reach, "the truth is I never married." He shrugged. "Warrior. No time. But I know a lot of women who know about babies. Ah yes, my friend, a *lot* of women."

"And what would you do if you were responsible for her?"

"Why, see that she was properly looked after, of course! See that she was in capable hands. Just like my own daughter. Right, cutie?" The baby giggled at Madmartigan.

Willow frowned.

"Psst! Willow!" Meegosh beckoned him back to the edge of the shade. "What are you *waiting* for? Do what you have to do and let's get *out* of here!"

"I don't *have* to do anything, Meegosh. I just don't trust him."

Meegosh looked to the east, where the army of Airk Thaughbaer had vanished. He looked west, down the empty road. He looked at Willow. He spread his arms. "Who else *is* there?"

Willow sighed heavily. He took out the braid of

hair Kiaya had given him and twined it through his
fingers. It didn't help. If anything, it made things
worse—made him feel more homesick for Kiaya and
the children.

He tucked it back into his pocket with the three
magic acorns. He looked at the child, who was laughing softly. "All right, Meegosh. You win. Madmartigan gets her."

In an instant Meegosh had hacked the lock off the
cage and Madmartigan had scrambled free, hopping
in a wild dance out into the sun.

"I thought so!" Willow said. "He's running away.
See?"

The man pranced in a big circle, whooping, kicking and stretching, slapping his rear end. The remnants of his clothes flapped like a scarecrow's tatters.
In a minute he was back. He patted both Nelwyns on
the back so hard they staggered. "Ah, my little
Pecks, you won't regret this. No sir! Madmartigan
remembers who his friends are. And as for *this* little
lady, you'll have no more worries about her. I guar-
antee."

The child shrieked in laughter as he lifted her.

"See? She loves me, don't you, little darling?"

"Here's her milk bladder."

"Any milk in there?"

"It's for *her*!"

"Of course it's for her. And I'll feed her well,
never fear."

"And keep her warm and dry."

"Of course."

"And clean."

"Certainly."

Madmartigan knelt down so that Meegosh could fasten the papoose-basket on his back, and Willow tucked the child into it and kissed her. A tear rolled down his cheek. "Bye."

"So long, boys." Madmartigan stood up and waved. "You've done the right thing. Go on home, now." He gestured south, toward Nelwyn Valley. "If you hurry you can catch your friends. No worries. Just forget about this little lady. Bye now. Bye." He was already marching north, whistling a soldier's tune.

"Take good care of her!"

"Word of honor!" Madmartigan shouted back.

"Come on, Willow." Meegosh tugged at Willow's sleeve. "Let's get away from this place. Let's go home."

Willow nodded, brushing tears away. Hastily they gathered their packs and turned south, crossing the road along which the Daikini army had just passed. "I *hope* we did the right thing, Meegosh."

"We did. We *did*. You'll see. When we get home, the High Aldwin will be waiting for you. Maybe he'll come out of a stone, or out of the river, or even out of one of your fields, Willow! And he'll ask, 'Boys, did you follow my instructions? Did you go all the way to the crossroads?' We'll say, 'Yes, High Aldwin.' 'And did you give the child to the first Daikini you met?' We'll say, 'High Aldwin, the first Daikini we met was very ragged and dirty. He was a scoundrel. He was imprisoned for having done something terrible.' The High Aldwin will say, 'Never mind all that. That was just a *test*. Did you give him the child?' And when we tell him that we did, why, we'll be heroes, Willow!"

"I don't want to be a hero. I just want to go home."

"You'll be the High Aldwin's Apprentice, at the very least."

"You think so?"

"No question! Just think, no more tricks with feathers! No more hiding pigs inside your coat! You'll learn real magic, Willow! Real sorcery! And as for me, why, I'll be a foreman at the mine!"

Real sorcery! Willow touched the acorns nestled in his pocket beside Kiaya's braid, the acorns that he had had no chance to use. Real sorcery! And, if he had that power, what would he use it *for*? Why, for good, of course. But what *was* good? What a hard question! On one hand, it would be good to charm his fields so that they would produce splendid crops every year, effortlessly; but, on the other hand, that would be merely selfish. On one hand it would be good to change Burglekutt so that he would not bully people anymore and steal the profits of their hard work; but, on the other hand, to do so might be to meddle in affairs of the soul which were better left to other powers. What dilemmas! But, surely, if one were a sorcerer with real power, it would not be wrong to destroy the Death Dogs! It would not be wrong to destroy the evil power of Nockmaar, which spread like a pestilence from the north over the whole land. Surely *that* could not be wrong. But how could one small Nelwyn be certain, even of that? Willow touched the acorns in his pocket, and as he did so he heard the High Aldwin's voice speaking to him again, echoing as if out of labyrinthine caverns deep in the earth. *Trust your own heart. Trust what you feel most deeply. . . .*

Willow stopped suddenly. "Meegosh, I'm going back!"

"What?"

But Willow had no time to tell Meegosh that he now knew with absolute clarity that he should not have given the child to Madmartigan.

He did not have time even to turn around.

They had been crossing a meadow to the west of the road, hurrying because it was an exposed place. As Willow spoke, a huge shadow fell across them, and at the same moment a sound like wind rushing before a thunderstorm enveloped them. Out of it swirled high-pitched laughter, tiny shrieks of perverse glee.

They froze. They looked up.

A stately eagle drifted over them. Mounted on it, his toes clenched in the feathers between its wings, was a person even smaller than the Nelwyns. He was dark brown except for spikey white hair and brilliant jade-green eyes. The slit of his mouth was twisted into a malicious grin, and as he passed them he pointed down, laughing wildly.

"A *brownie*!" Meegosh moaned. "Oh no! And look what he's *got*!"

Willow had already seen, and the vision struck him cold. Gripped in the eagle's claws was a familiar basket, and inside, wrapped in Kiaya's little blanket, was the child.

"Behold Franjean!" the brownie piped. "Behold Franjean's prize!"

"No!" Willow shouted. "Come back! Put her down!" He threw down his pack and tore wildly back across the meadow, smashing into rocks and bushes. He wanted only to be under the bird if the baby fell. But the eagle stayed just ahead of him. Fluttering the tips of its wings it glided on, toward a deep woods at the meadow's edge. The brownie twisted on its back and thrust a bony finger at Willow, cackling. "Fool! Hurry, Peck fool, else you will miss the brownie feast!"

"Meegosh! Help me! We've got to get her!"

The eagle drifted low over the trees, disappearing.

"Come *on*, Meegosh!"

It was dark in the woods, so dark that Willow could see nothing as he raced out of the bright sunlight. He banged into a tree and reeled back, blinking. He heard nothing but the frantic rush of his own blood and the insane cackling of the brownie, up ahead.

"This way, Meegosh!"

A path led off to the right, toward the sound. They plunged along. Suddenly Meegosh cried out in pain, and in the same instant Willow felt sharp stings in his shoulder and neck. They burned like biting flies, but when he swatted and brushed at them he discovered they were actually tiny arrows, no bigger than his finger. Running, he pulled some out, but dozens more rained down on him, from the limbs of the great trees, from the scanty undergrowth, and with them came a maniacal chorus of shrieks, chortles, shouts, and cackles, as if Franjean had been magically and horribly transformed into hundreds of other brownies, all equally malicious. All around, Willow saw mean, sharp little faces in the shadows of the foliage. He saw bright and baleful green stares fixed on him. He saw tiny busy arms reaching into quivers, stringing bows, launching arrows.

"Hey! Ouch! Ow!" Meegosh shouted, and each cry brought delighted screams from the brownies. Some were jumping up and down on the larger branches, hooting.

"This way!" Willow shouted. They came to a fork in the path and he swung right, certain he heard Franjean's laughter just ahead. But a black net of ropes and vines hung there, ready to drop. "Back! Back! The other way!"

Stinging darts struck home. Brownies whooped and jeered. Back and around the corner the Nelwyns raced. An open path stretched ahead. "Come on, Meegosh! We'll soon be out of this. We can . . ."

Go up here and cut back, Willow meant to say, but he never had a chance. The broad path was a trap. Dug across it, cunningly concealed with moss and supple branches, lay a deep pit. The next thing Willow Ufgood knew, he had crashed through and was falling down, down into a cold, dark place. All the panic and confusion of the past few minutes became a spinning oval of light, and all the chattering of the brownies became Meegosh's wild cry of alarm as he too tumbled into the pit.

And then Willow Ufgood knew nothing more.

CHERLINDREA

"**I**'m Franjean, King of the World!"

Someone was standing on Willow's chest.

He tried to move and couldn't. He ached in every joint and muscle. He burned all over from arrow wounds. His head throbbed as if he'd been hammered with hardwood mallets. Cautiously, he opened his eyes.

The brownie that had been riding the eagle now crouched on his chest, prodding his nose with a tiny spear.

"Ow! Stop that!"

Cheering and chattering, the swarm of brownies no more than nine inches tall appeared out of nowhere and jabbed him in the toes and fingers. Crisscrossing ropes bound Willow securely to the ground, and he could turn his head only enough to see Meegosh lying beside him, moaning that his arm was broken.

"Oh, Willow," Meegosh groaned. "We're doomed! You know what brownies do! They pluck out your eyes! They cut off strips of you and cook them!"

"Right!" exclaimed Franjean, prancing on Willow's chest. "And that's just the beginning. After that we'll . . ."

"Where's the baby?"

"Quiet!" Franjean slapped Willow's nose. "I'm speaking! I! King of the World!"

The other brownies jeered. "Hear that? King of the World! Gets one eagle ride, and it goes to his head!"

"Silence! Respect!" Leaping up and down in a sudden frenzy, Franjean poked Willow's nose until finally Willow sneezed violently and blew him backward, head over heels. He ended up sitting dazed on Willow's belly. "Wretched Peck! I'll . . ."

Suddenly the glade lit up with eerie luminescence, sparkling and darting. It flowed off the undersides of the trees and showered back on Willow where he lay. It felt like healing rain.

"Behave yourself, Franjean!" The voice that spoke was wind-soft yet clear. Like silver. Like ice.

"Yes, Your Majesty!"

"What a miserable brownie you are! I ask you to bring the two Nelwyns to me, our guests, and what do you do? Hurl them into a pit! Strike them and abuse them! Tie them up!"

The other brownies shrank back, bumping into one another. "King of the World, huh, Franjean?" they whispered. "Kings aren't supposed to be frightened, Franjean. They're not supposed to tremble and shake!"

One of them shuffled over beside Willow's ear, a slack-jawed and big-eared simpleton of a brownie. "Know who that is? That's Cherlindrea! Franjean's in trouble, now. We're *all* in trouble. Your fault!"

"Who . . . who's Cherlindrea?"

But the brownie had no chance to answer before the radiant cloud surrounded him. Willow saw to his astonishment that it was composed of fairies, hundreds of fairies, each smaller than the smallest butterfly. Their laughter rang like tiny chimes. When they circled his head their touch soothed like spring water and his headache vanished. When they surrounded his body, the brownie ropes fell away. The arrow wounds ceased stinging, and the throbbing in his joints and muscles vanished.

Willow sat up. He stood.

Meegosh rose too, more slowly.

"You all right?"

Meegosh nodded, frowning at his arm, which had been miraculously trussed up in splints and a sling.

"Bring the Nelwyns to me," Cherlindrea said, her voice like crystal wind. Willow and Meegosh felt the gentle pressure of hundreds of tiny fairy hands. The brownie circle opened before them and they were led to the edge of the glade, where the radiance was so bright they had to cover their eyes. "Oh, I'm sorry," Cherlindrea said. The light dimmed. "Is that better?" It dimmed more, still more, until they could open their eyes again.

Cherlindrea, queen of the fairies, hovered above them. Willow gasped, she was so beautiful. The fairies of his imagination had all been *old*—wizened and sharp-nosed crones. In the tales his mother told, they were pests and busybodies, forever making life harder for Nelwyns, forever stealing and casting irksome charms on crops and livestock. But Cherlindrea was young. Her tiny body was graceful and perfectly proportioned, and her radiance emanated not from it alone—and from her wings, and from her flaxen hair—but also from a gentle smile.

Near her laughing on a bed of moss, lay the child.

"Thank goodness!" Willow said. He started forward to take her up, but Cherlindrea's brilliance suddenly intensified and he fell back. "The child is well, Willow Ufgood, and you may hold her. But first, hear what I say."

"H-how did you know my name?"

"Elora told me. Elora has told me all about you." The light subsided, and Willow saw that Cherlindrea was gazing at the child adoringly. "Elora Danan. She is a very special child, Willow. She is the daughter of the sun and the moon, and the rightful empress of all kingdoms."

"Then you will look after her?"

"Oh yes. We *all* must look after her."

"And we can go home, Meegosh and I."

"Meegosh may go. We shall see that he has safe escort home. But your journey has just begun, Willow Ufgood."

"But, please, you don't understand. I want to go back to my family. I'm worried about them. They need me!"

"Elora needs you. That is even more important. She has chosen you to be her guardian on the journey she must make."

"Chosen me! But how could she? She's an infant."

Cherlindrea laughed. "A very special infant." Her light glowed brighter, and Willow shielded his eyes. With a gentle motion, she raised the baby off her bed of moss and floated her toward Willow, laughing. He took her into his arms. Sparkling light touched the inside of the child's elbow. "She has the Sign, you see." Then for a moment Cherlindrea fragmented and vanished, and the glade was lit only by the soft glow of moonlight and the dancing radiance of the other fairies. When she returned she was carrying a wand, like a crooked twig.

"Now, Meegosh," Cherlindrea said, "the time has come for you to part from your friend and begin your journey home. I must give Willow his instructions and tell secrets that are for him alone. You are a good friend, Meegosh. You have served loyally, and you shall be rewarded."

"*Must* I go?"

"Yes, you must."

"But will it . . . be dangerous for Willow?"

"Very dangerous."

"Then why . . ."

The radiance throbbed. Meegosh covered his eyes. "All right. I'm sorry."

Willow took his friend's hand. "Good-bye, Meegosh. Thank you."

"Willow, I don't think you really have to do this. The High Aldwin . . ."

Willow glanced down at the smiling child. "If I don't do it, who will?"

"Well," Meegosh sighed, "be careful, then."

Willow nodded. "You must tell Kiaya and the children that I love them. And Meegosh, tell them we had a nice trip. Tell them the country around the Daikini crossroads is very pretty. Don't tell them what it's *really* like."

Meegosh laughed. "I won't have to with Burglekutt around. Everything will be twice as big and twice as scary as it really was."

"Look after them, Meegosh."

"I will."

"Promise?"

"Promise. Round the bend!"

"Round the bend."

"He's a donkey . . ."

"I'm your friend." Willow hesitated a moment, grinning. Their childish ritual brought good memories flooding back—memories of long summery days spent fishing along the shadowy banks of the Freen; memories of days when there were no urgencies, no responsibilities, no terrors; memories of boyhood.

He watched Meegosh head south into the forest, a little cloud of fairies surrounding him.

"He will be well looked after," Cherlindrea said. "Now, Willow Ufgood, your way lies to the north, where you must take Elora Danan."

"North! Even beyond the Daikini crossroads?"

"Far beyond. You must travel the old road. You must take this child to Tir Asleen."

"Tir Asleen!" Willow sat down suddenly. "Do you mean there really *is* a Tir Asleen?"

"Oh, yes."

"But I thought . . . I thought . . ."

"You thought it was only legend."

Willow nodded.

"No, Willow. Tir Asleen is real. You must take Elora Danan safely there. And you must take something else, as well."

"But what? *Why*?"

"Ah," the brownies said, nodding to each other. "The Question." All around Willow they drew closer and sat down, folding their legs and laying their spears and bows on the moss.

"Ohhh," sighed the fairies, "the Question, the Question." The chorus of their voices whispered like breath in crystal. All around Willow silvery clouds of them settled on flowers and drooping leaves.

Cherlindrea smiled. She laid her wand beside her. Her aura diminished so that Willow could see her clearly. She nodded, looking a little sadly at him. "Yes, of course, when you go into the Daikini world you must *know*, mustn't you? Well, to answer your question, and to show you what you face I must tell you a story. . . ."

Cherlindrea's Tale

Long ago, the high castle of Tir Asleen reigned over all those lands—south even farther than the Nelwyn Valley, east beyond Galladoorn, and westward to the sea. In those days the Earth was wild and good. There was room in it for all, and a multitude of plants and animals flourished on it, woven together in ways that no mortal may understand. Daikinis lived at peace with one another and permitted the small folk to go their ways undisturbed. Fairies, brownies, Nelwyns and elves all lived out their lives in harmony with each other and with men. There was no time then, but only the slow round of the days, only the turning of the seasons.

For many generations the kings of Tir Asleen had kept the order of this land, not by decree, but by the wise channeling of will, so that disputes were quelled as if by magic, and enemies found themselves sharing the same currents of Life. Then as now, of course, all things died, but in those days we understood better how all things were reborn.

As well as the kings of Tir Asleen, there were in those days others with special powers, powers sometimes far surpassing the High Aldwin's. Often they began as mere tricksters, performers of magic acts for their friends. They crafted many devices—hollow feathers, hanging sleeves, hidden pockets. Some aspired to rise above these things and touch the infinite power of the Great Mystery; they longed to become true sorcerers. Only a very few achieved this end.

The youngest ever to become a sorceress was Fin Raziel. She was a wondrous child. From her birth, all who attended upon her mother knew she participated in the Mystery, for the animals came to her. Deer and elk emerged from the forest at dusk and waited in the fields to pay her homage. Hawks and sparrows settled together in the boughs of firs and uttered soft cries of greeting when the nursemaid brought the child to the lighted window. Salamanders and frogs struggled up from the marshes to see her and gazed upon her with large eyes.

While she was still a child, she often went far from home, and for many days. Her parents had no fear for her, because they understood that she must follow the urgings of her heart, and they knew that no harm would come to her. Where she went, what she did, whom or what she saw—they never knew, for the child would never talk. Some said that before she was five she had made great journeys on the backs of eagles. Some said that before the age of ten she had travelled to the farthest reaches of the kingdom and had made a pilgrimage to the Western Islands, where ancient ruins lay glyph-covered in their fogs. Everyone understood that when Fin Raziel departed on her journeys, she had been summoned by true sorcerers. They knew that she was being nurtured in the Mystery, and shown how to find her Way. They knew too that she conversed with all the small folk of the lakes and forests—with the lords of the elves, with the high priests of the brownies, and with fairy queens. Cherlindrea saw her often in those days and watched her grow. She was a radiant and beautiful child, pure as a still pond. . . .

But she was a woman also, and a Daikini, and hence subject to all the Daikini whims and passions. Neither spells nor solemn warnings could protect her from those passions, for they lay within. As a sorceress she was sublime; as human she was vulnerable.

And so she fell—down into danger, down into love.

The young man was beautiful, and good, and a worthy mate. He was a prince of Tir Asleen and next in line for the throne. All the virtues of that royal house were his—courage, kindness, generosity, patience, and wisdom. He was handsome besides, with regal bearing, and the broad honest face of his family.

Splendid red hair distinguished him, as it did them all.

Imagine him at the festivals where he rode among his people on his white horse, or dismounted to stroll and feast with them, to bless their provender, and laugh with them at the games and plays. How splendid he was! No wonder the young Raziel should fall hopelessly in love with him.

When autumn came, her pursuit of the Way became a halting thing. She grew reluctant to make the journeys, loathe to respond to summonses. For many days at a time she would close off all contact with her mentors in sorcery, and they could not know what was happening to her. She became private and secretive. She moved out of the currents of the Mystery, and into Daikini life.

Joyous was all that Daikini world! Their prince had found a princess as lovely as he was handsome, one whose virtues matched his own, who equalled him in majesty, who would join him in a long and fruitful reign. When their engagement was announced, what a festival was held in the valley of Tir Asleen! They bedecked all the castle with flags and flowers. They covered the whole broad avenue with blossoms. People from all the kingdoms journeyed to bestow gifts and blessings.

But the wedding was not to be. In the valley of Tir Asleen dwelt another young sorceress—Bavmorda! She too had once shown great promise. Creatures of the forest night—whippoorwills and owls, night herons and flying squirrels—had all attended at her mother's chamber in the hour of her birth. Like Fin Raziel, Bavmorda had received nurturing and tutelage from Cherlindrea and others of the Mystery. Upon her they lavished all their wisdom, urging her to find her Way. How they came to regret that! For Bavmorda's power found tides deeper than Raziel's and blended into darker seas.

Now, the great Mystery is eternal and beyond all persuasions. Those who draw upon it, either Daikini or other-than-human, must control themselves, and see clearly what is good and what is evil. Some few abandon that control; they lust for power as a traveler in dry land longs for water. Bavmorda was one of these. Her Way drew heavily on the powers of the Mystery, but it was restricted by no conscience. Selfishness drove her. Passions dominated her. So cunning was she, and so strong, that she concealed her purposes even from all her mentors' divination until too late, until she had passed beyond control.

Then she became enormous; she became an enormity!

She did not change physically. If anything, she grew sweeter on the outside and more charming as her dark and inward power grew. But sorcerers of all degrees from across the realms could *feel* what was happening. They could feel each other's consternation and helplessness, each other's foreboding.

When Bavmorda turned her wiles on the young prince of Tir Asleen, what protection did he have against her? None! In no time she had spellbound him, in no time aroused his passions to meet her own. In no time she had lured him away from Fin Raziel. For days they would vanish together, making love in caves and bowers that only Bavmorda knew, while her minions kept watch, turning back all creatures from their natural haunts and habitats. In no time the young man was besotted by her. And, as she controlled him, so she controlled Tir Asleen!

Poor Raziel! Too late she realized what had happened—too late, when her own Way had eddied into backwaters and disuse. She rushed frantically from one sorcerer to the next, pleading for help, but there was nothing they could do. They could not lend themselves to such a cause, to a mere struggle of the passions.

At last Raziel came to Cherlindrea. She asked her for her wand to confront Bavmorda, to win her prince back again, and when Cherlindrea refused she flew into such a passion of furious and inconsolable weeping that the fairy queen withdrew, leaving watchers to make sure she did herself no harm. The following day, when she had grown calmer, Cherlindrea talked earnestly to her, although she knew that reasoning with Daikinis was difficult at the best of times. Sometimes they listen and sometimes they do not, and even when they do listen, no one can be sure they understand.

Cherlindrea consoled Fin Raziel as much as possible, and made her this promise: that if she returned to her discipline and pursued her Way, and if Bavmorda's power grew, then, when the time came to confront that power for the sake of Earth and its creatures, Fin Raziel would have Cherlindrea's wand.

So, in the fullness of time, Raziel resigned herself to the loss of her love. She returned to the nurturing of her sorcery, and in the years that followed she did much good. She grew sublime, though sad. She rose over passion to compassion. She became beloved of all creatures—a healer, a true sorceress.

Bavmorda married the prince, though the event caused small rejoicing, and there was only token attendance at the feast. They had a child, Sorsha, who was said to have her father's red hair and gentle disposition, though she was bent early to her mother's will. Not long afterward the old king and queen died together, and some whispered that Bavmorda's spells had helped them go.

So she became Queen of Tir Asleen, and Tir Asleen became a mournful place. Where once there had been festivity and laughter, now there was only gloom and mourning. The real Bavmorda emerged from pretense and loosed her baleful power. The young king sickened. Animals fell ill. Crops waned and died. Retainers suffered. Those who had freely waited on the old king and queen were now constrained to serve and punished harshly for trifling faults, their every action narrowly watched by Bavmorda's guards and minions. Grotesque and alien creatures inhabited the palace moat and cesspools, the dark corners of the orchard, and the hedgerows beside the wilting fields of maize.

Tir Asleen filled with whispers.

Then, when she had sucked what she could from the castle and its lands, Bavmorda abandoned them like a husk. In a nearby valley, where the volcano of Nockmaar smoked and fumed, she built a towering new fortress. Much agony and grief its building caused. Many lives it took. It rose a dread, grim place—invulnerable. Its denizens were such creatures as only a will utterly depraved could summon into being.

When she withdrew to this place, Bavmorda surrounded Tir Asleen with a maze so convoluted that no one ever found their way back to that castle. The young king was never seen again. The child, Sorsha, Bavmorda took with her, to raise in her own manner. They say the little girl wailed so pathetically on the journey that the very birds mourned and drooped their wings as the drear procession passed.

Fin Raziel, when she protested Bavmorda's act, was defeated in sorcerers' combat and banished to an island in the center of a great lake in the north, where she has been imprisoned ever since. . . .

"And there, Willow Ufgood, you must go. You must take to Fin Raziel the wand which she requested long ago, for the time has come to use all means to challenge the power of Bavmorda."

"But . . . but Cherlindrea, how do you *know*?"

"Because of this child, Willow. Here is the Sign where Fin Raziel's prophecy said it would be. She is the child promised long ago, the child who will restore Tir Asleen and cause the downfall of Nockmaar."

"But why don't *you* take the wand to Fin Raziel? You have magical powers."

The fairy queen shook her head, smiling sadly. "I wish I could, but my presence cannot extend beyond my woods. Besides, the child has chosen you, and you have powers, too."

"Me? But I'm just little. I'm small even for a Nelwyn! This is a task for a warrior! For a whole army!"

"I cannot make you go, Willow. The final choice is yours. I must tell you again that the task is very dangerous. Bavmorda's troops are rampaging, searching for the child. If she is found in your presence, at least you will perish instantly. . . ."

"At *least*!"

". . . at worst, you will suffer with Elora Danan the Ritual of Obliteration."

"The Rit—What's *that*!"

The light of all the fairies dimmed. *"Worse, worse than death!"* they whispered.

"Far worse," Cherlindrea murmured. "It is the wiping-out of all you were since Earth began, of all that you are, of all that you have been.

Willow shuddered, wrapping both arms around Elora. "No!"

"Everything! So, the risks are very great, and I cannot make you accept them. I can tell you only that if you undertake this task you must bear my wand to the Lake of Fin Raziel and give it to the great sorceress herself." Cherlindrea leaned forward and offered the crooked shaft.

Willow swallowed.

Still trembling, he stepped forward and accepted it.

There was an instantaneous burst of radiance around him, the hum of fairy exultation, and the cool touch of myriad fairy kisses.

Cherlindrea smiled. "Remember," she said, beginning to vanish before his eyes, fragmenting into crystalline points of light, "you must give the wand only to Fin Raziel."

As Cherlindrea faded, so did the sparkling light of the fairies. It flowed like mercury in all directions back into the forest, together with the tinkling of their laughter, and Willow found himself alone with Elora in the center of a moonlit glade, surrounded by murmuring brownies.

Only one fairy remained, asleep under a drooping leaf. The large-eared brownie who had spoken to Willow earlier crept over and sprinkled silvery dust on her out of a tiny pouch.

"Rool!" Franjean said, bustling up, "where did you get that Dust of Broken Heart?"

"Found it! There!" He pointed to a hollow tree.

"Uh, I mean there!" He pointed to a little cave at the edge of the glade.

"Stole it, you mean! Give it to me!" Franjean snatched the pouch and tied it to his belt just as the fairy awoke, staring at him adoringly. Arms stretched to embrace him, she fluttered up to him, murmuring endearments.

"No!" Franjean squeaked. "Back! Help! Get her away!"

Cackling, one of the brownies doused her with water from a pitcher plant, and the little fairy fled muttering into the woods, her ardor cooled.

The incident caused much merriment at Franjean's expense. The brownies chortled and punched each other, pointing at him. With as much dignity as he could muster, he bowed to Willow. "Peck, I mean, Sire, I am to be your guide to the Lake of Fin Raziel."

"What? But you're the one who stabbed me in the nose!"

"I know, Sire." Franjean's green eyes twinkled mischievously at the memory. "Before I knew your mission. Now, you have been chosen by Elora Danan. Now, Cherlindrea has appointed us to guide you, Rool, and me."

"Rool?"

"Me! Me!" The grinning, big-eared brownie hopped up and down, waving both hands.

Willow took a deep breath. "When do we leave?"

"Now, Peck. I mean, Sire. Beyond the Woods of Cherlindrea, the way is very dangerous."

Rool nodded wide-eyed agreement. "Trolls! Brigands! Death Dogs!"

"We should travel at night. We should begin this night. Now."

"But the child . . ."

"She's been fed," Franjean said. "Fairies did that. Come!" He started northward, beckoning.

Rool followed, waving happily to his friends with both hands.

"Farewell, Rool!" they shouted in great merriment. "Try to stay on the path! Don't forget to eat, Rool! Look after the King of the World!"

Sighing, Willow tucked the wand into the long pocket of his coat where, once upon a time, he had hidden a piglet at the Nelwyn fair. He touched the three magic acorns and the braid of Kiaya's hair concealed near his breast. He picked up the papoose-basket with Elora Danan inside and followed his two guides into the forest.

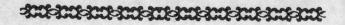

HILDA

Dawn found them north of the woods.

The landscape was the bleakest and most awful Willow had seen. Great fires had raged there, leaving charred rock and cadaverous forests. No flowers grew in that place; no birds sang. Noises echoed down sepulchral valleys, distorted and magnified like the groans of Earth itself.

Willow shivered. The brownies communicated by signs, speaking rarely and then only in whispers although, for miles around, they could see no other living creature.

They kept to the high ground; Willow was soon to wish they had been even higher.

Near noon, Rool crouched suddenly and hissed, slapping Willow on the leg. "Death below!"

They took cover in a shallow crevasse with charred shrubbery in front. Cautiously, Willow peered through this screen and down the slope. All morning weird sounds had echoed and rebounded, surrounding them with the clamor of a ghostly battle. Now at last the real battle swirled into view. Clutching Elora close, Willow watched in horror. The remnants of the majestic force he had seen pass through the Daikini crossroads were being driven down the valley in a rout. All semblance of order had vanished. The banners had fallen, the baggage train had been captured. Only the pennant of the commander was still aloft where Airk Thaughbaer and his standard-bearer, besieged by a sea of Nockmaar troops, fought desperately. All around them men died, pinned by lances, hacked by swords, crushed under thrashing hooves.

So horrified was Willow, and so loud was the clash of battle, that he was unaware of the approach of Nockmaar horsemen behind him until he heard a harsh bellow.

"No quarter! Kill the scum!"

Willow cowered over the child, expecting to be struck down the next instant, but when no blow fell on him he peeked around.

The man who had spoken was mounted on an enormous black stallion. The crimson ensign of the Nockmaar commander fluttered from the staff of his standard-bearer. A purple cape drifted from his shoulders. Black plate and chainmail covered his thick torso and his huge arms and legs. Splashes of blood stained his sword and gauntlet. But the most terrifying aspect of this man was not his size. Where a human head should have rested there rose a massive skull, a thing with glowering sockets and an immense, protruding jaw ringed with fangs. A scrap of rank black hair clung to it. A pair of iron horns arced from its forehead.

As Willow stared, the rider lifted off this terrible helmet to reveal a face almost as terrible—a face thickened and brutalized by savagery. A face scarred and broken. A face beyond all pity.

He was oblivious to Willow and the brownies. His gaze was riveted on the battle in the valley below. "Galladoorn scum!" he growled. "Clean them up! Charge when ready!"

"Yes, General Kael!"

One of the two adjutants with him wheeled his mount and trotted back along the ridge, shouting commands; the other raised a ram's horn to his bearded lips and blew such a resonant, throbbing blast that Willow felt the very stones quiver under him. Over the rise trotted a legion of fresh Nockmaar cavalry, dressing themselves in battle-order as they came. When their captain's sword arm dropped they surged down the slope and over the wretched Galladoorn survivors. The howl they uttered—pure blood lust—turned Willow cold.

Death Dogs charged with them, hot for the throats of men.

Willow cowered while the charge went past and

over him. The child shrieked such a long and piercing
scream that he thought they would surely be discovered, but even that cry was lost amid the cries of
dying horses and dying men, and the clang of steel on
steel.

As soon as the last rider had swept down into the
valley, the brownies were on their feet, tugging at
Willow. "This way! Hurry!" Choking in dust, they
clambered to higher ground and lost themselves at
last among great boulders, where horses could not
follow. Death Dogs might have tracked them there,
but they were busy with richer work below. They had
no noses, then, for two brownies, one small Nelwyn,
and a baby.

Gradually the sounds of slaughter faded. Gradually Willow and the brownies found their way down
through tortuous goat tracks among the crags, back
onto greener slopes. Birds sang again, drifting among
the trees. Gradually Willow stopped shaking enough
to comfort the child.

"A-awful!" he said, sinking down at the base of a
great tree.

Franjean's jade eyes glinted. "And they call brownies cruel! I tell you, Peck, no brownie would be part
of what you've seen today."

"Un-unh," Rool grunted, shaking his large ears,
eyes sorrowful. "Only Nockmaars kill. Only Galladoorns. Only..."

"Only the big people," Willow said. "Daikinis."

The brownies nodded.

Gradually their horror and fear subsided. They stayed safe in the tall woods until the exhausted child fell asleep in Willow's arms, and then they started down through lengthening shadows toward a lush valley in the distance. Lights twinkled there, although the western hillsides were washed with sun. "We've got to find food for her," Willow said.

Franjean nodded. He pointed to the lights. "An inn."

Three hours more they walked, down into darkness. Rain began, a steady drizzle that soaked them through and made it impossible for Willow to keep Elora dry. Wet and hungry and miserable, she wept pitifully, and by the time they emerged from the forest and reached the inn, Willow was not just worried about her, he was alarmed. "We've got to get her dried and warm," he said.

Franjean nodded, looking skeptically at the inn ahead. "You might do it here, Peck, if you keep your wits about you. But it's no place for brownies, I can tell you that!"

Willow's heart sank. It was no place for a Nelwyn, either. The inn hunkered into a hillside at a bend in the muddy road. It was a sprawling and ramshackle structure, with two long balconies hanging over the stableyard. Its thatched roof drooped, moldy and rotten. Raucous shouts and laughter spilled out of the banquet hall on the second floor. Dishes smashed. Fiddles and bagpipes played a lurching song. Even as Willow watched, two tattooed Pohas, snarling and grappling, sprawled through the door, fell over the railing, and plunged into the manure pile outside the stable. A Nockmaar deserter followed them, so drunk that when the huge man holding him by the collar let him go, he skidded down the steps bawling hysterically, loose as a rag doll. The bouncer on the balcony growled something unintelligible and shook his fist. Black hair hung over his ears and eyes. A thick beard brushed against an apron stiff with grease and grime. He growled again and lumbered back inside, bumping against another patron who, with a frowsy barmaid, was heading for one of the rough lodgings farther along the balcony. Underneath, tethered mules and horses stamped and shivered in the rain.

Willow shivered, too. This was a nest of cutthroats and brigands, no place for brownies, Nelwyns, or for the child in his arms. Still, he had to have food and shelter.

He took a deep breath and trudged down toward the inn. Franjean and Rool scampered up his clothing and dove into the coverings of the empty papoose-basket.

Through the muck of the yard he went, up the stairs, and into the main hall. The place was hot, noisy, and incredibly foul. Tallow stumps guttered in crude chandeliers. Swaggering louts and ruffians clanked tankards, arm-wrestled, reeled on tabletops. At the edges of the room, a few families huddled, travelers who had been caught at nightfall with no

other shelter. Watchfully, they munched the coarse
bread of that place and drank goat's milk from
earthen jugs. Willow pressed close to the wall in the
shadows, edging toward the nearest family. He tried
to be as inconspicuous as possible, but he had not
gone far before a drunken Poha spotted him.

"What's *this*? A Nelwyn, by the gods! A Peck!"

Another laughed harshly, thumping his fork on the
table. "Just in time! Just when we need meat!"

"Spit him!" shouted a third, lunging at Willow
with his dagger. "Throw 'im on the coals!"

Willow dodged and scrambled away between legs,
under chairs and tables, and the three let him go with
more laughter, quaffing their ale. Elora began to
shriek again, and he tried to hush her, although his
heart was racing. A boot kicked him and he sprawled
in a corner, stunned.

"*Get up!*" Franjean whispered from the basket.
"Get us out of here!"

"Oooooo!" Rool's head popped out of the blan-
ket, eyes wide at the sight of a buxom barmaid.
"Look at *her*! Franjean, quick! The Dust of Broken
Heart!"

"No! Get back, you fool! Get down! You can't
have it!"

"Yes!"

"No!"

"Ha! Got it!"

"Give it back, Rool!"

But Rool was already scrambling onto the edge of

the basket, gaze fixed on the barmaid, who was delivering jugs of ale to a nearby table. He pulled open the pouch of magic dust just as Willow heaved himself to his feet.

"Look out!" Franjean shouted, holding on. Rool toppled to the floor. Dust from the pouch spilled out into his eyes, and when he opened them again he found himself in love with a yellow cat crouched under the table. "Oooo," he crooned. "You're so *beautiful*!"

The cat was a tom, a rangy veteran of many brawls and scuffles. He was missing one ear, one eye, his tail, and two claws from his right forefoot. He fixed Rool with his good eye, spat, and clouted him with a left that sent him sprawling. He scrambled frantically up into Willow's pocket.

Willow edged close through the noise and confusion to a low table where a family sat munching pigs' knuckles. They were churlish folk. The mother and father glanced his way and kept chewing, but the son, a lout of ten or eleven, stopped and stared at Willow with a malicious grin.

"Excuse me. Could you spare a little milk? For the baby?"

Still grinning, the lad pushed a pitcher of goat's milk close enough for Willow to almost reach, then jerked it away. He chortled, wiping his mouth with a greasy hand. Again he pulled the jug close, but this time when Willow reached for it he tipped it and

slopped thick milk across the table and into Willow's
face.

"Thank you," Willow said, mopping the milk up
with his shirt tail while he kept a sharp eye on the
boy. "Very kind."

Then, as he put the end of his shirt into Elora's
mouth, the boy kicked him. Willow staggered back
against the wall so hard that the rotten boards gave
way and he fell through. He had no time even to cry
out before he was dropping into another room, hearing the guttural laughter of the boy's parents as he
fell. He shut his eyes and held Elora tight, braced for
the impact, hoping only to land on his back and so
cushion the child. He was ready for any landing—on
bricks, on timbers, even on the edges of mangers or
the tines of hayforks.

But he hit something soft. He bounced.

He opened his eyes. He had landed on a straw
mattress in the innkeeper's own bedroom. By dim
candlelight he saw clothes, men's and women's, hung
on hooks on the wall. A ring of keys dangled from a
peg near the door. Sounds from the revelry above
drifted through a high window, under which stood a
washstand. Near it, two women were hurriedly getting dressed.

"A Peck!" one of them exclaimed, pointing at
Willow. Her voice was curiously hoarse. She was a
large, big-breasted woman in an ample mauve gown,
one fold of which she pulled up to hide her face. A
shawl covered her head.

"Don't worry about *him*," said the other. "Hurry up! Llug's coming! My *husband*'s coming!" She was struggling into her skirt and blouse, kicking her petticoats under the bed, and trying to straighten her disheveled blond hair, all at once.

"Peck!" said the big woman, laughing oddly. "How do I look, little Peck?" She came close, grinning, packing thick powder onto her face.

"Madmartigan!"

"None other! Stick close to Madmartigan now, small friend. Nelwyns should keep clear of angry husbands." He snatched Willow off the bed and set him on the floor behind him. "What's *this*?" Franjean and Rool had stuck out their heads. "You're crawling with brownies!"

"Brownies!" the innkeeper's wife screamed. "I *hate* brownies!"

The door burst open and Llug stomped in, rolling massive shoulders. He stared at the rumpled bed and at his rumpled young wife. He glared at Madmartigan and at Willow cowering behind him with the child. He roared, "What the hell's all this?"

"This?" his wife said. "Why, Llug dear, this is my cousin, Hilda. She just arrived."

"*Hilda?*"

"Yes," Madmartigan squeaked, batting his eyelashes. "Just arrived."

Llug wiped his mouth. He leered at Madmartigan's bulging chest. He shambled forward, groping.

"Pecks!" Madmartigan exclaimed, bending suddenly and snatching Elora from Willow. "They make terrible nursemaids!" He pressed the child to his bosom.

"Here!" Willow jumped up and down. "Give her back!"

"Too excitable, you see."

Llug kept advancing, groping at Madmartigan's blouse. He snorted. A little drool dribbled off his chin.

"Charming," Madmartigan said. "You have a lovely husband, my dear, but we must be on our way, mustn't we, Peck." He dragged Willow with him by the collar. "Off to our room to feed the child. Don't bother to come with us, Llug. We can find . . ."

A Nockmaar trooper blocked the doorway. More crowded down the hall. They barged in, large and dark, smelling of sweat and wet horses. The whole inn had fallen silent. No more drunken shouts and laughter. No more revelry. Only the tread of heavy boots and the clear, stern voice of a young woman: "Check them *all*. Every child. And look carefully. The mark is very small."

"What are you *doing*?" Llug's wife pressed her knuckle against her mouth. "We're not hiding anyone."

The troopers laughed harshly. "I hope not," one of them said. "If the princess finds the child under your roof, that'll be the end of it *and* you."

Sorsha strode in. She looked cool, calm, dispassionate. Wisps of red hair spilled out around the edges of her helmet. In one glance she took in the whole situation. She pointed to Llug and gestured with her riding crop. "Get him away from her!"

Three troopers shoved the big man back against the wall, where he continued to leer at Madmartigan.

"Now then," Sorsha said, coming close to Madmartigan, "are you the mother of that child?"

"Certainly! Of course!" He had drawn a fold of the gown across his face and backed up as far as he could into the shadows.

Sorsha's eyes narrowed, searching his. "Uncover it!"

"No!" Willow leaped forward; she brushed him aside with her boot.

"Let me see it! I gave you an order, woman! Uncover that child *now*!" She grabbed for Elora, and Madmartigan flung out his arm, striking her across the throat and knocking her off balance. Her helmet clattered to the floor, and her long red hair tumbled free about her shoulders.

Madmartigan gasped.

Troopers surged forward, daggers at his throat, Sorsha waved them back. "You're very strong," she said, eying him. "*Very* strong. In fact, *you're not a woman*!" She pulled open Madmartigan's gown; two round bundles of rags tumbled out.

Llug growled. "*Not a woman!*" He shook off his captors and lunged. The blow he aimed at Madmartigan's head, with all the momentum of his charge behind it, hit the lieutenant beside Sorsha. Blood spurted. The lieutenant struck back, and the two men went down together, grappling. Madmartigan ducked under a stabbing lance, walloped a Nockmaar trooper in the belly, and shouldered his way through the door. "Outside, Peck!" he shouted. "The stables!"

"Hold on!" Willow said to Franjean and Rool. In one bound he was on the washstand. In another, he grabbed the windowsill and scrambled out onto the balcony. Just ahead of him, Madmartigan swung over the railing and slid down a rope, still clasping Elora in one arm. "Come on!" he shouted to Willow. He ran for the stables and the Nockmaar horses, only to find his way blocked by three troopers. They advanced, lances at the ready.

Madmartigan spun around.

In the gray dawn, a farm wagon came creaking along the road toward the inn. Skirts flying, Madmartigan dashed for it and vaulted into the seat. He pushed off the startled farmer, seized the reins, and snapped them, jolting the horse into action. Baskets of bread and cheese went flying. The wagon swooped in under the balcony. "Come on, Peck! Jump!"

Willow jumped, landing on the hay in the box of the wagon. The brownies spilled out of his pocket.

"Here! Take the baby! Put her under the seat! We'll have some fun, now!" Laughing wildly, Madmartigan whipped the horse into a snappy trot, then into a gallop. Franjean and Rool scrambled under the seat with Elora. Willow braced himself and looked back.

Sorsha shouted orders from the balcony. In the muddy yard troopers were mounting up. The first away jerked too sharply on his reins and his horse twisted and fell, legs thrashing, blocking the others.

In seconds, however, Nockmaar cavalry were in hot pursuit of the bounding wagon.

"How many?" Madmartigan shouted.

"Three!" Willow groaned. "No, four! And a war chariot!"

Madmartigan laughed. "Nothing to it! I thought for a minute we were in trouble!"

They raced north. The road soon dwindled to a cart track, and then to a rough trail through the fields. The wagon bounced and clattered, slamming against boulders, banks, branches. The riders gained on them fast, with the light war chariot close behind. The lead trooper unlimbered his bow and notched an arrow into it. At full gallop, he took aim.

"Madmartigan! Look out! Look . . . !"

The wagon hit a rock and bounded into the air. Intended for Madmartigan, the shaft struck the heavy tailgate and drove right through the splintered wood before it stopped, its flanged steel head inches from Willow's belly. Willow gaped at it, paralyzed with horror.

Then the troopers themselves were on them. The archer flung away his bow and leaped into the box beside Willow. Another galloped abreast on the op-

posite side, drawing a bead between Madmartigan's
eyes. Madmartigan whooped, threw up the reins, somersaulted backward into the hay. For a split second
the horse slackened. The archer pulled ahead and
had to twist in his saddle. When he shot, his aim was
off enough to miss the sprawling Madmartigan and
hit the belly of the other Nockmaar trooper, who was
raising his dagger to plunge into Madmartigan's
heart.

In a flash Madmartigan was up. He tore a post
from the side of the wagon and clubbed the dying
man out over the tailgate. Then, clinging with one
hand, he leaned out to smash the bow out of the
archer's hands as he was stringing another arrow.
Snarling, the man dove off his horse and clutched at
Madmartigan's throat. Madmartigan yanked him forward and rolled back, kicking into his belly, vaulting
him up and over the side. "The reins, Peck! Hold
that horse!"

And then the third trooper was on him.

Willow clambered up into the seat and groped for
the flailing reins just as the wagon smashed into a
huge root. The bump jolted him out of the seat and
he went airborne, arching over the horse's rump and
down between the traces, close to the thrashing
hooves. He grabbed desperately. The traces were
slimy with mud. Twice he nearly fell before he managed to get a leg up and over and climb back into the
seat.

The fourth trooper was waiting for him. He had

just jumped into the wagon. Now, while his cohort fought Madmartigan, he braced himself, crouched, and jabbed at Willow with his lance. Willow dodged and dodged again under a second thrust. He grabbed a mallet off the seat and swung hard—a well-aimed blow to his opponent's groin. The man gasped and straightened up, just as they hurtled beneath a low branch. There was a sound like a belly flop and he vanished. A moment later, Madmartigan knocked his man out and under the wheels.

"Four down, Peck! Only the chariot, now!"

But the chariot was the most fearsome antagonist of all. Low, rugged, fast, curved knives flashing on its hubs, it was a formidable war machine. And the driver knew how to use it. Lashing his horses relentlessly, he narrowed the space between himself and the fleeing wagon. When he came within range, he chose a horrible weapon from the arsenal arrayed around him. This was a circlet of polished steel, whetted razor-keen on the outside edge. Driving with one hand, he spun this ring aloft, twirling it with his fingers on the flat inside, and let it go. His aim was perfect. Hurtling in, this round knife would have sliced Willow in half where he sat on the driver's seat, had not Madmartigan deflected it at the last instant with a blow of a lance. It angled up and over Willow's head, snipped off several finger-sized branches, and dropped into the forest.

Then the chariot itself was upon them. The driver had drawn a great sword and was raising it to strike when Willow braced both feet and hauled back as hard as he could on the reins.

"Whoa! *Whoa!*"

The old farm horse reared back, half-crazed. The wagon halted abruptly. The chariot swooped by with the knives in its wheel hubs slashing air. A hundred yards ahead, the driver swerved out onto a broad meadow, turned, and came back.

"Down! Under the seat!" Madmartigan said.

Willow did what he was told, joining Elora and the two terror-stricken brownies on the floor of the wagon. He heard the terrible rumble of the machine approaching. He heard the snorting of the horses and the bloodcurdling battle cry of the Nockmaar driver. He saw Madmartigan brace himself solidly on the floor of the wagon and lift the lance. He saw him balance it, aim it, hurl it. He saw him fling up his arms in victory. None of the sounds changed, except the shriek of the driver. That cry became more awful, became the snarl of an enraged doomed man. The lance had driven clean through the center of his chest. As the chariot swept past, Willow saw the driver with his arms flung high. He saw him hurtle on that way for a hundred yards before the chariot veered to the right, struck a rock, and crashed. The horses tore out of their traces and galloped wildly away.

Madmartigan laughed, clapping Willow on the back. "Well done, Peck! Out now! Hurry up! Here come some more!" He scooped Franjean and Rool up in one hand and Elora in the other and kicked the side of the wagon hard. "Giddup!"

The horse bolted off and the little party scrambled into the undergrowth. A few moments later another squad of Nockmaar troops passed at full gallop, intent on the dust of the fleeing wagon. Sorsha led them. She rode easily, mounted on Rak, and her lips were parted in a small smile. She was enjoying this chase. She had left her helmet behind in the inn, and her long red tresses flowed free in the wind.

"Come on, my little friends," Madmartigan said when they had passed. "We can't stay here. As soon as they find out that wagon's empty they'll be back. Up in the hills, that's the safest place for us."

They climbed, and before long they were so lost in the dense forest of the slopes that no horseman could have found them. "We've got to stop," Willow said at last. "We've got to feed Elora. This is no way to treat a baby, Madmartigan. No way at all!"

But Madmartigan kept going till noon. Then they came to a cool glade, where a clean spring tumbled out of the hillside and the sun filtered through high leaves. Here they washed and rested. But the child was hungry, unsatisfied with water. "She needs milk," Willow said, as her restive whining became sobs.

"You're a magician." Franjean looked at him with bright eyes. "You've got Cherlindrea's wand. Get her some."

Willow slipped his hand into the deep pocket of his coat and touched the wand. It felt hot and cold, dry and wet, trembling with energy. It felt as big as all the green Earth, and Willow felt very, very small. "I don't know..." he said uncertainly. "You know, I'm not *really* a sorcerer."

"You don't have to be," Madmartigan said. "Look."

A doe stood in the dappled shadows, her newborn fawn at her side. Perhaps she had been there all along. Perhaps she had just arrived, summoned by Elora's cries. In any case, she came forward placidly and offered her milk to the child. When Elora had fed, the doe and her fawn vanished back into the woods.

Rool gaped.

"Never seen anything like it," Franjean said.

"Now *that*," Madmartigan said, laughing softly, "is a special child."

"I *told* you!" Willow said. "Why do you think I didn't want to give her to you back there at the crossroads? What a fool I was!"

"*What?*" Madmartigan spread his arms. "She's here, isn't she? I just saved her life five or six times!"

"Yes, but back at the crossroads you gave her to *brownies*!"

"Here! Wait a minute!" Franjean bristled.

"I didn't give her to those brownies. They stole her!"

Rool cackled. "Followed you! Waited till you got to the stream and put her down while you got washed!"

"Anyway, we had orders," Franjean said. "Cherlindrea commanded us. That should be obvious, Madmartigan, even to you! You think eagles just happen along whenever you want one?"

"Cherlindrea's a meddler."

Franjean turned red. He pointed. "Her meddling saved your skin! Two months ago. Down at Blackstorm Ford!"

Madmartigan rubbed his chin. "That was an elk, not an eagle."

"Doesn't matter! We got you out of a tight scrape. And this is all the gratitude we get. Thankless lout!"

"Lout!" Rool nodded, maneuvering behind Franjean, shaking his small fist. "Just want to save your own skin!"

"Look, if I just wanted to save my own skin, you wouldn't be here. You'd be meat for Death Dogs." Deftly, Madmartigan rebraided one of his long locks that had come loose during the chase. He tore off the upper half of the dress and belted on the skirt. "If you really want to help you'll find me some proper clothes. And a *sword*! Will you do that?"

Franjean folded his arms and shook his head. "You're reckless."

"Drive wagons too fast," Rool said.

Willow nodded. "And you don't know how to look after babies."

"I never said I did!"

"Yes, you did! You promised. . . ."

"I said I knew lots of *women* who . . ." Madmartigan stood up suddenly. "Look, I don't need to be pestered by a bunch of gnomes. I've got to find some *people*! And a sword!"

"Gnomes!" the brownies flustered. "Did you hear what he called us? Gnomes! We don't even have beards!"

"So long, skinny." Madmartigan tickled Elora under the chin. "You're not a bad kid, despite the company you keep."

"She's *not* skinny! Is she?"

"She certainly is. Look at her arms. Like sticks. One thing I know about babies is that you gotta feed them. So long, Peck." He strode off into the dusk, skirts swinging.

"Good riddance!" Franjean said when he had gone.

Rool nodded vigorously. "Better without him." A Death Dog howled in the far distance, on the edge of approaching night. "...I think!"

"We'll be all right." Franjean bustled about, gathering sticks for a fire. "They've lost the scent. Don't worry, Peck, I'll look after you and the little one. We don't need that stupid Daikini."

"But he *is* a good warrior. . . . Do you know him?"

"Of course. We know everyone. Light this fire, Peck!"

"I-I don't know. . . ."

"Try!"

Willow looked at them. He closed his eyes and

concentrated, pointing at the little pile of tinder. *"Strockt lachtnoq!"*

A flame glimmered in the dry moss.

"I did it!"

Rool patted him on the shoulder.

Franjean nodded with satisfaction, rubbing his hands together. "Wait. I'll get us food." He vanished into the darkness and in a little while returned with his arms full of mushrooms, watercress, and succulent tubers. "All is well," he said as they ate, noticing Willow's nervousness. "The stag stands guard. The owl keeps watch for us. Nockmaars are far off on a false scent. We'll not be disturbed this night."

Willow glanced in the direction Madmartigan had gone. "Still, I wish . . . *Is* he a good swordsman?"

"Madmartigan? Oh yes. The best." Franjean gobbled down two small puffballs and one morel. "At least, he used to be."

"What happened?"

"It's sad. It's a pathetic story."

"Tell me anyway, Franjean."

"All right." The brownie wiped his small hands on the moss. He burped. He tugged contentedly at one tufted ear. "Here goes."

Franjean's Tale

This is a tale of Galladoorn, the last of the free kingdoms of the north.

Madmartigan was born there in the full flower of that castle. In those days, Galladoorn was second only to Tir Asleen in splendor. Its king and queen were renowned in all lands for their kindness and readiness to give refuge to all whose own lands had been torn by strife. From the coasts of the south refugees came to Galladoorn, and from the west as far as the sea, and from the nomadic tribes of the great eastern plains, where the bison moved in their hundreds of thousands, and the panthers prowled in the canyons. Wherever their place of birth, all those who had been persecuted and uprooted dreamed of one day finding succor in fabled Galladoorn, and many had their dreams fulfilled.

All who reached the castle brought their customs and habits, and they were encouraged by the king and queen to keep those ways. So, Galladoorn became a wondrous mix of differences. Bog folk mingled with the plainsmen there; seafarers with farmers; mountaineers with forest dwellers. Children growing up in Galladoorn at that time were surrounded by a swirling blend of costumes, an infinite array of exotic foods and spices, skills acquired in faraway trades and arts, and travelers' tales of fabulous domains. Galladoorn's strength grew from that rich diversity.

Son of noblefolk, Madmartigan was given tutors early so that he might be trained for the administration of the kingdom, but he was a restive and truant child. He preferred to escape into the bazaars on the castle commons, hearing unknown languages, breathing rare perfumes. He liked to sail on the green lakes of Galladoorn even before he was big enough to properly handle a boat. Most of all, he loved to run along the hedgerows when the Eastern horsemen rode, and watch them out of sight from the hilltops, rapt by the beauty of each man and horse, so fluidly perfect that neither seemed complete without the other. Madmartigan lingered long near their corrals and beside the ranges where these men practiced archery. Eventually, when he was still a child they began to take him on excursions. So, he came to know early the free life of the camp and the hunt. He came to love the soft voices of those nomads beside their fires, telling strange tales that flowed, and shimmered, and shifted like wind in the tall grasses of the plains, without climax, without beginning or end. . . .

By the age of eight he was an archer. By ten, a superb horseman who could ride standing up, or backward, or swinging down to shoot from under his mount's neck. Like all plainsmen, he wore loose garb; like them, he let his hair grow long, weaving it into tight braids.

His parents disapproved of his way of life and feared for him. But they were Galladoorns: they advised him, they surrounded him with love, and they moved back and let him grow.

When he was eleven, Madmartigan fought his first battle. Warfare was rare then, but the lands were rife with scoundrels—churls and knaves of various ilks who marauded in gangs, raping and pillaging. One

night, Madmartigan's band was attacked by a gang of
Pohas after their horses. Surprise was complete. Far
in the wild, the Galladoorns had been careless, had
posted no guards. Suddenly the Pohas were among
them, snarling like boars, hacking with daggers, their
blue tattoos swarming like separate beasts in the fire-
light. Madmartigan saw two of his friends cut down
before they were even on their feet, and a third
stabbed and knocked back across the fire as he was
rising.

The boy had never used a sword. Compared to the
elegance of a fine bow, he had thought that weapon
crude, and an instrument of war as well, not of the
hunt. But now in his extremity, he grabbed the blade
of a fallen comrade and flourished it with a wild cry.
It was one of the light, curved scimitars of the East,
and he handled it with ease. Two Pohas he slew on
the spot, laying open the throat of one and the belly
of the other. With one bound he was on the fence of
the makeshift corral and, with another, on the back
of a piebald mare, urging her onward with a soft
whistle and a touch of his heels, over the fence,
through the melee, after a pair of Pohas who were
scampering away. On one side he hacked down between a shoulder and a neck; on the other he swung
low and stabbed up through the small of a back,
splitting a tattooed chest. He twisted, lifted the sword
clear, twirled it above his head. He uttered a long,
high wail, and he touched the mare's neck, wheeling
her back for more.

But the battle was over. Three of Madmartigan's friends lay dead. Nine Pohas had perished, four of them slain by the boy.

After that, he sought out the finest of trainers in the use of that slim sword. This was an old man too frail even to lift the weapon anymore. He had been borne on a litter to Galladoorn by his family when they fled their homeland ahead of Mongol hordes. Though his body was weak, his mind was keen still, and his will was like layered steel. His eyes narrowed when he saw Madmartigan wield the blade, and he nodded. Yes, he would instruct him.

And so the boy became an adept of the ancient and elegant swordwork of the far northeast, an art of which he was the last disciple. The difference between that art and the hefting of a broadsword was the difference between a wasp and a charging bear, between a viper and a raging bull.

Three swords Madmartigan ordered before the craftsmen of Galladoorn satisfied him with a blade of a thousand layers, finely tempered and polished, balanced and light, leather-honed to the keenest edge. *Sushin*, Madmartigan named that first sword, *Mosquito*. Like all later blades, he carried it on his back, so that at any time he might tip his head and feel the caress of Sushin's haft against his neck.

By the time he was twelve, Madmartigan was a knight of Galladoorn, dubbed by the king in solemn ceremony, and honored by his peers. But, although he was courteous with them and respectful of their

tastes, he spent little time with them in the mead hall
or on the jousting field where their horses shook the
ground with war games. He preferred the laughter of
the lithe men of the East or the solitude of a long
hunt in the foothills.

He had only one real friend among the other
knights—Airk Thaughbaer, a youth a few years older
than himself. A staunch friend Airk was, as loyal to
Madmartigan as to the kingdom of Galladoorn. His
oath bound Airk's very heart to Galladoorn until the
death. Although all knights swore that same oath, it
was not something Airk *gave*; it was what he *was*.

When Madmartigan fell in love, Airk tried to
counsel him. He had been through the agony of first
love and he had survived. Be cautious, he warned his
friend. Keep pure the core of yourself. Do not be
swept by passion, lest you mistake mere happiness
for joy. Stay mindful of your oath to Galladoorn.
Maintain the integrity that forged that oath.

Madmartigan heard but did not listen. What is ad-
vice to a young man in love? Words, words! As Airk
spoke so earnestly, Madmartigan heard his mistress's
laughter in the rapids of a brook, saw her skirts rus-
tling in the swaying boughs, smelled the perfume of
her bosom in the banks of flowers. She was all he
saw, all he listened to.

She was a princess from the East, a charming and
empty-headed child of breathtaking beauty. She
rarely finished what she began to say, except with a
careless laugh or gesture, as if thought could be

found later, if she needed it, as easily as she had
found her beauty.

Madmartigan's affair with her lasted several
months. Airk watched and worried, a conscientious
but helpless mentor. Probably it would not have been
serious, probably Madmartigan would have survived
to have grown into the man everyone expected him
to become if, in the middle of the affair, he had not
had his Dream. It was a very simple dream, and it
came easily to him, unlike those of others whose
dream-visions had to be induced by fasting and long
exposure on barren slopes.

In Madmartigan's Dream, a white stallion appeared out of the forest and told him that he was
destined to carry him one day triumphantly—a king!
But, said the horse, the vision and the prophecy must
be secret, never to be shared with anyone; otherwise,
it would not come true. With that, the horse vanished.

The next day, laughing, Madmartigan told his lady
love, from whom he had pledged to keep no secrets.

Even this, though it would have put an end to the
prophecy, would not have brought Madmartigan's
disgrace. That calamity occurred when the love affair
ended, when the girl derided him in the presence of
other knights, who turned away their faces in embar-
rassment, and when, in scorning his Dream, she revealed that he had told her of it and so had broken
his Oath of Knighthood.

Then Madmartigan knew hot shame and bitterness

thick as bile. Honor gone, what now was left to him? His friendship with Airk remained, to be sure, but tempered now by Airk's sad disappointment. His parents loved him still, but his shame was theirs, and under the burden of it they grew old before their time. His joy in the wilderness and the chase remained, but oddly lessened, compromised as were all other pleasures by his loss of pride.

He grew wilder. He grew more reckless. Old comrades in the hunt drew back from riding with him, and although Airk Thaughbaer sallied at his side into many foolish perils (and twice saved his life) he got small thanks from Madmartigan. The young man who had once avoided the companionship of the mead hall became now a frequenter of inns, and many serving-wenches in the realm of Galladoorn and beyond grew to know Madmartigan well. In time he became less welcome at Galladoorn, and at last he was rarely seen there. He became a vagabond, a wanderer. Where he wandered and what adventures he had we shall never know, though they were surely many. Those adventures, those passions, became his life.

Years later, the dark power of Nockmaar rose in the north and the plea went out from Galladoorn for all knights and warriors to rally to the defense of that kingdom. Airk Thaughbaer answered the call but Madmartigan was not with those who rode toward home.

In the inns and taverns, Madmartigan drank with

brigands; in the halls of Galladoorn, as Nockmaar power grew, there were good knights who wished him dead. . . .

Franjean recounted this tale with much gusto and gesticulation, interrupted often by comments from Rool. Elora Danan had long since fallen asleep in Willow's arms. Several times the fire had dwindled to embers and had been replenished.

"But what happened at Land's End?" Willow asked when Franjean had finished.

"Land's End! You heard about that, did you? Ah, a great betrayal, a great desertion! There Airk Thaughbaer led loyal troops against the Nockmaar army, though they were far outnumbered, and there Madmartigan deserted him in battle, after Airk had scoured the realm to find him and return him to honor and the Fold of Knights. A sad desertion! A sad conclusion to this sorry tale! No, Peck, you are well quit of that Daikini. Place your trust in us!"

"In us!" Rool echoed, slobbering down his chin.

Willow looked skeptically at the two of them. Far, far away, so far that it was no threat but only a reminder, a Death Dog howled.

FIN RAZIEL

At dawn, Franjean led them down into a long, wooded valley. For a while both brownies marched along briskly, but when the calls and growls of large, waking creatures began to echo in the woods they scrambled up into Willow's pockets. "Straight ahead!" Franjean ordered, ducking down inside. "Just follow the path."

And so Willow struggled on with Elora on his back and his pockets full of brownies, bending lower and lower under this load until at last he was looking almost straight down at the path.

He saw the feet first, in soft leather boots.

Then he saw the mauve skirt.

And then, staggering back, the rest of the body. "Madmartigan!" He sat down abruptly.

"Hullo, Peck." Madmartigan was leaning against a fallen tree. A sword-sized stick swung gently in his left hand.

"I thought you'd be far away! What are you doing *here*?"

"Resting. You caught up with me."

"Thank goodness!" Willow wriggled out of the papoose-basket. The brownies climbed out of his pockets and flopped into the moss beside him, wiping their brows.

"Hard work!" Franjean said. "Supervision! Directing! All that responsibility!"

"Madmartigan," Willow sighed, "we need you."

"Oh? I thought I drove wagons too fast. I thought I didn't know how to look after children."

Elora looked up out of her basket and raised her arms to Madmartigan. Smiling, he laid down the stick and picked her up.

Willow nodded. "Well, we still need you. *She* needs you. I can't protect her, Madmartigan. Not the way you can."

Madmartigan shrugged. "The little one's all right, and you're not a bad Peck, but I don't like *them*!" He pointed to Franjean and Rool. "Brownies! Aargh! *You* heard what they said to me. In fact, you *all* insulted me, except the little one."

Willow got to his feet. "Look," he said. "We're sorry. Aren't we sorry?"

Franjean and Rool nodded.

"And if you come with us we promise not to insult you anymore. We promise not to pester you."

"Hey!" Franjean exclaimed. "Don't go too far!"

Madmartigan rubbed his mouth with one hand and the top of Elora's head with the other. "Some crew! One Peck, one infant, and two gnomes! If we meet up with more Nockmaar troops, it's pretty clear who'll do the fighting, right?"

"Right!" Rool said.

"That's the point!" Franjean said.

Madmartigan sighed. "Well, we're almost at the end of the valley. Which way are you headed after that?"

Rool and Franjean spun into a weird little dance. Rool's knobby arms suddenly extended stiffly in front of him with the palms pressed together, like a weathervane. Franjean clasped his waist from behind and whirled him around this way and that, until finally they zeroed in on the northwest. "That way!" Franjean exclaimed. "To the Lake of Fin Raziel."

Madmartigan slapped his knee. "Bad luck! Exactly the way I'm going. Well, I suppose you can come with me as far as the lake, but no farther. Agreed?"

"Agreed," Willow said.

The brownies nodded. "Do you mind if we . . ." Franjean pointed at the higher, safer pockets.

"Yes! I do mind!" Madmartigan tucked Elora Danan back into her basket and picked up his stick. "I'll have enough to do without being cluttered with brownies! If you want a free ride, ask the Peck."

Willow nodded wearily and opened his pockets, and they hopped in.

After the end of the valley they climbed back to higher ground, angling northwest and keeping to the deepest woods. Twice they saw Nockmaar horsemen searching below, and once four Death Dogs at full run, hot on the scent of some unfortunate traveler whose path had crossed their own.

At evening they made camp in a secluded thicket. The brownies found tubers, gathered eggs and berries. Once again a nursing animal came close to provide Elora succor—this time a little vixen. She padded into the clearing, watched them with bright eyes while the baby nursed, and then slipped away as silently as she had come. There was no baying of Death Dogs, no distant clatter of Nockmaar harness that night. They built a little fire. Huddling close to it, Franjean and Rool quickly fell asleep, rear ends high in the odd position of sleeping brownies, and soon Madmartigan drifted off as well, cradling the sleeping infant in one arm.

Left alone, Willow drew closer to the fire, listening to the night sounds of the deep woods. He touched the magic wand in his pocket and felt a sudden surge of confidence. Emboldened by it, he drew the wand out. It gleamed with unearthly radiance, outshining the fire. He waved it, and the figure he inscribed hung in the air, a separate entity, until it crumbled to sparkling powder, glinting like fairy dust. Smiling, he wrote WILLOW UFGOOD in bold letters and admired the name until it too dispersed into gleaming dust. He wrote KIAYA, and RANON, and MIMS. MIMS hung in the air longer than any of the others, and it disintegrated in a curious fashion, growing larger and larger until it was no longer legible.

Willow was delighted. *Trust yourself!* Isn't that what the High Aldwin had told him? *You have the ability to be a great sorcerer.* Well, perhaps he did have that ability! Perhaps he really would become a sorcerer!

He stood up.

Gripping the wand in both hands, he braced himself, pointed it at a flowering apple tree, and repeated a chant he had heard the High Aldwin use to produce sudden, luscious fruit. *"Tuatha... lawkathok... tuatha...!"*

An explosion lifted him off his feet, somersaulted him, and draped him over the tree's lowest branch. He blinked. He shook his head.

Madmartigan was on his feet in a flash, stick-sword in hand. *"Willow?"* He looked at the wand glimmering beside the fire. He peered into the darkness. "Ah, there you are! Made a mistake, huh?" He lifted the dazed Nelwyn down out of the tree and set him back beside the fire. "Please, no more magic games now. Gets too noisy."

That night Willow dreamed horrific dreams in which he was chased by Death Dogs, trolls, and ravenous monsters. They all caught him. Several times

Madmartigan wakened him, saying he was shouting and screaming. In the morning he felt exhausted, confused, and grumpy. Right away he picked a quarrel with Madmartigan, who was feeding Elora a tuber the brownies had found.

"That's blackroot!" Willow shouted.

"Of course."

"You should *never* feed a child blackroot!"

"Nonsense. Mother always fed me blackroot. Puts hair on your chest, right, Sticks?" He shook the child and she gurgled happily.

"Her name isn't Sticks! It's Elora Danan. She's an empress, and the last thing she'll need, Madmartigan, is hair on her chest. Give me that!" Scrambling over, Willow seized the root and hurled it into the underbrush. "Now let's get going. The lake can't be too far ahead. I hear the waterfall."

The two brownies stared at him in astonishment.

"Well," Willow said. "Can't you hear it? There. When the wind blows."

He was right. Two hours later they came to a cliff top and gazed down on the lake below. It was a spectacular sight. It wound like a long silver ribbon through the hills, narrowing gradually until it funneled into the cascade at the south end. Here it plunged out and down, falling in a thin plume wrapped in clouds of spray. Mist from this cataract drifted back over the lake and the small island that lay like a child in its two long arms, still far below the rays of the rising sun. Mist covered the marshes and the wooded shores, and the long beach on the eastern shore, parting only long enough for the travellers to glimpse a hodgepodge of small thatched rooftops.

"Fishing village," Madmartigan grunted.

"We can get a boat there," Franjean said, hopping out of Willow's pocket. "I'll lead the way!"

"Franjean," Willow asked, his brow creased with worry, "are you sure Fin Raziel's there?"

"Certainly. You heard the legend! Cherlindrea told you."

"But . . . but it was a long, long time ago. She may have died."

"*Died?* Impossible! What a stupid Peck you are! Of course she isn't dead. Sorceresses never just *die*!"

"Never!" Rool said, looking at Willow as if he were an idiot.

"But what if . . ."

Franjean waved his arms. "No more! No more! I haven't got time to answer a lot of stupid questions. Hurry up! You'll see for yourself when we get there."

They emerged into the misty dunes of a broad beach, crossed to the water's edge, and followed the shore toward the village they had glimpsed from above.

It was very quiet. Uneasy, Willow held Elora close, trying to peer through the dazzling clouds of mist. At home on Ufgood Reach, morning was the noisiest time of the day. Fish jumped, dogs barked, cattle moaned to be milked and fed, and myriad birds greeted the dawn from high perches. But here there was no sound, except the distant rumble of the falls. No children shouted from the beach in front of the village. No oars creaked in the mist. No animals announced their presence.

It was too quiet. It was eerie.

Madmartigan stopped them when the first houses appeared. "Wait here," he said softly. "I'll be back." He had tied the skirt into a loincloth. Naked except for this and his boots, he moved across the beach and vanished into the mist like a hunting animal, soundlessly, crouched low. They didn't wait long. In a few minutes he was back, loping along the water's edge. "Deserted," he reported. "Every last house. A long time ago. Plates on the tables, weapons on the walls. See?" He displayed a stiff leather buckler and a rusty sword—no warrior's weapon, but the sort of implement a farmer or a fisherman might keep. "There are some boats that might still float. Come on, we'll have a look." He led them into the center of the village.

Here fishermen once landed with their catch. Here the boats were hauled up, the trout cleaned, the nets strung on drying-posts in the breeze. Once the place had been filled with life; now, it was strangely still. The drying-posts vanished like a line of sentinels into the mist.

"Let's try this one," Madmartigan grunted. He kicked the side of what appeared to be a sound little boat. Unlike most of the others, which had been abandoned to the weather and had rotted, this one lay overturned on logs. Madmartigan flipped it right

side up. Oars clattered inside. He skidded it down to
the lake and launched it. Some water seeped in
through the dried-out seams, but it floated. "In you
go, Peck. Best of luck to you and the little one. As
for these wretched brownies..."

"Glad to be rid of you," Franjean grumbled.

"You eat too much," Rool said, scrambling into
the prow of the boat. "And you make too much
noise!"

Willow stood in the sand, dismayed. "But you're
not coming *with* us?"

Madmartigan laughed and shook his head. "No,
little Peck. You're safely here, and this Fin Raziel,
this sorceress, will look after you." He peered into
the mist, where the first sun was touching the tree-
tops on Fin Raziel's island, and he shook his head
again. "Sorcerers, enchantresses, magic wands...
No, my friend, I'm a warrior, and what should a warrior do with all of that? You deal with Bavmorda in
your way, and I'll deal with her in mine." He patted
the sword. "Hop in, now, and I'll push you off." He
touched the child's head as Willow climbed over the
gunwale, and then he sent the boat gliding out onto
the mirror surface of the lake. He stood a moment
with his fists on his hips. Then waving farewell, he
strode up among the huts. Soon he was lost in the
mist.

"I'm going to miss him," Franjean said.

"Me too," Rool said.

"Teasing a Peck just isn't the same as insulting a Daikini!"

Willow unslung the papoose-basket and settled Elora safely on his lap. As the boat drifted farther out he fitted the oars into their locks. The lake was still quite shallow, and both brownies, Rool in the stern and Franjean in the bow, were gazing down through the limpid water at strange markings on the bottom. So preoccupied were they, and so busy was Willow struggling with the oversized oars, that none of them noticed a young boy appear suddenly out of the lake.

"What are you doing?" the boy asked.

Both brownies vanished in a flash, under the seats. Willow dropped the oars and reached for Elora. The boy was smiling radiantly. He was fair, and tanned, and blue-eyed. He stood waist-deep in the lake, his palms brushing its surface.

"We're just borrowing this boat," Willow said. "To row out to the island. We'll return it. There was no one home. We thought..."

"That island's cursed, didn't you know?" The boy kept smiling, blue eyes fixed on Willow. He brushed little ripples toward them.

"Cursed?" Franjean's head appeared above the gunwale. "The legend says nothing about a curse."

The boy laughed innocently. "Oh yes. All this lake is cursed. Queen Bavmorda's powers control the elements here. Venture on it at your peril!"

"Fin Raziel..." Willow began, but the boy was

gone. Only a little whirlpool remained where he had been, sucking the ripples back into its vortex.

They stared at this whirlpool. They stared at the island. Except for the very tops of its trees it was still dark and misty, although the rest of the lake was bathed in sun.

"Odd," Franjean said. "Odd boy."

"I don't think Elora should go out there," Willow said.

"I don't think *we* should go out there," said Rool.

"Aha! Idea!" Franjean held up a finger. "Of course *you* should go, Peck."

"Of course," Rool agreed.

"That's your mission, after all, to deliver Cherlindrea's wand to Fin Raziel. But you're right about the child. Crossing the lake might be, uh, rough."

"Winds," Rool said, nodding.

"Waves. So leave her with Rool and me. Back there. On shore. In one of those huts."

"You'll guard her?"

"With our lives! Right, Rool?"

"Right!"

Reluctantly, Willow rowed the small craft back to the beach and carried Elora into the nearest hut with a sound roof. "Sleep well," he said, kissing her. "I won't be long, and they've promised to look after you." He gave Franjean a small bladder of the fox milk he had gathered the night before. "Give her this if she wakes up, and keep her warm."

"Of course."

"And dry."

"Certainly."

"And *safe*."

Franjean peered out the door, up and down the empty beach. "Nobody! Deserted! What can happen in the time you row out there and back? Off with you! Stop your silly Peck fretting."

So, Willow rowed alone to the island. The lake had changed. It was no longer silvery, no longer clear and sparkling. It had become opaque, darkening to the color of lead. And it had thickened, too. It dragged on the boat, and when Willow dipped his oars they got so heavy he could hardly lift them to pull again. The island, which had seemed so close to the shore, now receded as he approached.

It was slow, hard rowing, and by the time the prow ground into the gravel of the island beach, Willow was exhausted. Worse, he was frightened. The morning had grown ominously black during his crossing. Rumbling thunderheads moved in from the north, and strange winds came scudding down the valley, swirling clouds of sand around the mainland beach. He could no longer see the hut where he had left Elora with the brownies. Soon, he could no longer see even the mainland.

The island was eerily still.

Willow scrambled up the bank and laid his hand right on the face of a brown skull.

He screamed, lurching back. "Fin Raziel! Where are you? Come out, please! Help us!"

The black clouds closed down around the island. A flock of dark birds swooped low, hard eyes all fixed on Willow.

"Please! Fin Raziel!"

"Go home! Get away! Are you *mad*?"

He spun around. He had backed against the trunk of a large tree, and the voice came from overhead. A furry creature hung there by its tail, snarling. It had a skinny tail, black legs, and squirrellike claws. It was alert, intelligent, and energized.

"Are you mad?" it asked again. "Who are you?"

"I-I'm Willow Ufgood, and I'm here to find Fin Raziel, the great sorceress."

"That's me! I'm Raziel!"

"What? No! It can't be true!"

"It *is* true. It is!" Chattering, the creature swung in furious little circles. "Bavmorda transformed me! First she imprisoned me on this island and then in this wretched body."

"But the legend didn't tell . . ."

"*I* can't be responsible for the legend! Well, why have you come here? Why have you risked your life?"

"Because of this," Willow said, drawing out the wand, which glowed and shimmered in the growing darkness. "From Cherlindrea."

With a wild shriek the little creature leaped off the tree onto Willow's chest, her claws digging through his shirt and into his flesh. "Cherlindrea! Then the prophecy has come true? The Empress Elora has been born?"

"Yes. She's here. On the shore. And she needs you, Fin Raziel."

"*Here!*" The little creature howled a bitter cry of rage and fear. She scrambled up onto Willow's shoulder and peered toward the shore, now invisible behind the clouds and spray of the wind-lashed lake. "Hide the wand! Bavmorda knows she's here! She'll destroy you if she can, and the child! Hurry! Into the boat! We must get off this island and into shore!"

"But the lake! The storm!" Willow shouted over the howling wind.

"Don't think! Trust me! Into the boat, quick!"

She scampered across the shore and into the little craft, one paw beckoning Willow to hurry. He launched them out into the maelstrom. "Row for your life, Willow Ufgood! Row for the Empress!"

With all his might, the little Nelwyn strained toward shore. "Oh Mims," he whimpered. "Ranon. Oh, Kiaya!" If he had had a free hand he would have taken his wife's braid from his pocket and pressed it to his lips, for he was certain he was doomed. Never, never would he cross that lashing strait and reach the mainland safely. Never again would he see his beloved family.

"Kill him!" Fin Raziel shrieked suddenly. "Kill him!"

"What?" They were in the middle of the lake,

driven toward the falls by winds and towering waves. The mainland was invisible, the island had vanished.

"Kill him!" Fin Raziel screamed again, pointing at the prow of the little boat.

Willow turned.

The boy he had seen earlier, in the shallow water at the village, was climbing over the gunwale. He was as radiant and as innocent-looking as ever, his face creased in a broad smile, his flaxen hair windblown.

"What? But he's a child!"

"No, no!" Raziel shrieked. "He's no child! Look!"

The boy now had one foot in the boat, but it was not a foot. It was a webbed fin. And although he was still smiling, the smile revealed sharklike teeth. His innocent eyes had reddened with the lust for blood.

Willow swung an oar and jabbed it as hard as he could into the middle of this creature. Laughing, it flipped into the churning lake, bobbed porpoiselike, and vanished.

"Too late!" Fin Raziel wailed, her voice tiny in the roar of the wind.

Back the creature came! He was huge, now. His furry back foamed through the troughs of the waves. His eyes glowed red out of the depths of the lake. His jaws with their rows of glittering teeth, yawning open to engulf the boat, loosed a gagging stench of death and decay. Willow choked, tumbling back, seeing the front half of the boat vanish into the creature's maw. He had time only for one solid crack with the oar on the thing's snout, and then he was overboard and sinking, his legs tangled in the old fishnet and rope that bound him to the monster. So fast was the creature's downward rush that Willow's lungs were bursting before he found his knife and slashed himself free of the beast.

He bobbed through the surface like a cork, sputtering and gasping. Huge waves rolled him over. Clinging to the wreckage of the boat, Fin Raziel shrieked unintelligible warnings, but Willow was too far gone to hear her properly. In fact, he heard nothing. All had gone silent for him. In silence the great breakers rolled over him. In silence the maw of the returning monster yawned open to gulp him down. And in silence, with the last of his meager strength, Willow groped into his pocket, fumbled out one of the magic acorns, and threw it.

No force lay behind that throw. Had the monster not been rushing forward, the acorn would have fallen short. As it was, it looped up and dropped straight down his gullet.

Sheer momentum carried the beast over Willow and a few feet farther. But the horrible hairy scales that brushed against the Nelwyn were not soft now, but rock-hard. The dreadful red eye was fixed forever in gemlike brilliance, and the jaws with their quartzite teeth would yawn through eternity. The acorn had done its work.

Bavmorda's monstrous guardian had been turned to solid stone. And like a stone he sank.

"Willow!" Fin Raziel was crying. "Hold on!" He

heard her voice like a glimmer of light in darkness. Reflexes kept him alive, kept him afloat, kept him paddling while breakers foamed over him. Reflexes opened his eyes at the sound of her voice, and drove him forward with his last energy to clutch the end of the oar shoved out from the ruined boat. Clinging to that oar and to the sound of Raziel's voice, Willow lost consciousness.

He was not aware when the wind fell, when the waves subsided and the sky cleared. He was not aware when the hulk of the little boat to which he and Fin Raziel clung was drawn away from the precipice of the falls and borne on friendly currents to the beach, or when Franjean and Rool hurried anxiously down to drag him up on shore.

The first thing Willow Ufgood knew after his defeat of the monster was the laughter of Elora and the delighted clapping of her small hands.

"I don't know why she's so happy," Franjean grumbled. "You just ruined a boat and nearly killed yourself. You didn't even bring Fin Raziel!"

"I *am* Raziel, you idiot! Willow, tell him! And stop this lout from poking at me!" She swatted away Rool's hand with a tiny paw.

"Talking possum," Franjean grunted. "All we need."

Willow choked and coughed. He struggled to sit up. "It's true," he said. "She is Raziel."

"What! Why is she so fuzzy?"

"Why so small?" Rool asked.

"Bewitched, that's why," Willow said. "By Queen Bavmorda."

"Satisfied, you two? Now then, Willow, you must undo the spell. You must transform me back again. Thank goodness you've come! Go ahead, speak the charm."

"What?"

"Use the wand. Speak the charm."

"What charm?"

"What charm! You mean you don't *know*? You're not a sorcerer?"

"Well, not really. Not yet. I'm a farmer. I know a few tricks. If you tell me what to do . . ."

"Farmer! Tricks!" Squealing, the small animal scampered in tight circles.

"Hysterical possum," Franjean said. "Ouch!"

Raziel nipped his ankle. "Idiot! Cherlindrea sent you, Ufgood, and you're not even a sorcerer! What was she thinking of? What madness . . ."

"Just tell me what to do," Willow said. "I'm willing to learn. Honest. It can't be *that* hard."

"Of course it's hard! Why, if you misspoke a charm . . ." Raziel shuddered. Her tail twitched.

"Well then," Willow said, *"teach me properly!"* He punched the dirt floor of the hut and rose shakily to his feet. "Abuse! That's all I've had since I started this trip! I've been laughed at by fairies, mocked by brownies, persecuted by Daikini louts, and half killed in seven different ways. Now I get a scolding from an irrational squirrel!"

"I'm *not* a squirrel!"

"I don't care! If what you say is true, Raziel, and if you want to be human again, settle down and teach me to be a sorcerer!"

The brownies sat abruptly, blinking.

Fin Raziel stopped running in circles and stared. Again the only sound in the hut was the soft laughter and light applause of Elora Danan.

"All right," Fin Raziel said. "I'll teach you."

"You will?"

"Of course. You're right. It's our only hope. Come outside and bring the wand."

Willow staggered after her out of the hut, groping for the wand in the long pocket of his cloak. Fortunately for all of them, he had not drawn it out before he emerged.

Sorsha was waiting on the beach. Behind her stood three Nockmaar troopers, arms at the ready. A dozen more held their horses at the edge of the village.

On his knees in front of them, his face bloody and his arms bound tight at his back, was Madmartigan.

SORSHA

"Hullo, Peck. Would you please cut these ropes? I'd like to strangle this hag, this . . ."

"Quiet!" Spurring up, a Nockmaar sergeant thumped the heel of his boot between Madmartigan's shoulderblades and sent him sprawling into the wet sand.

"Don't kill him yet," Sorsha said.

Raziel shrieked and scurried along the beach, but a trooper easily overtook her and snatched her up by the tail. At arm's length he carried her back, dangling and struggling. "A little rat for the dogs." He laughed.

Willow ran into the hut and snatched Elora out of her basket. But there was no escape. Sorsha strode in behind him, drawn by the child's screams. "I'll take her."

"No! You won't! Help, Franjean!" But the two brownies were nowhere to be seen. Sorsha easily overpowered Willow, holding him with one hand while she yanked the papoose-basket away from him with the other. Dispassionately, she opened Elora's clothing and exposed her left arm. She smiled when she saw the Sign. It was an expression of relief and of triumph. But it was a sad smile too, the kind of haunted smile that sometimes came to Sorsha's face at the end of a long, hard hunt, when it was time for the kill. "Get out, Peck!" She booted Willow off his feet and sent him sprawling through the door. "Tie him up," she said to her sergeant. "Put him on a pack mule."

"Your Highness," the man asked, "is that the child?"

"It is."

"Then why should we be bothered with this Peck and this Daikini scum? Why not slay them now?"

Sorsha considered. She stared at Willow. She looked at Madmartigan and her chin lifted slightly. "No. My mother may want them for the Ritual. Who knows what powers the child may have given them."

"More than Bavmorda has, Sorsha!" Fin Raziel shrieked, still dangling from the trooper's fist. "You'll see! More powers than exist in all of evil Nockmaar!"

Sorsha drew her sword and tipped up Fin Raziel's head with the point of it, gazing into her small, smoldering eyes. "Look at you, Fin Raziel. What a pathetic creature! How can you talk of power? You will have a special place in Bavmorda's Ritual, I think."

Around her, the Nockmaar troopers chuckled. Sorsha thrust a foot into her stirrup and swung up onto Rak. "Throw her into a cage. Put her on the mule with the Nelwyn. As for him," she nodded to Madmartigan, who had struggled to his feet, "let him walk."

Madmartigan grinned up at her, squinting into the sun and spitting sand. "Good idea! Why don't you come down and walk with me, Princess? You and I, we'll take a little walk back into those woods . . ."

Sorsha spurred Rak and the great horse lunged forward, smashing Madmartigan back onto the beach. "Come!" she said, beckoning to the troopers. "We have a long journey." Rak trotted along the water's edge, hooves splashing, and Sorsha gazed on the dilapidated huts and sheds as she passed them. At the far end she wheeled and casually flung her arm in the same gesture of destruction that she had seen Bavmorda make many times. "Burn this place!"

When the last troopers had flung their torches into the village and galloped northward, Franjean and Rool emerged from their hiding place in the woods. Pyres blazed and ashes smoldered where the fishing village had been, and smoke hung in a heavy pall over the windless lake and the island of Fin Raziel.

"We ran," Rool said.

"Certainly we ran. We're not idiots, Rool! Do you know what sport those Nockmaar thugs would have had with two brownies?"

"But we promised."

"To protect the child. You're right."

"And they've got her."

"And the Daikini. And the Peck."

"And Fin Raziel. Franjean, we should help."

"Don't be honorable, Rool! It's not what brownies *do*. Say rather, 'We should continue this adventure, Franjean!'"

"We should continue this adventure, Franjean."

"You're right, Rool. Let's get started. You heard what the princess said: it's a long walk."

"Maybe we could find an eagle."

"Maybe a hawk."

"Maybe a seagull?"

They looked hopefully up and down the beach, out across the lake through the drifting smoke. But as far as they could see, there was no life at all.

"Again!" Fin Raziel hissed. "Try the chant again!" She pressed her face against the bars of a crude cage, gaze fixed desperately on Willow.

"Hear her?" he asked. "It's Elora. She's crying. She's cold and hungry." He struggled against his bonds to see over the head of the plodding mule, past the thick bodies of Nockmaar troopers. "Sorsha's not looking after her up there. She doesn't *know* about babies."

Raziel bounced and quivered. "Don't worry about her *now*. The *charm*, Willow! It's the only hope for the child or for any of us! Get it right!"

"Cut these ropes and give me a good sword and I'll show you another hope," Madmartigan muttered. He was plodding beside the mule, a rope around his neck tied to the pommel of the Nockmaar sergeant. The sergeant was occupied, busy sharing some joke with two of his men.

"She's cold. She's . . ."

"*The charm!*"

"Oh, all right. Let's see. *Tanna . . . looth . . .* I can't remember the middle part."

"*Locktwarr!*" Fin Raziel hissed. "That's the word that pleads for change."

"*Locktwarr, locktwarr . . .*" Willow murmured, eyes shut tight.

"Look out! Quiet!"

Willow opened his eyes to see Sorsha approaching, riding beside the file of soldiers. Beyond her, only a few miles ahead, rose the snow-capped peaks of the mountains. She rode calmly, confidently, her red hair free, surrounded by her own frozen breath and the horse's.

"Witch!" Madmartigan said.

"Quiet!" The sergeant jerked the rope, suddenly efficient in Sorsha's presence.

"Young woman," Fin Raziel squeaked as Rak

came alongside the mule, "you reminded me of your father just then. He, too, was a . . ."

"Silence!" Sorsha's riding crop cracked across the bars of the cage. "You insult me! My father was a weakling! A fool! An enemy of Nockmaar!"

Raziel cringed but continued. "So your mother says, but it was not true, Sorsha. Enemy of Nockmaar perhaps, but fool and weakling? Never!"

"Princess Sorsha," Willow pleaded, "please, let me help you with Elora. She needs food. She needs warmer clothes in this cold."

Sorsha hesitated. She glanced at the head of the column, where the child was wailing pitifully in the embrace of the lieutenant. For a moment she seemed about to relent, but instead she shook her head. "We'll feed her soon enough, when we bivouac. As for warmth, she'll have all she needs in my mother's Ritual."

Gritting his teeth, Madmartigan twisted around against the pressure of the rope. "Do you know what you are, Princess? You're a nasty, mean-spirited little . . ."

The sergeant cursed and yanked the rope, and Madmartigan staggered, strangling. "And if you're not careful," he croaked, "you'll grow up just like your damned mother!"

Sorsha flushed scarlet. She spurred Rak around the plodding mule and raised her riding crop.

"Go ahead!" Madmartigan wheezed. "You and your boys do your worst!" He twisted again, running

sideways against the pressure of the rope so he could
look up into her eyes. His jaws were clenched, but he
was grinning. "And I promise you, when my turn
comes I'll do my best!"

The whip wavered, fell; but instead of landing
across Madmartigan's face it struck Rak's haunch.
The stallion surged forward, carrying Sorsha beyond
earshot, cantering to the head of the column.

The sergeant laughed hoarsely, yanking Madmartigan's rope so tight that he could say nothing more.
"You'll pay for that. At Nockmaar you'll pay and
pay. Ah, you'll give us all good sport, you and this
little Peck."

"*Locktwarr*," Willow murmured, his eyes shut
tight again. "*Tanna...*"

"*Looth,*" Raziel whispered. "*Tanna looth...*"

Up they went, and up, winding ever higher into
the mountains. Squalls and flurries swept down the
slopes. As they went they were joined by other
Nockmaar squads and search parties, summoned out
of the valleys by the triumphant bellowing of the
ram's horn, sounded by Sorsha's bugler. Many had
Death Dogs. These froze Willow with terror as they
trotted beside the mule, eying him. Their thick
shoulders bunched and rippled. Their snouts wrinkled to show long fangs. Their hairless tails twitched.

Most of the other groups stayed with Sorsha's
party only long enough to congratulate her on the
capture of the child, and then they trotted ahead to

the main Nockmaar encampment in the mountains, weary from their long search and anxious to rest.

At evening on the third day, Sorsha's men brought their prisoners to the encampment. It lay in a high valley near a fork in the road. To the left, an old and disused track had once taken travelers to Tir Asleen; to the right, the broader road led straight to Nockmaar. A camp of a hundred or so tents had been set up by this fork, growing steadily as the Nockmaar soldiers marshaled and prepared to return to the castle. It was a heavy place, all gray and black in the trampled snow. No music played there. No banners flew. Men drank in hunkering groups beside sullen fires. Most of their shelters were small; some, mere skin tarpaulins propped on sticks. Some were more spacious, with enclosed sides, and a few—the officers' quarters—looked almost comfortable.

General Kael rode out to meet them with two of his brigadiers. "Hail!" he greeted Sorsha as he approached, raising his mailed fist. "Your mother will be pleased!" He tried to smile but managed only to show his teeth. Seared, scarred, broken, his thick face could no longer express any real emotion. All its lineaments were set fast in that awful grimace. He looked like that when he gazed on a beautiful scene or a lovely creature. He looked like that when he watched the torturing of a child. He would look like that as he watched his own death come.

"Kael!" Madmartigan whispered, crouching down

and hiding his face as well as he could against the jerking of the rope. "All I need!"

"You *know* him?"

"We've met. Years ago. A small misunderstanding, but enough for him to remember me."

Kael gave the prisoners only a cursory glance before wheeling his horse in beside Sorsha and the lieutenant and roughly pulling back Elora's blanket. The child howled as he twisted her small arm to see the Sign. "That's it," he grunted. "That's the one. Send word to the queen."

One of the brigadiers spurred back to the camp, and by the time Sorsha and her prisoners arrived, a messenger on a fast horse was cantering off on the frozen road to Nockmaar.

That night was the most awful of Willow's life. Guards clamped an ankle manacle on him and tethered him to the wheel of a barred cart like those used to haul pregnant women to Nockmaar. They threw Madmartigan inside and hung Fin Raziel's cage on the corner, where passing troopers could jeer and poke at her in the torchlight. All three of them got only scanty gruel to eat, and no shelter at all from the wintry winds of the plateau. Worst of all, Elora was taken away to Sorsha's tent somewhere on the other side of that dark camp, and Willow could no longer see her or even hear her.

It began to snow.

Wet, cold, despairing, thoroughly miserable, Willow crept under the wagon and huddled there, whispering the names of his wife and children, and touching the braid of Kiaya's hair like a magic amulet.

"Have faith, little friend," Madmartigan said softly from above. "All will be well. This isn't the first cage Madmartigan's been in, and I promise you it won't be the last."

"Practice!" Fin Raziel hissed. "Work the charm! Work the earth!"

"All right," Willow said. "I'll try." Creeping to the edge of the wagon, he gathered some mud into his food bowl and stirred it into a soupy mess with wet snow. He held the bowl up in both hands and looked toward heaven, but there was no moon, there were no stars. The only light came from the flickering torches and dim fires of the camp.

"Bah!" Madmartigan said. "That stinks!"

Willow shrugged. "Earth, water, sky," he said to Fin Raziel. "What's next?"

"Fire."

"I can't do it, Raziel. I can't get fire. It's all too far away. They've got me chained here!"

"Don't give up, Willow! A way will come, I promise. Repeat the incantations."

"Hither walha, bairn deru, bordak bellanockt. . . ."

"No sword," Madmartigan grumbled. "Just gibberish and a stinkpot!"

"It's not gibberish!" Fin Raziel hissed, shaking her small fist. "It's the charm for the life-spark. All we need now is the fire."

Boots sloshed toward them through the icy mud. "Look out!" Willow whispered. "Kael!"

Madmartigan faded into the shadows of the wagon, but not quickly enough. "You!" Kael growled. "I know *you*!" He strode up and grabbed the bars. "Come out here where I can see you!"

"Know me? No, sir. I'd remember you. Oh yes, I'd..."

"Madmartigan!"

"*What?* No! My name's Runge. Elbert Runge. But I knew Madmartigan. Oh yes, sir, I knew that scoundrel! And I'm glad to tell you he's dead."

"Good! He stole one of my women!"

"One of mine, too! That's why I killed him. What a fight that was! Took half an afternoon before I skewered him. He was a good swordsman, I'll give him that. But I'm better. I'm a master, General Kael. Let me out of here, and I'll win this war for you."

Kael's fist jabbed through the bars and seized Madmartigan by the throat, jerking his face against the bars. "This war's already won! Bavmorda'll decide what to do with you, you scum!" He flung Madmartigan onto the floor of the wagon and slogged away toward his tent.

"Willow?" Fin Raziel said when he had gone, and when Madmartigan had stopped cursing. "Are you all right? Are you practicing?"

"I can't, Raziel. I'm shaking too much. And I'm too worried about Elora."

"You must practice! Worrying won't help her.

Only action will. Only the charm. You must make the wand your own and transform me now. Tonight!"

"Tonight! But I'm not ready!"

"You have to be, Willow. *You have to be!* Watch out, now!"

Sorsha's lieutenant came trudging up through the mud. He gave Raziel's cage a shove that sent it swinging wildly, slamming against the wagon and toppling the little creature inside. He laughed at her confusion, and bent to unlock Willow's manacle. "Come on, Peck! You're wanted!" He seized Willow by the collar and hauled him off.

"The bowl," Raziel moaned, still swinging. "Take the booowl."

Somehow Willow managed to do that, concealing inside his coat the mixture of earth, water, and sky that needed only fire to be a magic potion.

The lieutenant had a firm grip on his collar, and he dragged him unceremoniously through the mud of the camp. Crouched around their fires, drunken troopers shouted as they passed. "A Peck! Just what we need! Let's have him, lieutenant. We'll gut him and spit him!"

Horses stomped in the darkness. From somewhere amid the tents came the sounds of a brawl. Willow bit his lip in terror, but he clung to the bowl.

Sorsha's was the only round tent in the camp. It stood apart from the others, on higher ground. Its roof sloped from a central pole down to other poles supporting a wall twice as high as Willow. The shields of Sorsha's personal guard ringed its periphery. Her pennant surmounted its peak, drifting in the smoke from inside.

Willow heard Elora crying as they approached, and the sound struck fear into his belly. It was no ordinary crying. It was the desperate, choking wail of a very sick child. He knew it too well; Ranon had made that sound after he fell through the river ice and hovered five days between life and death. And Mims also had made that sound when she was an infant with such spasms of coughing that for awful moments she had stopped breathing entirely.

"Your Highness, I've brought the Peck."

"Send him in."

The lieutenant let him go, and Willow straightened his coat and pushed aside the flap. The tent was dry and warm, lighted by several large candles and a fire in a brazier in its center. Freed of her armor and in looser garb, Sorsha sat cross-legged on a thick sleeping-carpet, with Elora beside her. She looked tense and worried. She glanced at Willow and then back at the screaming and coughing child on the floor.

"I've tried everything. She won't eat, won't drink, won't stop this howling. What's wrong with her?"

Willow took off his coat and laid it beside the brazier, keeping the bowl with the mud potion upright in its pocket.

"Well, all this time you've been hounding us she's been wet, and cold, and hungry. For another thing, these clothes are too tight. She's half strangled. *There*, Elora. Is that better?" The baby stopped thrashing and sobbing, but she was coughing still. "And for another thing, Princess, babies like to be *held*."

"I'm not a mother. I don't want . . ."

"Here. Against your shoulder. Like this." Willow placed Elora in her arms. The child's fretting subsided a little. Her hand brushed Sorsha's cheek.

The princess almost smiled, but then her brow clouded again. "This child must be kept alive. . . ."

"Oh yes!"

". . . for a time. My mother needs her for the Ritual."

"She won't die. I promise you. Not if I can help it. Please, rock her while I warm some milk." Willow turned and busied himself at the brazier with the bowl of milk that Sorsha had laid out before his arrival. Behind, after a bit more coughing, Elora laughed, and when he looked around, the princess was smiling.

"That man, Peck. Your companion."

"Madmartigan."

"Madmartigan, yes. Who *is* he?"

"Just a warrior, Your Highness. A renegade."

"A wanderer."

"Yes. Please, give me Elora now." Cradling the child, Willow dipped his finger into the warming milk and fed her. She hiccupped, waving her tiny fists for more. He smoothed her wisps of hair; she was coughing still, very hot and flushed.

Sorsha yawned.

"I'll look after her, Your Highness, if you want to sleep."

"Ha! Steal her, you mean!"

She went to the door and summoned her lieutenant. "Check often," she told him, "and when this child sleeps, take the Peck back with the other prisoners."

"Yes, Your Highness."

Sorsha loosened her belt, turning back toward her bed. She hesitated as she passed Willow and the restless child. "You've fallen into deep waters, haven't you?"

"Yes, Princess."

"Far from the place safe for Nelwyns. Tell me, is it true that in your valley the Freen flows pure and clean, and that great fishes might still be caught in it?"

"Oh yes, Your Highness. At our village we fish every day."

"And is it true that in the woods there, wild boars still roam?"

"Wild boars! It certainly is true! Why, one morning on the bank of the river, right beside Ufgood Reach . . ."

Sorsha smiled, yawning again. She waved her hand. "No more." She lay down on the rug, drew her furs over her, and was soon fast asleep.

When he had fed Elora until she would take no more, Willow cautiously slipped the bowl containing the muddy mixture out from inside his coat. Into it, he dropped a small coal from the brazier. Instantly the potion flashed so brilliantly that Sorsha tossed and murmured in her sleep. When the glow had subsided, only a strange dust lay in the bowl, gleaming like dull silver. Particles clung to his fingertip when he touched it; they tingled, now hot, now cold. Willow's arm felt suddenly very strong—as big and strong as any Nockmaar warrior's. On impulse, he touched the fingertip to Elora's forehead.

Instantly, the last of the child's fretting ceased. Her fever vanished. She grew cool. She slept.

Willow stared in awe. "I-I've done it," he murmured to the child, to the shimmering coals, to the magic ash. "I *am* a sorcerer!"

"She asleep?" The lieutenant stuck his head around the flap.

Willow nodded.

"Put her down then. There."

Willow barely had time to pull his coat back on and hide the bowl of dust inside it before the lieutenant seized him by the scruff of the neck and hauled him back through the camp.

It had grown colder, and winds had piled snowdrifts against the side of the cart. The lieutenant clamped the leg-iron on Willow and hurried back to his fire.

Fin Raziel lay curled in a tight ball in her cage.

Madmartigan huddled shivering in a corner of the wagon. "What happened?" he asked.

"Elora was sick, but she's going to be all right now."

Raziel stirred. "Did you fire the potion?"

"Yes! And what's more . . ."

"Good! We're ready, then. You must transform me. Quick, get me down!"

"How can I? I'm chained to this wagon!"

"That stick! Madmartigan, you can reach it. Knock this cage down!"

Madmartigan did as she told him. Two blows of the stick and the furry little sorceress crashed to the ground. The bars splintered open and she scampered out, tearing in small circles. "Free! Free!"

"Great!" Madmartigan muttered. "Can't get out myself, but I can set loose this muskrat!"

"Muskrat! Do you realize how close you are to freedom, Daikini oaf! Minutes! Seconds! When I change into my former self! When I use Cherlindrea's wand . . . Willow, quick!"

"Ouch! Why'd you bite my finger? Look, blood!"

"That's why! Put three drops into the potion. You have to make it your own."

"You could have warned me!"

"Now, mix it up and rub it on the wand."

"Yes. And now?"

"Now, Willow Ufgood, you must tell me: What is a sorcerer's greatest power?"

"His will."

"Good. Use it now. Hold on to it. There will be pain, and only your will shall hold the charm. You must not lose your concentration. Ready?"

"Yes."

"Say the charm I taught you!"

Willow raised the wand over Fin Raziel, who crouched trembling. He closed his eyes. *"Hither greenan, bairn claideb, lunanockt...."*

"Hello there, everybody!"

"Brownies!" Madmartigan groaned.

"Made it!" Franjean and Rool staggered up through the muck. "You're saved!"

The wand wavered. Willow opened one eye.

"Quiet, fools!" Raziel hissed. "Start again, Willow. The Words for Overcoming!"

"Avaggdu ... suporium ... luatha ..."

Madmartigan gazed skeptically out of his cage at the conjuring Nelwyn and the furry creature on the ground. "Raziel, what'll you look like if this works?"

"Quiet! Quiet!" Raziel scampered in furious circles. "Don't interrupt!"

"... luatha danalora ..."

"Young," Franjean whispered to Madmartigan.

"Very beautiful!" Rool added.

"Really?"

The brownies nodded. "More beautiful than you can imagine."

Madmartigan grinned. *"Concentrate,* Willow!"

"Danalora avalorium, greenan luatha, danu, danu, danalora luatha danu...."

"No, Willow! Forget the pain! You're drifting! You're losing me! You're . . . Awk! Grawk!"

"Oh-oh!" The brownies ducked underneath the wagon.

The wand flashed, knocking Willow head over heels. Raziel's body contorted, soft fur becoming black feathers, and with a squawk she changed into a hulking raven.

Madmartigan grimaced. "Wrong charm, Peck. Nice try, though. You all right?"

Willow nodded. Sitting in the mud, he nursed his bruised arm and stared at the bird, who glowered back at him. "*Now* how'll we escape?"

"Escape?" Franjean asked. "That all you want? Easy. We pick the lock." He climbed up the bars and went to work with his tiny spear.

"Sorry, Raziel," Willow said.

"My fault," Fin Raziel croaked, dolefully examining her new body. "Too much rush. You weren't ready. Farmers! Cherlindrea sends me farmers! Never mind, Willow. Put the wand away for now. We'll try again later."

"Back!" Franjean exclaimed, swatting at Madmartigan, who had leaned close to watch what he was doing. "Stupid Daikini! Out of my light! Back, I say!"

At that moment the lock clicked and the door swung open. Madmartigan tumbled out into the mud, and Franjean fell on top of him. His tiny spear and knapsack went flying. The fairy dust, the Dust of

Broken Heart, spilled out of the little pouch on his belt and right into Madmartigan's face.

"Me, too!" Willow cried, thrusting out the foot with the shackle, and Franjean grabbed his spear and scrambled over to free him also. "Come on, Madmartigan! Let's get Elora! Let's get *out* of here!"

Croaking excitedly, Raziel rose on her new wings and flew toward Sorsha's tent.

With brownies close behind him, Willow dashed through the wakening Nockmaar camp. He had run a considerable distance before he missed Madmartigan and spun around to see him lagging far behind. "What's wrong with *him*?"

"Dust of Broken Heart," Franjean said. "That's what's wrong."

"Oh no!"

Grinning stupidly, in love with everything, Madmartigan was ambling through the camp with his arms spread wide, as if it were a flowery meadow. "Beautiful!" he called to Willow, pointing at the sunrise.

"Come *on*, Madmartigan!"

"Adorable! Lovely!" Starry-eyed, Madmartigan tottered toward a mud-caked and sneering mule.

"Come *on*!"

"Ah! Love of my life!" Arms wide, Madmartigan tried to embrace a swarthy and hungover trooper who was just then lurching out of his tent. The man cursed and reeled back inside.

"*Now* you've done it! Come on!" Pulling and

prodding, Willow and the two brownies managed to hurry him the rest of the way to Sorsha's tent.

"Leave this to me," Madmartigan whispered when they had slipped past the sleeping guards. "I've had experience with these things. I know *all* about it."

"What are you going to do?"

Madmartigan leered.

"No! The baby, remember? The baby!"

"Right!" He winked and vanished through the flap.

Both princess and child lay asleep as Willow had left them. However, it was Sorsha who drew all of Madmartigan's attention, as Willow had feared. Curled in the furs, her splendid red hair tumbling free, she looked innocently beautiful. Even if one had not been bedazzled by the magical fairy dust, it would have been hard to believe that she was Bavmorda's daughter. It would have been hard to imagine her engaged in the business of death. She radiated life—glowing, pure, and exuberant.

Madmartigan crept up and kissed her gently on the cheek. "I love you," he said.

The princess stirred but did not waken.

"No!" Willow hissed, pointing from the doorway. "The baby, Madmartigan! Elora!"

Shouts and alarms rose from the camp behind.

"Sorsha," Madmartigan said. "My dearest Sorsha, waken from this hateful sleep that deprives me of the beauty of your eyes." Again he kissed her.

This time she woke. She came up swinging. One

arm slammed Madmartigan so hard across the neck he fell sideways. The other whipped out of the furs, clutching a short dagger. "One move!" she said.

Flat on his back, Madmartigan spread his arms. "You are my moon, Sorsha! My sun! My starlit sky! Without you I dwell in darkness! I love you!" He began to laugh helplessly.

Outside, Fin Raziel took flight, croaking, "Doomed! All doomed!" The brownies vanished. Willow scrambled into the tent and headed for Elora Danan, who had awakened and was adding her delighted laughter to Madmartigan's.

"I love you!"

"Stop saying that!"

"But it's true! How can I stop the beating of my heart?"

"*I* can stop it!" Sorsha said, bringing the dagger close.

"Go ahead. Kill me! The touch of your hand is worth a thousand deaths." He seized her free hand and pressed it to his chest.

The point of the dagger wavered, faltered.

Willow snatched up Elora.

At that moment the whole side of the tent split open under the thrust of a mighty sword. Kael pushed through the opening, with half a dozen troopers at his back. He smiled with terrible satisfaction. He hefted his black sword. "So. It *was* you, Madmartigan. Now, by the gods, you'll pay!"

AIRK THAUGHBAER

T hen Willow Ufgood, Nelwyn farmer, saw truly what it was to be a warrior.

He knew Madmartigan the wheedler and cajoler, Madmartigan the womanizer, Madmartigan the adventurer and braggart. During the escape in the wagon, he had seen Madmartigan the fighter. But he had never seen Madmartigan the swordsman, the master that Franjean had described.

Now he saw that person.

Madmartigan laughed in Kael's face, even as the general lunged through the torn tent. With one arm he pulled Sorsha down to kiss her. With the other he groped in her bed until he found the sword concealed there. He drew it out, flinging the scabbard off. "Ha! A *real* sword at last!" Before Sorsha twisted free, before Kael's sword slammed down into the bed, Madmartigan had somersaulted backward and up on his feet. The blade flashed and sang above him like a living thing. His first blow missed Kael's neck but struck his epaulet so hard that the Nockmaar dropped to one knee. His second blow severed the arm of another warrior charging at him. His third cut clean through the tent pole, dropping the skin structure on a writhing human mass.

"This way, Willow!" The sword flashed again in the darkness, slicing through the roof, and Madmartigan scrambled through the gap, pulling the Nelwyn and the child after him.

"Run! Run!" Fin Raziel shrieked, circling frantically above them. "Up here! Up the path!"

The camp was fully aroused and chaotic. Some troopers were struggling into their armor while others had found their weapons and were racing toward the fallen tent, answering Kael's bellows of rage. Trainers dashed to loose Death Dogs straining at their leashes. In no time, Madmartigan faced enemies on three sides.

Willow ran after Raziel. A little path, a goat path, wound up from Sorsha's tent to the face of a sheer precipice. There was no way through. Within a hundred yards the path had narrowed to a ledge so small that he dared not go farther despite Raziel's urgings. Perhaps a mountain goat, calm and surefooted, could pass along that ledge, but Willow knew that both he and Elora would certainly plunge to their deaths.

And horrible deaths they would be.

Willow's knees went weak when he looked down. Almost sheer, the cliff fell away below his feet. Far, far down, in the darkness and mists of the valley, huddled a little village, so small in the distance that the smokes from its chimneys hung like merest threads, like the filaments of spiderwebs. Between Willow and the village lay an awful chasm. Ridges of fallen rock reached through the snow of it like waiting claws. The black mouths of its caves and caverns yawned open, glinting with icy teeth. Far below, an eagle circled. Willow pressed back against the rock wall. "No!" he said. "Oh no!"

Even Fin Raziel squawked and flapped back when she drifted over that abyss.

But there was no place else to go.

"Go on, Willow! Out on the ledge!"

"I can't, Madmartigan! I can't!"

Madmartigan was fighting brilliantly, holding off a swarm of dogs and lancers while he retreated slowly along the narrow track to where Willow cowered with the child. His sword leaped and slashed, whirled, stabbed, cut. Blood flew from it. A trail of bloody snow led up to him, and the bodies of a dozen dogs and as many men lay dead or sorely hurt along the track. But time was against him. More troopers crowded in; and he was tiring. Even as Willow watched, Madmartigan twisted a split second too slow, and a lance grazed his neck, drawing blood. The talons of a Death Dog raked his hip, and its jaws were snarling open for his belly even as his sword plunged down its throat. Sorsha and Kael thrust through the melee, shouting for room, and Willow saw clearly that the exhausted Madmartigan would be no match for the fresh and enraged general.

Willow groaned.

Better armed troopers came surging forward. One of them, a bear of a man, howled his war cry as he pushed through ahead of Kael, knocking his companions aside with a gigantic bronze shield. His sword flashed around its edge, and the whites of his fierce eyes shone over its top. So fast and powerful was his charge that he misjudged and his first swing sliced right over Madmartigan's head, striking a chunk of rock off the cliff above. The shield slammed into Madmartigan as he ducked, and the two men went down, both roaring. Willow did not see what happened under the dome of that great shield, but a terrible shriek emerged, changing instantly into a coughing gurgle. The Nockmaar warrior's huge legs pumped and thrashed. Other men shrank back in horror, and in that instant Madmartigan bounded free, flipping the bloody shield off the dying man and spinning it up toward Willow. "Get on!"

Willow faltered, but Madmartigan screamed again, running toward him with swords jabbing at his heels, and Willow jumped. The next instant Madmartigan flopped beside him on his belly. The shield skidded and spun under the flailing Nockmaar lances.

"Archers!" Kael shouted above the uproar.

The shield spun as a bolt from a crossbow ricocheted off its rim. An arrow whistled into loose snow inches from Willow's head. Then they skidded onto the glare ice leading down to the precipice.

They were going over.

Madmartigan sat up and spread his arms wide as the shield hurtled into space. For that moment he was fully vulnerable, a perfect target. Incredibly, he was laughing! Willow glimpsed Sorsha only yards away, her feet braced and her eyes cold, leveling a fully drawn war-arrow at Madmartigan's chest.

"Sorsha! I love you!" he shouted.

The arrow stayed in its bow.

The shield swooped over the edge and dropped.

Madmartigan's laughter changed to a strangled scream. All Willow's insides leaped into his throat. He tried to scream too but couldn't. He tried to see where they were going, but the world tipped horribly; it became only a craggy cliff looming over them, and Fin Raziel folding her wings for the plunge, her eyes shut tight. Willow shut his eyes, too. He hung on to Elora. He hung on to the spinning disk.

Only the child watched everything.

Only Elora laughed.

Down they went, glancing off boulders, bounding over snow crests, swooping through icy tunnels and crevasses. Rock talons snatched at them. Looming walls almost toppled them. Snowdrifts slowed them slightly before they punched through and whirled like a top out the other side. At last, when he felt the shield steady a bit, Willow dared to open one eye. They were no longer spinning. Straight as an arrow, they were hurtling toward the forest where the valley began. Thick and dark, the tree-wall loomed ahead. Willow glimpsed the village on the other side, but he saw no way through.

He hugged Elora. He took a deep breath and said Kiaya's name, and Ranon's, and Mims's. He got ready to die.

With his eyes shut tight, he felt the shield veer right, but did not see it zip into the mouth of an icy tunnel, a smooth greenish slide that angled through the forest and then back again, crossing the slope several times in ever-more gentle zigzags out onto the floor of the valley. Miraculously, it took them safely to the last slope above the village, where laughing children were playing on skin toboggans.

Here, in the last stage of that dizzy flight, Madmartigan fell off. Willow scarcely had time to miss him. One minute he was there; the next, gone. Willow and Elora were skidding alone down to the village, finally slowing to a stop as the slope flattened near the first houses, and the children swarmed up to them. Elora had laughed all the way, and she was still laughing.

Willow staggered off the shield and reeled a few paces before collapsing. The village, the mountains,

the children, all tilted and rocked, steadying slowly.
He became aware of Fin Raziel shouting something
overhead. He saw that some of the children had
raised the shield and were bearing it and Elora
triumphantly toward the village. Others were pointing at the slope, where a large snowball was rolling
down. It slowed as it crossed the field and broke
open against a woodpile, spilling out a limp and dizzy
Madmartigan, still clutching Sorsha's sword.

Willow ran over to him.

"Peck, where are you?"

"I'm here."

"What *happened* up there?" He thumped his tem-
ple with the heel of his hand.

"You don't *remember*?"

"Nothing! Last I remember, I was in that cage and
the brownie was picking the lock. I got something in
my eyes."

"Fairy dust. Dust of Broken Heart."

"That's all I remember."

"Well," Willow said, heaving a big sigh. "Quite a
lot happened. You tried to make love to Sorsha. You
had a big fight. You skidded here on that. . . ."

"What?" Madmartigan shook his head incredulously. *"Sorsha?"*

"You kissed her. You said she was your moon and
stars and sun."

"Impossible! I hate that woman!"

Willow shrugged. "Well, that's what you said.
Then . . ."

"Kael! Kael!" Fin Raziel screeched overhead. "Coming!"

Madmartigan shot to his feet. Down the winding road to the village rode a troop of Nockmaar cavalry with Kael and Sorsha at their head. They were less than half a league away and coming fast.

Children milled around them, pulling at their hands.

"Hurry," they said. "This way!" They led them behind woodpiles and stables, through the back lanes of the village. "We'll take you to the others."

"Others?" Madmartigan asked. "What others?"

"You'll see," the children answered. "Hurry! The Nockmaars are almost here!"

It was a poor village, far poorer than Willow's. The houses were small for Daikini houses, the barns dilapidated. Word of their arrival had spread fast, and people emerged from every house to surround them, quickly hiding them in a crowd.

Ahead, Willow saw the child-borne shield with Elora Danan on it vanish into what appeared to be another ramshackle barn. As he drew closer, however, he saw that it was a large meeting hall at one side of a village common. Up and in they went, hurried along by the crowd. A white-bearded elder scuffed aside thick straw and heaved open a trapdoor in one corner of the floor, while the other villagers and the children began an impromptu meeting. One man proclaimed loudly as if in mid-speech, and the rest listened, shuffling, mumbling agreement or dissent. All kept glancing at the road.

The last Willow saw was General Kael in his terrible skull helmet, rounding the bend and driving toward the village at full gallop. Sorsha rode close behind, her red hair free and the bow still in her hand. After her, well spread out, came thirty or forty Nockmaar troopers.

"Down!" someone hissed. A hand pushed hard on the top of Willow's head, and he skidded down steep steps into darkness. The trapdoor thumped shut, and boots hastily scuffed straw into place on top of it.

Willow found himself in a large, cool cellar, a storageroom for perishables. It smelled of cheese, fresh milk, and vegetables. At first he could see nothing at all, but then as he struggled to find Elora in the gloom, his eyes adjusted, and by the dusty light filtering through the cracks in the floor he saw that they were not alone. The cellar was crowded with men. Weary men. Hurt men. Beaten men. Sitting on barrels, lying on straw pallets, they looked warily at the new arrivals. Some had drawn swords and daggers and were gazing up toward the thunder of hoofbeats and the unmistakable roaring of Kael.

Only one was standing. A large man with an auburn beard. Willow blinked, squinting into the darkness and into the tumultuous jumble of memories since his journey had begun. He *knew* this man. He remembered a proud army with banners aloft. He remembered . . .

"Airk Thaughbaer!" Madmartigan whispered, stepping forward and laying his hands on the big man's shoulders, shaking him gently. *"You left me in that rat trap to die!"*

"I knew you'd get out. You're a cat with nine lives."

"What happened to you, Airk?"

"Slaughtered. Too many of them, too few of us."

"You see! You should have given me . . ."

"Quiet down there!" someone hissed from above. "They're here!"

The shouting and hooting of the sham meeting died away. The shuffling stopped. The crowd fell silent.

Heavy boots crunched across the floor of the hall. "You have a choice, you scum!" Kael's voice rang out. "Tell us where you've hidden that Nelwyn and the child, or have your Prefect killed and your village burned!"

The crowd gasped.

"You wouldn't *dare*!" the Prefect declared, thumping his staff of office on the floor so hard that dust swirled down onto Willow's face. He was the elder with the flowing white beard who had held the door for Willow to scramble down the steps—a Daikini version of the High Aldwin. He was shorter than most Daikinis, and Kael towered over him. He tipped back his head and jutted out his jaw as he spoke, his face flushed. "Enough! For years you've kept us in fear, you Nockmaars. You've taken what you wanted from our valley. You've done what you wanted with our people. You've forced us to pay fines and taxes. You've kept us poor. And now you interrupt our meeting with threats of burning and murder! And I say to you you can't! You won't!" He advanced on Kael as he spoke, thumping his staff. "You wouldn't dare, Kael. I tell you . . ."

No one would ever know what the agitated little man intended to say, because he never said it.

He died.

Kael swung his sword.

The blow sliced off the Prefect's head as a birch switch might take the bud from a flower stalk. It dropped into the straw, eyes still blazing at the general. The body twitched convulsively where it fell, arms and legs striking out. Blood trickled through the cracks in the floor onto Airk's men underneath, who cursed softly, fingering their weapons. A moan like wind through tall pines rose from the crowd, and in the midst of it came a cry shriller and higher than any other: Elora Danan. The baby's gaze was fixed at the place above her where Kael stood, and her cry was a shriek of outrage.

"Whaaat?" Kael said. He looked around. He looked down. The hiding men drew their weapons and prepared to die fighting. Even the most sorely wounded struggled to their feet.

But Fin Raziel saved them. Squawking in a perfect imitation of Elora's cry, the raven came swooping in through one window and out another, narrowly missing Kael's head.

The general laughed gutturally. "Next!" he thundered, waving his sword at the silenced crowd. "Who else wishes to defy the power of Nockmaar?"

No one spoke.

"Where do you hide these fugitives?"

Still no one spoke.

"Very well! Princess, you and your men search and burn this miserable place. Start here, with this barn. You men come with me. Spread out through the woods. Remember, I want them all alive!"

His boots ground across the floor, and a moment later the hiding men heard the jingle of harness and the clatter of hooves galloping away.

"What I wouldn't give for a score of those mounts!" Airk Thaughbaer hissed.

"Shh!" Madmartigan said. *"The princess!"*

In the turmoil that followed Kael's departure and the rounding-up of the village councillors, Sorsha dismounted and came up into the building with her lieutenant.

"Torches!" the lieutenant shouted to his men. "There, and there!"

"Wait," Sorsha said.

She crossed the floor and then back again, her bow tapping her thigh, her footsteps echoing. "There's something odd. There's something . . ." She kicked aside the straw and found the trapdoor. "I thought so! Open it!"

The lieutenant leaped to do her bidding. He flung the door back. Then, sword drawn, he descended into the cellar where Airk's men crouched. Sorsha came close behind him with her dagger in her hand.

Airk struck first, looming soundlessly out of the shadows. In two quick blows he had knocked the lieutenant's feet from under him and slit his throat. He was raising his sword to strike at Sorsha when Madmartigan prevented him, pinning the princess as she started back up the steps.

"Down here!" she cried.

The stairway swarmed with Nockmaar troops.

"Drop your weapons," Madmartigan snarled, his knife to Sorsha's throat. "Drop them, or I kill this redheaded witch!"

"Don't believe him!" Sorsha said, pointing at Elora, who was howling in Willow's arms. "Get the baby!"

But seeing Sorsha captured, seeing themselves surrounded by desperate fugitives with swords drawn, the Nockmaars suddenly lost their fight. They did as Airk told them. Moments later, they were in the cellar with a heavy wagon overturned on the trapdoor, and Airk's men were upstairs in control of the meeting hall. Madmartigan had dragged Sorsha up with him, his arm across her throat.

"One word," he said softly, peering out at the contingent of troopers who were holding back the villagers in the square, unaware of events inside. "One word and I kill you!"

"You'll never . . ."

He clamped a hand over her mouth.

Beyond the village, they could see Kael's men scouring the woods, appearing and disappearing among the trees.

Willow scrambled into the hay in one corner of the building and attended to Elora, changing her and calming her as much as possible, given his own terror. Nothing frightened him more than the Nockmaar troops, and now here they were again, right here on the other side of the barn wall! Soon they'd know something was wrong. Soon they'd come looking for their comrades. So intent was he on them, and on keeping Elora quiet, that he did not notice Airk Thaughbaer approaching until the big man laid a hand on his shoulder.

"What does Bavmorda want with this child?"

"She's Elora Danan," Willow told him. "She's the Empress who'll defeat Nockmaar. We're her guardians."

"We?"

"Madmartigan and I."

"Where are you taking her?"

"To Tir Asleen," Willow said, without even thinking.

"Tir Asleen! Impossible! Nobody's been there in years. Besides, even if you could find the way, you'd never get past the Nockmaar army. Never."

"Airk," Madmartigan bent down, whispering, his hand still clamped over Sorsha's mouth. "We should move for those horses. Otherwise those Nock-maars..."

"I know. Listen, what's going on here, Madmartigan? Since when did you become a crusader? I've had half an army slaughtered fighting Bavmorda, and now you and this Peck plan to take her on? *You?* I don't believe it."

"Well then, come along and see."

Airk shook his head. "Look at us. We've been in the field for months since Bavmorda tricked us away from Galladoorn. We're tired, Madmartigan. We'll go with you as far as those horses. After that..."

"After that what, Airk? Will you keep running?"

Airk seized Madmartigan's free arm. "By the gods...! Someday, Madmartigan, one of us will stand on the other's grave!"

"Think, Airk! There's no Galladoorn to defend anymore. You have a force of men. What *good* will you do with them?"

Willow had stood up, holding Elora. The child gripped one of Airk's large fingers with both hands, laughing softly.

"Think!" Madmartigan said again, nodding. "Ready, Willow?"

"Ready."

"Then we go!" He hauled Sorsha out through the door toward the horses. She managed to twist her face and scream a warning to the lieutenant in the square. He whirled, saw what was happening, and ordered his men forward. They charged. Madmartigan boosted Willow and Elora up into the saddle of a big bay mare and slung Sorsha over the neck of another horse. "Ride!" he shouted to Willow. "Get out!" And he slapped the mare's rump just as the first troopers reached him. "Closer," he said, the dagger pressed against Sorsha's throat, "and she dies."

They hesitated long enough for him to swing into the saddle and back the horse through the square until he was clear. Then he wheeled and dashed after Willow, who had already reached the outskirts of the village.

"Ride! Ride!" Fin Raziel shrieked overhead. "This way!"

Fleeing at full gallop, aware only of the open road in front of them and of the shouts of Kael's outriders from the edge of the wood, Madmartigan and Willow would never know what happened behind, in the village.

The lieutenant ordered his men in pursuit, and some reached their horses. Some actually mounted them. But none rode out. Their way was blocked by people, the same people whose village they had been preparing to burn, whose Prefect Kael had just beheaded. Their Prefect had spoken their sentiments exactly: they had had enough Nockmaar oppression. More than enough. It was going to end—not later, when they might be better organized, or might have better leadership or weapons. It was going to end then. Right then. They had only the crude implements of the field—picks and hoes, sickles, scythes and shovels—but they knew those tools well.

Still, determined though they were, these farmers and craftsmen would have been no match for a charge of Nockmaar cavalry and, seeing that, the lieutenant laughed. "Mount up!" he commanded. "Line abreast!" He was still laughing as he wheeled to face these bumpkins with their tools.

But they were no longer alone. A rank of staunch soldiers had appeared in front of them—Airk Thaughbaer's men. Some were sorely hurt. All were tired. But they were an army still. An army of men who had also had too much of Nockmaar. An army that needed horses.

Airk signaled them forward. Behind him, his ensign unfurled his standard.

The Nockmaar lieutenant's laughter died with him.

TIR ASLEEN

"**A**ncient path!" Raziel cried. "This way!" She led them east away from the village, away from the encampment near the crossroads above.

"But that's the way to Nockmaar!" Madmartigan shouted.

"Ride!" screeched the bird. "Trust Raziel!"

They rode. Willow wrapped his arm around the pommel of the saddle and held on to it and to Elora for all he was worth while the great warhorse surged under him. He was terrified lest the child be thrown off and crushed on the rocks or under the hooves of Madmartigan's horse, coming hard behind. Madmartigan held Sorsha on the saddle in front of him. She laughed when she saw the direction they were taking, and Kael in hot pursuit less than half a league behind. "Straight to Nockmaar! There's no other way!"

But there was another way, known only to Fin Raziel. It led up into the snow of the mountains, and through the ice caves of the elves. Many years had passed since she had visited those caves, and so cunningly had the elves concealed their entrance that now, after a cold and anxious ride, Raziel had trouble finding it. She flapped back and forth across a precipice of sheer ice, muttering and squawking.

The clatter of iron-shod hooves echoed up the canyon behind them.

"Hurry!" Madmartigan said. "Another minute and they'll be here!"

Suddenly Raziel disappeared into the ice, only to emerge a second later. "Here!" she hissed, and vanished again. The tip of a black wing beckoned.

Urging his horse close, Willow saw a narrow opening, so tall that its top was lost in frozen mist, and so positioned that the mirror-walls of ice utterly obscured it. In they went, leaving Kael and their pursuers behind.

A tunnel led into the last domain of the northern elves, before they had finally been annihilated by the mountain trolls. It was a still, vast network of ice caves. Dim light filtered down from apertures high in the cliffs, and the scene glowed with the muted radiance of a winter evening. Workshops and equipment stood ready for use, just as they had been left, for these elves of the mountains had been armorers and metal workers, the best in all the kingdoms. Now, their forges were cold. Narrow ladders stretched up to their dwellings, high in the ice walls. Chains and ropes hung from winches and scaffolds, glimmering like crystal snakes.

Nothing lived in that frozen place. At last, the trolls had found it and invaded it, and the horrible remnants of the final battle lay where they had fallen. Corpses sprawled everywhere—elves slaughtered even as they were stripping off their leather aprons and reaching for their swords. The bodies of women and children hunched where they had been dropped. Raziel uttered plaintive cries as she drifted above this carnage. But in spite of the surprise the elves had acquitted themselves well, for there were many troll corpses too, their gruesome fingers splayed, their faces frozen forever in the grimaces of death.

They moved slowly, letting the horses pick their way. Behind, Kael's roars of rage echoed as he galloped back and forth, unable to find the entrance. Ahead, the caverns opened one into another, in what seemed an unending maze. Fin Raziel, however, remembered the way from long ago. She soared on, a black shadow in the eerie light, occasionally hovering to point a change of direction with her wingtip, and at last she led them out again, through another magically hidden opening, onto a black slope.

She fluttered her wings for silence. "Nockmaar Valley!" she hissed.

There before them, the volcano growled and grumbled. Sour smoke drifted down from it, and as Willow looked a plume of hot ash shot up and reached toward them. He felt sharp dread, as if some troll like those whose corpses lay in the caves had sunk talons into his belly. He knew how Vohnkar must have felt, perhaps at this very place.

Acrid and sulphurous, the smoke moved sluggishly, clearing enough for Willow to glimpse parts of the castle. It looked as if it had torn itself out of the ground through sheer, malignant will. Guttering flambeaux burned on the ramparts. Massive corner towers loomed with their loopholes and sluggish banners. Bavmorda's black tower rose in the center like a dragon's head, watchful in all directions.

"Oh Elora," Willow said, holding the child close. "What an awful place! I hope I never see it again. I hope you never have to come here again. Ever!"

To his surprise, the child was not whimpering. She was gazing at Nockmaar through solemn and unblinking eyes.

"Wait!" Fin Raziel hovered, holding them back, watching the drifting smoke and mist. "Bavmorda will feel us. She'll know we're close. If we're not careful, she'll see us, too."

"See us!" Madmartigan exclaimed. "But the place is two leagues distant!"

"She has ways," Raziel croaked. "Ways other than human eyes."

Sorsha suddenly lunged, making a try for freedom,

but Madmartigan gripped her tight. "Fool!" Sorsha hissed. "She's right. The bird's right. The dogs are already on their way. Soon they'll be here!"

"This way," Raziel beckoned. "Now!"

Smoke had hidden the castle again, and they hurried across a half-league of open space and into cover before it cleared and left them visible to watchers in the black tower.

"Ride on! Straight ahead." Raziel circled back to make sure that there were no Death Dogs on their trail. When she returned she drifted down beside Willow as he rode. "The next passage will be hard, Willow."

"What is it?"

"The labyrinth. The maze that Bavmorda created long ago around Tir Asleen. No one has been through it since that day. I have never been through it. We shall have to pick our way carefully, and there may come a time when you shall have to use your sorcery."

"I—I'd rather try to transform you again, Raziel. I'd rather let you . . ."

"No, no. We have no time now for that. I shall try to lead you through the passages, but if we encounter an obstacle, be ready to work a charm."

Willow swallowed hard. "I—I'll try."

The way grew tortuous. The canyons became craggier, steeper, narrower. Snakelike they twisted back upon each other, and only by peering far ahead was

Fin Raziel, hovering high, able to guide the little party through them.

Sorsha complained bitterly all the way. "You're holding me too tight!" she said, after striking her head on an outcrop. "Let me duck, at least."

Madmartigan laughed. "Oh no. I'm not letting you get away, Princess."

"Why? Because I'm your sun? Your moon? Your starlit sky?"

"Did I really talk such drivel?"

"Yes. You said you loved me, too."

"Unbelievable! I remember nothing of that!"

"So you lied."

"No. I mean yes. I mean, I wasn't myself last night."

Sorsha laughed sarcastically. "Enchanted, I suppose. You were helpless against my spell!"

"Yes. Sort of."

"And then what happened?"

"It . . . went away."

"Went away? 'I dwell in darkness without you,' and it *went away*?" She elbowed Madmartigan hard in the stomach and twisted against the arm clamping her tight. "You're a jackass!"

"Not anymore." Madmartigan laughed. "I told you, I'm fine now! My normal self! Handsome, intelligent, and the best swordsman in the world!"

The canyons had become much tighter, like narrow, twining passageways. The horses stumbled often. But from her vantage point high above, Raziel insisted they were on the right track. "A barrier!" she called down. "A wall of thorns ahead, and the way broadens beyond it. Get ready, Willow!"

"Can you at least tell me what's happening?" Sorsha asked. "Am I a hostage? Are you going to trade me for something you *really* want?"

"I told you. We're taking you to Tir Asleen. To see your father."

"And I told *you*: you'll never get past my mother's barrier. Kael will hack you up for dog meat!" She rode a little way in silence. "Besides, I don't even remember my father."

"He's a great king. When Tir Asleen is set free..."

"Kael!" Raziel warned, pointing back down the canyon they were wending their way through. Madmartigan twisted around. In the same instant his horse stumbled and Sorsha slammed her elbow into his stomach again, this time hard enough to tip him off balance and break free. The next moment she was running back down the canyon toward the hoofbeats they could all now hear, coming fast. Madmartigan leaped out of the saddle and after her, despite Raziel's frenzied warnings. He caught her just as she was crossing a muddy stream. He tackled her and they splashed down together, Sorsha kicking and punching viciously, Madmartigan gradually overwhelming her. At last he dragged her out of the water and pinned her to the ground.

"Leave her!" Raziel fluttered down. "Hurry!"

Madmartigan hesitated, then ran for his horse. When he looked back, Sorsha was on her feet, looking after them in silence.

In minutes they reached the wall of thorns Raziel had seen from farther down the canyon. It seemed an impenetrable barrier. Massive, spikey vines rose thickly intertwined as far as they could see.

Madmartigan cursed. "Impossible! No one can get through there! You've brought us all this way to . . ."

Raziel swooped down. "Quick! Light three fires three paces apart!"

Madmartigan did that, hurriedly using flint and steel from the saddlebag to chip sparks into a tinder of dried leaves and grass. Three frail flames wavered at the bottom of the wall.

"Now Willow! The Fourth Chant of Unity! Join the flames!"

"Tuatha lum . . ."

"Use the wand!"

"Oh yes!" He dug into his cloak and found it, holding it out with both hands. *"Tuatha luminockt tuatha!"* It burned and trembled in his palms, but the fires grew only a little.

"Too slow! Both of you!"

Madmartigan whirled around. He had drawn his sword, ready to fight the Nockmaars, who were almost upon them. "What, *me*? Charms?"

"Yes! Say it!"

"Tuatha luminockt tuatha," Willow chanted again, pointing the wand.

Madmartigan imitated him. *"Tuatha...loom...* What is it?"

Already the combined charm had begun to work. Flames stretched up from the fires like reaching arms.

"Together!"

"Tuatha luminockt tuatha!"

Now the flames leaped and the wall blazed, opening a smoking arch. They urged their frightened horses through. As soon as they were inside, the whole wall blazed, and moments later, when Sorsha, Kael, and the Nockmaar troops arrived, they faced an inferno. Their horses reared away from it.

"There must be another way!" Sorsha shouted above the roar of the flames.

Kael cursed. "None! Unless we go back and around, a full day's ride. No, they've escaped us, Princess, but not for long. We'll trap them in the castle and kill them like rats! Besides, we need time for our reinforcements to come up from Nockmaar." He waved his men back. "Dismount! Water your horses!"

Beyond the fire, Willow crouched low over his mount's neck, drawing a blanket across Elora's face to shield her from the whirling smoke. He could hear Madmartigan coming close behind and Raziel calling encouragement from ahead, but he could see neither of them. Choking in the smoke, he gripped the pommel and gave the horse its head.

"We'll soon be there, Elora. You'll be safe there,

at Tir Asleen. The good king will protect you. Maybe
someday, when it's safe again, we'll all come to see
you, Mims and Ranon and Kiaya and I. Meegosh
too. And Vohnkar."

The child stared up at him, apparently oblivious to
the swirling smoke. Looking at her, Willow felt again
the strange sensation he had had often since Elora
came into his care—that time itself had ended. He
felt that he might go on living forever, perhaps not in
the form of Willow Ufgood, but part of all that had
been and would ever be. He felt as if he were ex-
panding infinitely, growing larger than any Daikini,
larger than Bavmorda.

The child laughed, and although he was filthy, and
exhausted, and very frightened still, Willow laughed,
too.

So, laughing, they rode through the last wisps of
smoke and into the valley of Tir Asleen, a place that
fulfilled all of Willow's dreams. It was rich and fer-
tile, as green as Nockmaar was dark, as abundant as
Nockmaar was sterile. Great pastures stretched up
the gentle slopes of the mountains, dotted with oak
forests and beeches in the lower regions, fringed with
pines and firs toward the top, tonsured around the
peaks with the low shrubbery of mountain meadows.
The road to the castle lay as it always had, gleaming
white, paved with marble cut centuries before from
the quarries of the elves. Willow could imagine how
welcoming was that broad and tree-lined avenue to
all the pilgrims who had trekked to Tir Asleen. He

could imagine the gatherings of their tents in the meadows, and the festivities that would go on for days, with music and wine and fellowship, while the good king passed freely among his people.

So it would soon be again!

"Tir Asleen, Elora! There it is! We're safe!"

Fin Raziel uttered a long, falling cry of ecstasy, and drifted down over the valley.

"Come on, little friend," Madmartigan said. "Let's ride!"

And so they did, urging their tired mounts into a trot, they rode the last half league down the road and onto that marble avenue.

The castle rose ahead, the most magnificent structure Willow had ever seen. Built of the same marble as the road, it glowed so pure and white under the full sun that it seemed a source of light itself. Two corbeled towers rose like welcoming arms beside the lowered drawbridge. Sunlight glinted on the banners on their flagstaffs, and on the crenels and merlons of the battlements. Sunlight flashed on the silver surface of the moat. It seemed to Willow as they approached that a party of knights must come riding out to welcome them.

But there were no knights. There was no welcome. The closer they came to the castle of Tir Asleen, the more Willow's joy and relief shifted to foreboding and unease. No birds sang in the oaks through which they rode. No animals moved in the fields and forests. Although a breeze coursed through the valley, the king's banner did not flutter on its staff. *Frozen*, Willow thought. It hung as if it had been frozen, beyond any warmth in the natural world to thaw it.

Most disquieting was that they saw no people. No one waved from the gardens. No one stood in the doorways. No horses ran beside them in the fenced meadows. No cattle grazed. No sheep raised browsing heads to watch them pass.

"Something wrong here, Peck," Madmartigan muttered as they rode. "Not what we expected. Slow down! Watch out for trouble!"

Not until Fin Raziel had swooped over the castle walls and uttered a long and despairing cry at what she saw, and until they themselves had clattered across the drawbridge and into the courtyard, did they understand the depth of the horror that had befallen Tir Asleen.

"Cursed!" Raziel shrieked, flapping in little circles in the dust. "Bavmorda has frozen everything!"

It was true. Although the sun shone and the breezes were fair, arctic cold hung in that place. It came from several large blocks of crystal quartz standing here and there in the courtyard, on the steps leading up to the king's apartments, beside the well, around the winches that raised the drawbridge.

"No," Raziel moaned, flitting from one of these blocks to the next, finally settling on one of them. "Oh no!"

A human being stood inside.

A trapped woman, one of the servants of Tir Asleen, was captured there in the act of drawing water from the well, exactly as she had been at the moment of Bavmorda's awful curse. She was a young woman, and pretty. She had been lifting her head, smiling up at a lark or a lover on the parapet just as the curse struck.

All the inhabitants had been similarly trapped in their everyday tasks. Here was the blacksmith in the act of shoeing a horse, his hammer raised. Here was a milkmaid bent against a mild brown cow, and a pair of children running forever together in a game of hide-and-seek, and a thatcher at work on one of the roofs. Here were soldiers, and matrons with babes in arms, and farmers bringing harvest from the fields, and chambermaids shaking blankets through the high windows. One by one Willow and Madmartigan inspected them, shivering, for the air close to them was filled with deathly chill.

All their eyes were happy.

"No warning," Madmartigan said. "Never knew what hit them."

Willow shook his head, horrified and disbelieving,. "Will they be like that . . ."

"Forever," Fin Raziel wailed, her raven's cry of anguish filling the courtyard and rising out over the green valley of Tir Asleen. "Forever, or until Bavmorda is destroyed."

"Oh Elora," Willow said, holding the child close in his trembling arms. "I'm sorry. This is a terrible place!"

"Peck, why'd I listen to you? 'Everything'll be all right when we get to Tir Asleen,' isn't that what you kept saying? 'There's a good king with a great army that will protect us.' Well, I don't see any king at all, and the only army I know about is the one that'll come charging down that valley any moment— Kael's!"

"I'm sorry. Cherlindrea said we'd be safe here."

"Safe! Do these people look safe to you? Besides, look at that! Troll dung! There are trolls here! Probably watching us right now. Bah! I hate them!" Madmartigan fingered the hilt of his sword and peered up at the towers.

Again Raziel cried out, this time as if her heart was breaking. They hurried over to a staircase where she had found yet another of the quartz blocks. Inside this one was a handsome man of perhaps thirty-five, with bright red hair and calm, wide-spaced eyes. He had been calling greetings to someone across the courtyard when Bavmorda's spell had struck, and his hand was half-raised. "The king!" Raziel wailed.

"Sorsha's father?" Madmartigan leaned close.

"Yes. Oh Willow, draw the wand. The wand! You *must* transform me now!"

"Raziel, I don't think . . ."

"You must try! Trust yourself, Willow! And concentrate!"

Madmartigan grunted. "We'll need more than charms, Raziel. You go ahead, Peck. I'm going to find some real weapons." He strode across the draw-

bridge of the moat around the central keep and into
the armory on the ground floor. All the arsenal of Tir
Asleen lay ready. Covered in a heavy layer of dust
and cobwebs, the weapons rested as the defenders
had left them—longbows and crossbows, spears,
pikes and halberds, bolts and arrows of all descrip-
tions. Scores of hauberks and suits of armor also
waited for knights to put them on. On a pedestal in
the center stood the king's own armor, crafted of
bronze and tempered gold, tailored long ago by elfin
workmen. Madmartigan smiled. It was as if the king
himself stood there with one arm outstretched to
welcome him. Madmartigan walked admiringly
around that armor. He tried a golden gauntlet on his
own hand. It fitted. He took one of the golden
greaves and strapped it to his own calf. Again, it fitted perfectly. He raised the golden helmet, shook its
white plumes free of dust, and placed it on his head.
It felt as if it had been designed for him. Quickly he
strapped on the other parts of the suit—the neck
guard and the pauldrons, the breast plate, the skirt
and the tassets, the cuisses and sollerets. When he
was dressed, Madmartigan picked a good sword and
a crossbow from the arsenal. He gathered several
bolts. He hesitated beside the golden shield, but decided against it, for it would be too cumbersome for
the work he had to do.

Thus resplendent, he strode back out onto the
drawbridge of the keep. "Here they come!" he

shouted, pointing through the gates and down the avenue of Tir Asleen.

Willow was halfway through the Chant of Transformation when Madmartigan's warning rang out. "*Avalorium*," he said, his eyes closed tight in concentration, the trembling wand clenched in both hands. "*Greenan luatha, tye thonda, peerstar...*" And Fin Raziel, crouched in front of him, had begun to change from a raven into something else.

Willow whirled around. The spell snapped. Raziel popped into the form closest at that stage of her transition—a white goat—and pranced across the courtyard, bleating plaintively.

Neither Madmartigan nor Willow had time to notice what had happened to her. Their attention was riveted on the charge of Kael's troops through the meadows and down the avenue.

The Battle of Tir Asleen had begun.

"Arm that catapult!" Madmartigan shouted, pointing to a huge mangonel that stood ready on the parapet, lacking only its charge of spears.

Willow tucked the wand into his pocket, snatched up Elora, and hurried up the gate-tower staircase to obey the order. He ran out onto the battlement. After that, events came so thick and fast that he would never remember them clearly, or remember their proper sequence. For him, the battle was a night-terror, a livid and horrible dream.

Bolts and arrows sang around him, nipping at his clothes, ricocheting off the stone crenels, thumping into the hardwood of the mangonel. He reeled back, shielding Elora with his body and scrambling for the cover of the tower. Below in his golden armor, Madmartigan rushed to slam and bar the gates, just as Kael thundered across the drawbridge and drove his boot against them.

"Battering ram!" Kael roared. "That tree!"

Troopers hurried to obey, and soon a thick beech toppled. The Nockmaar force fell back and regrouped while this work went on, and through the slits of the tower Willow saw Kael and Sorsha on their prancing horses, pointing at the castle and discussing tactics.

Down in the courtyard Madmartigan rigged booby traps and triplines and then, with the help of Raziel, who butted rocks across to him, loaded a catapult aimed right at the gate. "Spears, Willow!" he shouted up. "Load that catapult!"

"But there *are* no spears!"

"There! In the armory!"

A bridge led straight from the gate-tower to the second floor of the keep, designed so that troops and ammunition could get to the battlements fast. Madmartigan was right; there would be spears over there. Lots of them. Willow laid Elora down in the safety of the tower and ran onto the bridge, heading for the open door of the armory.

He never reached it. Up over the railing, blocking his way, scrambled a troll. It was a hideous creature —its nose cleft, its face a mass of pustulant sores and wrinkles, its bulbous lips curled back to reveal scraggly teeth. Lank hair hung to its waist; it slapped and scratched itself with long fingers. "Hungry!" it said, staring with red eyes at the gate-tower. "Me take baby!"

"You will not!" Willow exclaimed. "Not unless you take me too!"

The troll nodded eagerly. Its long fingers reached out. "Me take little man!" It advanced.

"The wand, Willow!" Fin Raziel bleated from underneath. "Use the wand!"

Willow looked down. Nockmaar troops had begun to batter through the gates. Already they had snapped the old bars. Lances jabbed through. Madmartigan crouched behind his catapult, ready to fire.

"The wand!" Raziel bleated again. She was jumping up and down in a frenzy.

With the troll's obscene fingers only inches from his face, Willow groped desperately in the big pocket of his coat and drew out—not the wand, but one of his magician's feathers, a leftover from the fair! "Oh no!" There was no time to reach again. Instead, he flourished the feather inches in front of the troll's nose, making it disappear and appear again, making it perform a mesmerizing, swaying little dance in the air.

The troll stopped. His eyes crossed. He gaped, beguiled by the antics of this magic feather. He grabbed for it and missed, grabbed again and missed. Groping for the wand, Willow waved the feather lower and lower until at last, when his hand closed on the magic weapon inside his cloak, the troll's head was bowed in front of him.

Willow whipped out the wand and raised it in both hands. *"Avaggdu strockt!"* he cried, and whacked it down on the troll's head.

There was no recoil, no searing pain. Instead, Willow felt tremendous energy roll through him and out of him. In the panic of the moment he had used a broad charm for the smiting of Evil, and so had no idea what the effect would be. The results astonished him. The troll turned to jelly. It became a gibbering, jiggling mass of shapeless goo, like a squashed polliwog. Hair, eyes, fingers—all vanished into a quivering glob. He kicked it off the bridge and into the moat below. The turgid water churned where it hit.

Whunk! Madmartigan's catapult cut loose, launching its charge of boulders into the massed Nockmaar forces at the gate. Several men screamed and crumpled like broken dolls, but others came on, driven by Kael behind them. Several died in Madmartigan's booby traps and two more fell to bolts from his crossbow. Then the others were upon him, thrusting and jabbing, and he was into swordplay. He laughed. His golden armor shone and the white plumes on his helmet waved above the black uniforms of the Nockmaar troops. "So long, Peck!" he shouted up to Willow on the bridge. "At least we tried!"

Relentlessly, the mass of men pushed him back toward the moat.

But Madmartigan was not to die on their swords or spears, or to be brained by Kael's mace as the general pushed through to strike him. Long ago, Bavmorda had summoned another guardian to that moat. Out of the night she had summoned it, out of the thick and murky air above the swamps where primeval creatures struggled into life. Out of the darkness she had summoned it, out of the chaos beyond all time. It had risen to do her bidding. Into the moat of the Tir Asleen keep she had sent it, and there it had lain, waiting in the mud, feeding through its skin, breathing through the spiny fins that rose above the surface. It lay in wait, its claws sunk deep in earth to sense its trembling under the hooves of horses, its ears touching the surface to hear the clash of arms. It knew nothing of right and wrong, good and evil. It cared nothing for the conflicts of humanity. It knew only that men were now disturbing the malevolent tranquility it was summoned to preserve.

The guardian's four eyes opened. Its two necks tensed. It rose through the scum of the moat, inhaling so hugely that gales whipped the courtyard.

"An Eborsisk, by the gods!" Kael shouted above the roar and clamor. "Kill it! Forget the man! Slay the beast before it breathes!"

Too late!

Madmartigan spun to see the dragon's two great heads loom above him, its two mouths yawning to belch fire into the Nockmaar horde. Never had he pitied the Nockmaars, but he had pity now. He had pity for the poor wretches caught directly by that blast and changed to white ash, whirled away by the wind. He had pity for those who lived an instant or two, whose skin bubbled and writhed as if there were living creatures under it. Most of all he had pity for those whose clothing was ignited by that fiery belch, who spent the last moments of their lives shrieking and rolling in the dirt while their skin charred.

One head swung up toward the bridge, while the other drew breath for a second blast at the courtyard. Madmartigan found himself recoiling with Nockmaar troopers from the beast, found himself bumping into an armored body in the melee and looking into the frightened eyes of Sorsha. He grasped her. "Are you all right?"

She nodded.

"Down! Get down!" He pulled her behind a buttress just as the gout of flame smashed into it, spilling around it, sucking away all oxygen. Both fell gasping to their knees. On and on the blast went, roaring like a hurricane across the mouth of a mountain tunnel. When it ended, more screams of agony echoed around them as men and horses shriveled to crisp and unrecognizable shapes. For a split second in that chaos, Sorsha's eyes held Madmartigan's and her hand touched his arm. Then he was off, sword flashing, taking the tower steps two at a time, rushing out to that place on the burning bridge where Willow was being pushed back toward the fire by two more trolls. Before Madmartigan got to them, Willow had struck at one with his wand and missed. He had thrown the second of his precious acorns, and missed. With two blows, Madmartigan cut them in half and kicked the parts into the moat behind the Eborsisk.

"Back to the tower, Willow! Get Elora!"

Willow scrambled around him, but Nockmaar troops had already reached the top of the stairs and were advancing reluctantly onto the bridge, cringing from those swaying dragonheads. Kael drove them on from below. "Attack! Attack, if you know what's good for you! Kill that man and find the baby!"

Madmartigan moved to engage them, and Willow shrank down, caught between the fire and the fight.

Several Nockmaar arrows bristled in the necks of the Eborsisk. Viscous pus drained from the wounds. The maddened monster hissed and lunged, churning the foul waters of the moat, twisting one of its heads to blast the combatants on the bridge. The Nockmaars retreated to the tower, but Madmartigan leaped onto one of the creature's heads and, with a mighty two-handed thrust, drove his sword straight down through its skull. Then, as the gasses gathered in the creature's throat for another gout of fire, and the head rose with the sword plunged in it to the hilt, pinning its jaws shut, Madmartigan leaped off, seized one of the gargoyles' heads projecting from the tower, swung to a ledge lower down, and dropped to the ground. Above him, the dragon's fire turned inward, and its head blew away in a fountain of flame and foul liquid.

Howling in agony, the other head lashed itself against the stone wall of the keep, drooping lower as the beast died, until at last it collapsed into the courtyard.

Chaos reigned below. Dead and dying men littered the courtyard. The putrid odor of the dragon, the roasted flesh, the excrement of horses, the rankness of the moat—all mingled in a fetid stench in Sorsha's nostrils. She staggered away from the fray, gagging. This was not the clean thrill of the chase, the purity of fair combat. This was something mindless, something inhuman, something woefully beneath any honorable warrior!

She staggered up a flight of stairs as the dragon died, and came face-to-face with her father. She knew him at once, although he was encased in the crystal cast by her mother's curse. His hair was hers. His frank and broad-spaced eyes were hers. And in his voice, very faint and distant though it was, the princess heard her own.

"Sorsha . . ."

"Father . . ." She laid her hand on the stone, beside his cheek.

"I'm alive, Sorsha. Help me. Help me . . ."

"Oh, Father!" Her knees went soft. Memories came flooding back that she had not dared to recall all her life—her father laughing, running beside her while she rode her first white pony through the orchard; her father holding her hand while he accepted the acclamation of the multitudes in the broad flowered valley of Tir Asleen; her father teaching her to row her own little boat in the upper reaches of the Freen, so quietly that she disturbed neither the water birds, nor the frogs drowsing on their lily pads, nor the speckled trout suspended in their dark pools. She remembered her father's compassion, his generosity. She remembered his laughter and his love. In one great rush of emotion she remembered all that had been, and might have been, and might still be . . .

She wept.

"Sorsha, only you . . ."

She turned back to the slaughter. She saw the little Nelwyn clinging to the burning and collapsing bridge. She saw Kael striding across the charred bodies of men toward the gate-tower where the cries of a terrified infant rang clear. And she saw Madmartigan in her father's golden armor, hard pressed by a knot of troopers flailing at him with swords and spiked maces. Even as she looked, he went down.

Suddenly, things clarified and changed for Princess Sorsha, as a troubled sky might clear at evening, or a lake grow calm after a storm.

She hefted her sword. She strode forward. She loosed a high-pitched battle cry to warn the troopers assailing Madmartigan of her intent. And then she gave no quarter.

Two of the troopers ran away from her immediately. Two others offered token resistance before fleeing. Two more turned to confront her, and as they turned, Madmartigan twisted catlike and cut their legs from under them. His sword and Sorsha's sliced across their throats together.

She offered her hand to lift him; silently, Madmartigan took it.

Three things happened at once.

First, the bridge burned through and collapsed, dropping Willow hard against the wall of the tower and to the ground. Nockmaar troopers converged on him. They had time for only one glancing blow at Willow's head before Madmartigan was among them and they were dying, gripping stabbed bellies, gurgling through slit throats. The quick sword flashed— nine slashes, nine men dropped in their tracks or staggered off to die. Then Madmartigan was beside Willow, wiping the blood off his forehead.

"I—I'm sorry," Willow said. "There were too many. Elora . . ."

"Hang on, Peck." Madmartigan scooped him up in his right arm like a child.

At the same moment Kael's roar of triumph echoed out of the tower and through the courtyard. He appeared in the doorway with the tiny figure of Elora Danan lifted high in a mailed fist. Out of the death's-head helmet he roared again, in fury this time, seeing Sorsha at Madmartigan's side. He waved his great sword at them, and at Willow. "We have the child! Kill them! Ride with me to Nockmaar!"

Spearmen and swordsmen drew back from Madmartigan's blade. Archers notched arrows to do Kael's bidding.

But the shafts were never shot. At that moment the last event in that extraordinary battle occurred. In the silence after Kael's command sounded the clear note from a stout ram's horn; then, the rumble of horses charging.

Willow wiped the blood from his eyes. Through the open gates of Tir Asleen, past the Nockmaar troops scurrying for their horses, he saw the fluttering banner of Galladoorn, with chargers spreading into the meadows as they came on, gaining speed, and in the center a huge, red-bearded figure, sword pointed straight at the gates of the castle.

"Airk Thaughbaer!" Madmartigan whirled his sword and whooped ecstatically.

Faced with that grim charge, the Nockmaar troops broke and fled for any horses they could grab. After what they had been through, they had no stomach to meet Airk's men.

Kael's horse was the first through the gates, trampling a knot of fugitives too slow to scramble aside. The general had wrapped Elora in his cape. He rode furiously, bent low over his horse's neck. Four officers followed hard behind him.

Airk dispatched a squad to give chase, but with a sinking heart Willow could see that Kael had already gained too much distance. He would outflank his pursuers to the east and be clear to Nockmaar before anyone could catch him.

In the next few minutes, the remainder of the

Nockmaar force fell under the charge of the Galla-doorns.

Willow slipped out of Madmartigan's embrace and turned away, leaning against a pillar. He could not watch. He did not want to see them slaughtered. He felt too sick, and he had seen too much of senseless death and horror. He wished fervently to go home, back to the tranquility of Ufgood Reach, where he could sit on the banks of the Freen and let the gentle river cleanse this memory of horror. He wanted only to protect Kiaya and his little ones from all knowl-edge of this mad Daikini world. Forever. Yet, through all the beautiful thoughts of Nelwyn Valley burst the searing image of Kael in his death's-head, astride that black horse, holding Elora Danan aloft like a prize in his great mailed fist. Willow knew that he could never protect his dear ones so long as such men drew breath, so long as the forces remained that made them what they were.

So, when Airk Thaughbaer's bay mare galloped into that scene of carnage, Willow Ufgood wiped the blood off his face and cried, "Airk! We must ride on Nockmaar!"

Madmartigan sat down and pulled off the golden helmet. He grinned wearily up at his old friend. "Out for a little ride in the country, Airk?"

"Thought you might be lonely, but I see you're not." Airk gestured at Sorsha with his sword. "What's this?"

"She saved my life, Airk. She rides with us, now."

Airk grunted.

"But we must hurry!" Willow said. "Now. To Nockmaar! There's no time to lose! Bavmorda will destroy the child!"

A shrill clamor of agreement rose out of Airk's saddlebag: "Right! Absolutely right! The Peck knows what he's saying! Must ride! Attack! Charge!"

Franjean and Rool popped out.

"Greetings, Willow!"

"Never fear, Willow! We're here to take care of you, just like always!"

A white goat trotted up. "No delay!" Fin Raziel said. "To Nockmaar!"

BAVMORDA

Airk's scouts, riders of the East, pushed Kael hard. They rode light, unarmored and free to use their bows. Six of them pursued the five Nockmaars closely through the valley of Tir Asleen and out through the labyrinth of canyons. One Nockmaar officer fell to their shafts before they had cleared the canyons, and a second on the slopes of the mountain of the crystal caves. By the time they galloped out onto the black shale and ash of Nockmaar Valley, only Kael and two of his guard were left, and the mounts of the two henchmen had begun to flag.

Kael abandoned them. Roaring at the sentries to lower the drawbridge, he dug his spurs into the already bloody flanks of his stallion, and whipped the creature savagely with his crop. At the limits of his endurance, the horse hurtled down the last stretch of road and thundered across the moat, with Kael bellowing to the keepers to raise the drawbridge behind him. They obeyed, heaving on the ironwood windlass, and the dark bridge rose, dangling tentacles of slime.

It was most foul, the moat of Nockmaar, fuming with the noxious gasses of the volcano and laden with the relics of Bavmorda's flawed charms. It stank of sulphur and rot, of excrement and acid. Nothing could live in it. Sometimes bored sentries on the parapets amused themselves by dropping living things into it and listening to their howls as their flesh dissolved.

Screaming desperately for Kael to wait, to hold the drawbridge, the first of the Nockmaar riders flew over the stiff forelegs of his horse and under the edge of the rising bridge, headfirst into this moat. He vanished without a sound. The scum closed over him. The other rider had a few seconds more of life, although he did not enjoy them. He sprang off his mount on the moat's edge, leaped for the drawbridge, and grabbed it with one hand. So he dangled as the bridge rose, struggling to get a grip with his other hand but unable in his exhaustion to do that, kicking desperately as the angle of the bridge grew steeper and his hand slipped in the slime, until at last he fell.

The drawbridge clanged shut.

Loosing shafts at the battlements, loosing exotic

war cries that Bavmorda heard even in the recesses of her tower, Airk's riders fanned out in both directions along the walls before breaking off and galloping a safe distance back up the valley. Here, a short time later they met Willow, Sorsha, Madmartigan, and the rest of Airk's force.

Airk glowered down the valley, peering into the deepening shadows. There it lay, bleak and smoke-swept: Nockmaar. Spears crowded its battlements. Guttural commands and creaks drifted up the valley to them as the mighty war engines were winched into place. Iron braziers guttered and flamed on the parapet and in Bavmorda's dark tower, flickering on the queen's flag, with its lightning bolt piercing the curve of life.

Franjean and Rool moaned as they looked at Nockmaar, and slid back into the depths of Airk's saddlebag.

"Make camp!" Airk ordered. "We'll need battering rams. Assault towers. Ready them tonight!" His commands were confident, but he shook his head when he looked at those looming walls.

Madmartigan nodded grimly. "I know what you're thinking. We'll need more than good equipment for this job. We'll need good fortune, too."

"Even more!" said Fin Raziel in her bleating goat's voice. "We'll need strong sorcery. Willow, you must ready all your powers, all your faith, and all your concentration. You must go deep, deep within yourself, Willow. To the very source. This time you *cannot* fail!" Raziel's large and glowing eyes turned away from the dark battlements of her ancient rival and looked at Willow. "Forget all you know, all you think you know. You must prepare *now*! Quickly!"

"Fin Raziel," Madmartigan said, seeing Willow's exhaustion, "it's getting dark. Surely he can rest a bit. In the morning . . ."

"No! There's no time!" The goat jumped up and down on stiff legs. "Do you think that Bavmorda is not preparing even now? Do you not see Kael striding in triumph to her tower, placing Elora Danan in her hands? Do you not see her, hear her laughter? Do you not see her priests hurrying to begin the Ritual of Obliteration? See them! Scouring the bowl! Purifying the altar! Readying their chants! Oh no, she will not wait for dawn. Bavmorda will act *now*, Madmartigan!"

As if to confirm what Raziel had said, all the window slits of Bavmorda's tower lit up like fiery fangs. Exultant lightning cracked out over the balcony and smashed into the distant hills, rolling in fireballs down the slate slopes.

"Hide!" Fin Raziel cried suddenly, butting Willow into the cover of a large rock. "Quick! Say the Shelter Chant for yourself!"

"But why . . . ?"

"*Say* it!"

Willow clasped the magic wand, closed his eyes, and concentrated. "*Helgafel swathben, helgafel claideb, danu locktwarr!*"

"Good! Now the others!" Raziel pointed her snout at Airk and Madmartigan, who were listening attentively to Sorsha as she drew a plan of the castle. "Quick, Willow!"

But Bavmorda was too fast. With her three priests, she had already appeared on the battlement. Her mocking laughter stabbed out at them across the darkening space. The horns of her crown loomed large in the glare of the flambeaux borne by lackeys along the parapet. In that weird light, she undulated and grew huge, blending with her shadows. She was awful, and Willow shrank back at the sight of her. Yet there was a splendor about her, too, a grave and malefic aura.

"Army?" Bavmorda shrieked derisively. "They told me there was an *army* laying siege to Nockmaar. But *this*," she flung her arm and lightning cracked and stabbed above their heads, "*this* is no army!"

Only Airk and Madmartigan stood their ground, feet braced. "We've come for Elora Danan!" Madmartigan called up. "Give her back to us!"

The queen's laughter echoed through the valley. "Fool! Impertinent fool! You are not a man, you are a *pig*!" She flung out her hand again, this time with level fingers pointed at Madmartigan.

"Mother! No!"

"Pigs! You are all pigs! *Kothon lockdar bahkdt*!"

Willow Ufgood had seen many dreadful things since he had ventured among Daikinis, but what happened next was the most horrible. Airk's troops, and

Airk himself, and Madmartigan, all turned into the pigs that Bavmorda commanded them to be. Nor was their transformation a swift and painless thing, as in some fairy tale. It was agonizing. Men screamed and writhed as their bones changed—contracting, joints cracking and twisting into new shapes, skulls flattening, toes and fingers fusing into small hooves. Men howled as their skin peeled off and tightened around new rib cages. Men screamed and snuffled as invisible hands gripped and reshaped their faces, twisting them into long snouts.

Then, men squealed, finding they were no longer men but swine in the shreds of clothes. And among those who had once been men were Madmartigan and Airk.

"Oh, Mother, no! No!" Sorsha sank to her knees, her eyes filling with tears at the sight of Madmartigan, who grunted, and grinned, and stared at her out of little pigish eyes.

"And *you*, Sorsha! I warned you never to disobey me! So, you've made your choice!"

"Moth..." Then Sorsha also was screaming, squealing, her bones cracking, her skin splitting and reshaping around the flesh of a fat sow.

When Bavmorda's laughter faded from the battlement, when Willow dared look again, he could see only pigs rooting in the slaggy ground, including two piglets—Franjean and Rool.

"Oh, Raziel, it's horrible!"

"Yes," the goat said, "but it is not the end. You've

done well, Willow Ufgood, but you must do even better now."

"No, no, I've come all this way and now Elora Danan's going to die!"

"It's worse than death she faces, Willow, unless you save her. You know that. And we can still defeat Bavmorda."

"She's too powerful, Raziel!"

"No! Transform me! The hexagram!"

Shaking violently, Willow picked up Madmartigan's sword and scratched a hexagram in the dirt around Raziel. The goat stood with her head bowed. Then he drew forth Cherlindrea's wand, clasped it in both hands, braced his feet, closed his eyes, and gave his whole attention to the transformation. He spoke the magic words, and then: "Elements of eternity, above and below; balance of essence, fire beget snow!"

The wand trembled. Fin Raziel's goat-form began to change.

"Don't give up, Willow! Be strong!" Her voice stretched and echoed through long tunnels of time. Willow concentrated, pouring all his remaining strength into the wand, and it took that strength, and drained him. *"Locktwarr danalora luatha danu, tuatha, tuatha, chnox danu . . ."*

Willow's knees sagged, but he clung to consciousness. He concentrated.

Had his eyes been open, Willow would have seen Raziel pass through many changes in those moments.

From her goat-form she became an amorphous protoplasm, neither vegetable nor animal, and yet pulsing with blood; and then she became a stately deer; and then human—a child, a girl, a beautiful young woman....

Opening his eyes, Willow saw Raziel as she had been those years ago, when she and Bavmorda and the king had been young together, with all their lives ahead of them. For several moments she lingered in this state, smiling radiantly and beckoning as if she longed to speak, and then before his eyes she changed again, slowly and finally, into an old woman. Her flaxen hair grew glistening white; her shoulders hunched, her face creased and furrowed; her breasts and belly, once full and rounded, sagged into pouches of flesh.

Willow covered her with a smock. "Oh, Raziel...."

Sadly she looked down at her gnarled hands, her knobby feet. "It's been so long," she said. And then she gathered her concentration. Her eyes focused with purpose. "Give me the wand. We have a task, Willow, to undo Bavmorda's sorcery, and time is short. Quickly, now! And quietly!"

Willow hurried alongside as she passed among the pigs in the darkness, touching each on the snout with the wand and whispering the countercharm to Bavmorda's curse. *"Tuatha grain chnox, y foel famau...."*

One by one, painlessly, they changed back into

their human selves, huddling in fearful little groups, glancing at Nockmaar's battlements.

"Demoralized!" Airk said when they had gathered in his tent. "The whole camp! We'll never get through the gates of Nockmaar with these troops!"

"She cannot transform you again," Raziel said firmly. "My spell has protected you."

He stared skeptically through the gloom and drifting smoke. He shook his head. "Too well defended. We should retire, Madmartigan. Regroup. Come back another day."

White light flashed at the top of Bavmorda's tower, the clang of a gong echoed down the valley, and a tiny scream drifted out to them, the cry of a child in pain and mortal terror.

Willow groaned.

"We must attack tonight," Sorsha said. "Otherwise it will be too late."

"She's right." Raziel's face was pale but resolute. "Bavmorda has begun the Ritual. If we do not save her, Elora Danan will be gone on the thirteenth ringing of the gong."

"Then we've got to fight!" Madmartigan said. "Raziel, can you use your magic to get us into the fortress?"

"No."

"Hopeless, then," Airk said. "We haven't the men or the machinery to storm those walls."

Willow had been walking in little circles, biting his lip, pounding his fist into his palm. Now, as he gazed at Nockmaar and the ground before it, his eyes lit up. "Wait a minute! Back home we have a lot of hedge- hogs!"

Madmartigan and Airk looked at one another. "Willow," Madmartigan said, "this is warfare, not agriculture."

"I know, I know. But I have an idea how we can get inside the castle. Listen!"

Hurriedly, while the weird light glowed again in Bavmorda's tower and the gong rang again, Willow outlined his plan.

"Impossible, little friend!" Airk said when he had finished. "Too much work to get done by dawn."

"Besides," Sorsha said, shaking her head, "Kael would never fall for it."

The gong sounded again.

"Madmartigan, tell them! Elora needs us!"

"The chances aren't good, Willow."

"But at least it's *something*!"

"He's right." Raziel looked around at the group. "If the child dies, all hope for the future will be lost. It's a desperate chance, but we must try it. Other- wise..." She held out her hands to Bavmorda's tower, as if giving over the world.

Silver light flickered there; the fourth blow on the gong echoed across the slate hills of Nockmaar.

"I'm going to fight!" Willow said.

Airk smiled sadly down at him, but Madmartigan laid his hand on the Nelwyn's shoulder. "It's time to

decide who is going to fight and who is going to re-
treat."

In the tower conjuring room, the dark Ritual had
begun. As soon as they had seen Kael rush into the
courtyard with Elora Danan held triumphantly above
his head, the three priests began to prepare. They
summoned guards to clear the room of trolls, who
protested vehemently, slobbering and cursing as they
were dragged downstairs. They freed the night
herons, who rose through the opening in the roof,
circled, then turned thankfully toward the marshes of
Galladoorn. They prepared the copper altar, inlaid
with its bloodred rubies, and chanted incantations
over it, and laid the leather thongs upon it. They
cleansed and readied the great stone crucible, and
swept clear the platform around it. They tossed the
skulls and bones from other ceremonies into a basket
in an alcove ossuary, lest any clinging auras distract
the queen from the great business at hand. They
poured the bowl of blood from a bronze pitcher, with
all proper ceremony. They readied on their pedestals
the five small crucibles. They scoured the queen's
great shield with fire, burnishing it until its bolt of
lightning gleamed. They chanted the solemn spell to
open the secret recess, and when the hinged dolmens
swung back, they bore out the bronze gong and set it
in its place of honor. They ignited the flambeaux in

the wall sconces. They arranged and sanctified the Thirteen Tapers.

When all was ready, they notified the queen. Alone, Bavmorda came out of her apartment. Alone, she climbed the stairs of the tower. When she stood before the altar, her gown wrapped tightly around her, they brought her the child. Then they sealed the door of the chamber.

Bavmorda nodded to the altar, and the priest bearing Elora laid her on it and bound her down with the crisscrossing thongs. The child screamed.

"Your Majesty..." For a moment the old priest faltered.

"Silence! Move away!"

The Ritual began.

"Come thunder," Bavmorda murmured, drawing her hands out of her cloak and reaching toward the opening in the massive granite ceiling. "Come lightning. Touch this altar with your power."

Sheet lightning shimmered down, wrapping queen and child with baleful radiance.

Elora shrieked again, struggling helplessly against her bonds.

The gong sounded once; flame glimmered on the wick of the first of the sacred tapers. The tallow burned with the scent of death.

Bavmorda smiled. "Dark runes, dark powers! Blend and bind, bind and blend this night of Nockmaar with the universal Night!" From her sleeve she drew a thin knife taken from the elves long ago. A perfect knife. A knife that never needed sharpening, never lost its razor edge. She drew it gently across her palm and, sliding close to the bound child, cut three locks of her brilliant red hair and placed them in the first of the five small crucibles.

"Black fire forever kindled within, let the second rite begin!"

The priest at the gong swung his muffled hammer twice, and the repercussions swelled through the window slits, blending with the swirling smoke of the volcano. Another priest lit the second of the Thirteen Tapers.

A cold wind blew through the tower. The candles guttered. The gong swayed on its straps, moaning as the wind crossed its embossed face.

The priests shivered. One of them glided forward to daub Elora with livid paint—feet and hands, brow and heart.

Bavmorda plunged her hands into the bowl of blood and raised them toward the opening in the roof, toward dark stars which only she could see. Blood streamed down her arms. Inside the folds of her gown it coursed over her breasts, trickled across her belly.

The gong sounded, thrice.

The queen trembled. Her lips twitched. She muttered incantations unknown to the priests. She was growing darker as the Ritual proceeded, thicker, uglier at every stage, as if the energy to summon the powers for this destruction were being drawn from the marrow of her bones. Her eyes sank deeper. Cords stretched in her neck. Skin drew tighter about her teeth in a grimace increasingly hideous.

"Ocht veth nockthirth bordak!" She gestured upward, and the small body of Elora Danan, magically freed of bonds but clenched in the grip of the charm, rose off the copper altar.

The gong sounded again, four times. Four dark tapers burned. The air sucked in to feed them whistled through the window slits. . . .

Through the first light, through drifting smoke, alone on an empty field, Willow and Fin Raziel walked toward Nockmaar. In one hand, Willow carried a drum on a tripod, and a stick. In the other, he held the braid of Kiaya's hair.

"Your wife, your family will remember this day, Willow," Fin Raziel said, seeing the braid clutched in his small fist. "And I shall remember. I've waited all these years to face Bavmorda, and you have made it possible. Thank you."

"Oh, Raziel, do we still have time? That was twelve blows on the gong!"

"Yes. If our plan works we have time. The last stage of the Ritual is the longest and hardest, and the child is safe until the very end."

Just beyond arrow-shot from the castle wall they stopped. Willow set down the tripod and the drum. On both sides, the slate and barren hills of Nockmaar

loomed over them. Behind, where Airk's army had
bivouacked in the cold winds the night before, there
was now nothing but flattened tents and abandoned
equipment. Ahead, stood the dark fortress.

Raucous laughter echoed down from the parapet.
Summoned at first light from his carousing, Kael had
climbed up to the battlements to savor his victory. He
gazed out over the desolate litter on the plain deserted by the broken and demoralized rebel army. He
laughed coldly with his lieutenants, slapping the cold
stone.

So insignificant were the two small figures of Willow and Fin Raziel that at first no one saw them. Not
until more light had spilled into the valley did one of
Kael's officers point them out.

Kael leaned forward, squinting.

"Surrender!" Fin Raziel commanded.

"What?"

"Surrender!" Willow shouted. "We are all-power-
ful sorcerers! Give us the baby or we will destroy
you!"

Kael and his men laughed incredulously. They
roared, enjoying this good joke. And then, when he
had grown tired of laughing, Kael brushed his hand
outward as if at a pesky fly. "Kill them!"

Fin Raziel clasped her wand, Willow his drum-
stick, watching the bridge descend across the fester-
ing moat.

"Ready, Willow!"

"Courage, Raziel!" he answered, managing a smile.

And then, as the drawbridge fell and a squad ran out to do Kael's bidding, Willow turned and struck his drum. The sound boomed down the valley.

Kael roared in laughter again, slapping the parapet. "Is that your magic, little man? Is that your fearful sorcery?"

"Yes!" Willow shouted back. "I bring warriors out of the ground! Like hedgehogs!"

Suddenly the valley came alive. With a surging cry, men and horses threw off their coverings and lunged up out of shallow pits. Some had trained their mounts so well that they had lain down still in the saddle, and horse and man now rose as one. So fast were they, and so complete was the surprise, that before Kael even had time to shout, "Raise the bridge!" the first of Airk's men had charged over it and was inside the Nockmaar courtyard. The assassins who had come out to kill Raziel and Willow were slain in their tracks.

Airk bent down and scooped Willow onto his saddle, and Sorsha lifted Fin Raziel onto hers. Madmartigan had been one of the first inside, and by the time Willow reached him three gatemen lay dead at his horse's feet and a fourth was gaping at blood spurting from his arm. In no time Kael was on his horse and roaring his battle cry, rallying his defenders at the top of a long ramp which led up to the tower. "Form your line there! Loose the dogs!"

Sorsha slipped Fin Raziel off her horse at the foot of a broad staircase and then dismounted herself, giving Rak a slap on the rump that sent him back out through the gates and away from the fighting. A moment later, Madmartigan found her there. He was laughing as he leaned down and reached to embrace her. "Sorsha, you are my moon, my sun, my stars!"

"What? Not again!"

"I mean it! You are!" He drew her close and kissed her.

Then the Nockmaars sallied down the ramp and the fight swirled close. His horse shied and pranced away. Airk galloped up and lowered Willow to the ground. Then the two friends rode together, roaring in laughter, their swords whirling, cutting down a charge of five Nockmaar troopers.

"Willow! Raziel! There's another way to the tower. Here!" Sorsha hurried them through a doorway and into a dark and narrow corridor.

Behind, Airk waved his bowmen forward. He pointed up the ramp where Kael had marshaled a phalanx of troops. "Let's squash 'em!" he yelled, and he and Madmartigan led the charge.

For Franjean and Rool, cowering in the very bottom of Airk Thaughbaer's saddlebag, all was confusion—a mayhem of blows, and lunges, and the terrible sounds of dying. They knew only that men and horses were perishing around them, and that this was a fight without pity or quarter. Airk's great horse took a Nockmaar bolt in the thigh, and another in the neck, launched from crossbows on the parapet, and at the same moment a pikeman danced close and laid open its stomach, spilling its intestines into the mud. The beast fell, shrieking. Franjean and Rool were thrown out of the saddlebag and into the thick of the fighting. They found themselves surrounded by plunging hooves and singing arrows. They scampered for safety under a flight of stone steps and ventured out only once for the rest of that battle— to hamstring a huge trooper who had cornered Madmartigan. The man dropped to his knees and Madmartigan ran him through. "Thank you!" he shouted, waving under the steps. "Maybe you're not so bad!" Then he was challenged again and drawn back into the battle.

Roaring like a bull, Airk Thaughbaer had meanwhile fought his way out of the mud, up the steps, and along the parapet to a cauldron of boiling oil. Directly below, a squad of Nockmaar troops had linked their shields together and were now advancing, a formidable human machine, threatening the flank of Airk's brigade. Straining mightily, Airk reversed the apparatus of the cauldron and tipped it, spilling boiling oil down on this armored unit. Men died hideously beneath those shields, flayed alive, broiled in their breastplates. Their awful wail rose above the clamor and drew Kael's attention from across the courtyard. His gaze locked with Airk's; their war cries clashed. Kael gripped his sword. He hefted his mighty axe. Airk strode down to meet him.

Their combat went unseen in the melee by every-one but Franjean and Rool. For decades afterward, as their beards grew long and white, they would de-scribe that fight to circles of wide-eyed brownies in the Woods of Cherlindrea: how Kael fought like a demon possessed, raining blows so thick and fast on Airk Thaughbaer that his arms blurred and his axe struck fire off the stones of Nockmaar; how Airk fought bravely under that savage attack, ducking, weaving, striking back, until at last Kael maneuvered him to the top of the ramp and forced him down; how Airk Thaughbaer lost both balance and life in that muddy place, hacked by Kael's axe, pierced by Kael's sword; how Kael kicked him without honor over the edge and into the mud below; and how Madmartigan, seeing this last act, hurled his sword spearlike into the antagonist he was facing and ran to his old friend . . .

"Airk!"

"If you . . . ever stand . . . on my grave, Mad-martigan . . . I'll haunt . . ."

Madmartigan wiped the blood and mud from his friend's face. He held Airk while life faded from his eyes. He freed the hilt of Airk's great weapon from his locked fingers. "Give me your sword, old friend, and I'll win this war for you."

Kael was not the first to feel the bite of that sword that day, but he was the last. Madmartigan fought his way through to him, and when at last they came face-to-face on the parapet, they were directly beneath the queen's tower, in the first rays of the rising sun. Their duel was even more spectacular than Airk's, but this time it was Madmartigan who rained the blows on his opponent, swinging Airk's broadsword as if it were a mere rapier, battering that grim death's-head helmet, knocking the axe spinning from Kael's left hand, slicing into Kael's side above the hip bone. The general fought with all the desperate strength left to him, but he was, finally, merely human. He was tired in body, tired in soul, tired of life—tired, perhaps, even of killing.

Perhaps (Franjean and Rool would suggest when they told this tale to admiring fairies) enough of his heart remained for him to know the wickedness of his cause, to know he should make an end. Perhaps that was why, at last, he did not strike when Madmartigan gave him an opening by lifting Airk's sword high with both hands. Next instant, it plunged down through Kael's breastplate and ripped open his heart. Kael's last sound, as he fell backward over the parapet and into the moat, was laughter.

Swiftly after that the battle in the courtyard ended. Nockmaar troops threw down their weapons. Officers fled. A few witless trolls continued to shriek and gibber from niches in the battlements, hurling poisoned darts until they were picked off by archers. A few Death Dogs, loosed in the depths of Nockmaar by their trainers, hurtled into the last of the fray and onto the weapons of Galladoorn lancers. But

soon the fighting ceased. Except for the moans of the
wounded, the courtyard fell silent.

The rising sun went dark.

The real battle, the one in the conjuring room,
was about to begin.

Grimly, Sorsha had led Willow and Raziel through
corridors and up staircases that she knew well. Once
she beheaded a troll who leaped snarling from an alcove, and once a Death Dog that came pelting in
silence, eyes fixed on her throat. Soon they were
climbing the corkscrew stairs that wound up to Bavmorda's tower. Below, horses roared and men bellowed. Steel struck steel. Steel struck stone.

Willow's heart had faltered as he peered down
through the arrow-slits into the courtyard and saw
Kael, saw the strength of the Nockmaar force. Yet he
climbed doggedly, following Sorsha, followed by Raziel.

At the top, harsh light throbbed under the oaken
door of the conjuring room and spilled down the wet
stairs. From behind the door came Elora's small wail,
and overriding it, killing it, the shriek of Bavmorda.

Willow faltered utterly at that sound. His heart
urged him on but his body failed him. He sank trembling to his knees. "No. I can't go on."

"It's all right," Raziel said, laying a hand on his
shoulder as she went past. "You don't have to, Willow."

She murmured a chant to the barred door and it slammed open, sucking such a draft of air up the stairway that it flattened Willow where he knelt and snuffed the flames on the sacred tapers.

Bavmorda stood lost in the distant intricacies of the Ritual, her arms lifted to the dawn. The wind swept around her, whipping at her sleeves and the hem of her gown. "Raziel!" she said, turning slowly.

She had begun to change in the earlier stages of the Ritual, and now, toward its end, she had become unrecognizably grotesque. Her eyes had sunk into dark pools; her mouth twisted in a snarl of frightful depravity. Bereft of grace, bereft of dignity, her body had grown taut, her movements tense and quick, like those of spiny creatures in the froth of the sea. Crouching, she turned. "Raziel..." Her laughter was like the grating of pebbles. "Good! Now you will witness my greatest triumph!"

Sorsha stepped forward and halted abruptly, frozen by the icy wall of Bavmorda's hatred. "Mother..."

"You! Get back! How dare you speak to me! You're pathetic!"

"She has discovered kindness," Raziel said from the doorway. "She has discovered love."

"So!" Bavmorda hissed. She crept closer, arms stretching, fingers spread like talons. "Then you have seen your father."

"I have seen what you did to him. But he's alive in spite of you!"

"Traitor child! I shall destroy you now as if you had never been! You will become less, now. Ever less! Less than a child, less than a seed, less than a single germ!" Bavmorda signaled the three priests from the shadows and they slid forward like one body, beginning in unison the Chant of Infinite Diminishment.

Sorsha cut them down. She did it cleanly—three strokes of her sword across their necks. She stepped across their bodies toward the altar where Elora Danan lay, whimpering pathetically. "You will not kill this child!"

"Away! *Avaggu strokt!*"

The rising sun vanished. Lightning struck through the roof, paralyzing Sorsha. Bavmorda's curse lifted her off her feet and hurtled her backward toward a wall of spikes where traitors were pinned, where truculent trolls and laggard servants were skewered, where all those were hung who gravely displeased Bavmorda in the circle of her conjuring room. But, before Sorsha could be impaled, a second spell slid between her and the spikes, and against its blessed cushion she slipped to the floor, unconscious.

So, she did not see the last battle. Only Willow saw; Willow, quaking in mortal terror but summoning enough courage to creep to the top step and peer over.

"You have gained strength since we last met!"

"I have Cherlindrea's wand. See." Raziel raised her hand, and an axe which Bavmorda had conjured and sent hurtling toward her halted in midair, and hung. "You cannot defeat our combined powers, Bavmorda!" She turned the axe and sent it flying back. "Elora Danan will be empress! The prophecy will be fulfilled!"

Bavmorda exploded the axe with a gesture of her fist. She scuttled behind her stone crucible. She swayed, muttering, claws beckoning. Stone gargoyles on the wall behind Raziel grew flesh, writhed free, slid from their perches, reaching for her.

"*Bellanockt!*" Raziel spun and blasted them. They burst, splattering like jellyfish.

The queen laughed. "You believe you are my match? Never! My Ritual has undone the prophecy! The child's energy will be obliterated! *Strockt!*"

Charms, chants, countercharms—all flew thick and fast, and with them such berserk violence that Willow cringed whimpering against the steps. He watched.

"*Avaggdu suporium avaggdu!*"

He saw Raziel enveloped in fire which could not consume her. He saw fireballs and lightning bolts carom wildly off the walls, narrowly missing Elora.

"*Furrochk! Furrochk lithrak!*"

He saw the room plunged into a deep freeze, howling with arctic winds, and Bavmorda clenched in a block of ice so cold that smoke rose from it. He heard her laughter echoing, saw the ice shatter, felt the searing blow of her curse as she hurled Raziel to the floor, toppled a pillar on her, and scuttled forward, whipping cords of fire across Raziel's face. He saw Raziel struggle to clasp her fallen wand, lift it, and hurl Bavmorda against the ceiling, against pillars and the wall of spikes, against buttresses and gargoyles' claws until Willow was sure that the queen must be cut to ribbons.

"Hither walha! Tuatha la!"

Up Bavmorda rose, blasting the wand out of Raziel's hand and sending it spinning on the slimy floor. Ghastly creatures sprang out of whatever it touched. A chair turned into a five-headed coil of snakes, each with an agonized human face, a thing so appalled at life that it swarmed to a window and hurled itself out. A table became a gelatinous mass with myriad teeth that slid gnashing at Willow. He pounded out its life with a bronze candlestick.

"Elora..." Willow murmured. Without thinking he crept into the room and crawled along the wall toward the altar where the child lay.

Torn and bloody, whirling in the chaos they had created, the two sorceresses at last came to grips with one another. In that final encounter it was Bavmorda who drew quicker on untapped reserves of strength. It was Bavmorda who triumphed. Her nails raked Raziel's face. While Raziel groped blindly, her eyes full of blood, Bavmorda's hand closed like iron claws on her throat and wrung out the last of her consciousness.

Raziel sank to the flagstones.

Bavmorda uttered a hoarse cry, part laugh, part curse, part howl of triumph.

The door of the chamber slammed shut. The winds ceased.

Stiff, hunched, arms spread and bent, Bavmorda turned in the silence and faced Willow with Elora in his arms. "Bring back that child! And who are you?"

He held the child tight, her small head against his heart. She gave him strength, enough to say clearly. "I am Willow Ufgood. I am a sorcerer greater than you, Bavmorda."

"Ha!" Bavmorda stared at the destruction and the horrors the fight had spawned. "Put her on the altar!" She gestured at the twelve candles and they sprang into flame. She pointed to the gong, and a ghostly reverberation echoed—the thirteenth. She pointed to the thirteenth candle. "*Avaggdu tuatha. . . .*"

"Wait!" Willow groped for the last of the magic acorns given to him by the High Aldwin, found it, and threw it.

Bavmorda caught it.

She watched her hand turn to stone, watched her arm begin to petrify. Her eyes rolled back, white orbs in black sockets. She groaned. Her teeth ground together. She reached down a final time, down into the depths of sorcery for the means to confront this threat. She uttered a charm like the cry of a waking reptile.

Willow watched her wrist bend as flesh and sinew

returned. He saw her fingers clench, pulverizing the acorn. He saw her hand open and brown powder drift across Fin Raziel's body.

"Is *that* the extent of your power, fool? Now you will see *my* power. Now you will see the Ritual completed. Place the child on the altar!"

"No! You hag! You murderess! With my magic I'll send Elora into . . . into a realm where Evil cannot touch her!"

"There is no such place."

"*Helgafel swath! Ben helgafel!*" Willow chanted. "*Bairn off danu famoww. . . .*"

Bavmorda grunted contemptuously.

"You're no sorcerer! You're a charlatan! A clown! You will go with the child!" She turned and beckoned. Cherlindrea's wand flew from Raziel's limp hand and into hers.

In that instant, Willow whipped his cloak and Elora vanished.

"*What*! Impossible!" Bavmorda scuttled forward. "Lightning!" As she lifted the wand, her gown brushed against the lip of the last bowl laid ready on the platform of the great crucible, and thick fluid spilled over and around her feet. She had only an instant to realize what had happened; an instant to understand that her conjuring, driven by weird fate, had twisted back upon her. An instant to know that she herself—all that she had been or would have been—was the victim of her Ritual of Obliteration.

In that instant she cried out her fury and frustration, and something even more terrible—an echo of lost innocence, a sound like water gurgling over stones, or like the laughter of a child. . . .

Then the lightning struck, a single, quivering, jagged spear that pierced Bavmorda from head to foot and stayed, writhing above and through her.

She neither exploded nor flamed. She incandesced. She turned white hot like some magic metal, and when her flesh had gone her skull and skeleton hung intact in that white aura before they also vanished, leaving only drifting particles of ash.

The lightning became a ray of sun; the thunder, a roar of victory from the courtyard.

Sorsha revived as Madmartigan rushed in and gathered her into his arms. Fin Raziel returned to life as Willow touched her hand. "Willow . . . where's the child? Where's Elora Danan?"

"Here," he said. "Safe." He reached into the secret inside pocket of his cloak and drew out the smiling child. Wonderingly, he gazed at her and at the surrounding death and chaos caused by the sorceresses. "It . . . it was just the old disappearing-pig trick," Willow said.

EPILOGUE

After the defeat of Bavmorda, all those lands grew natural again, even the black slate valley of Nockmaar. Renewal came like the thawing after a hard winter, so gently that no creature could be sure when it began. All living things felt it, and responded, and added their songs to the resonant hymn of Earth. Old rhythms returned. Old cycles revived.

Fresh winds blew over Nockmaar, sweeping away the stench of death. Bright wildflowers sprang up on the crags and in the slate crevasses. New shrubs and bushes bloomed. Clear springs welled up from deep underground to sweeten the caustic moat.

Despite this revival, no one stayed at Nockmaar. So dreadful were the memories of it, and so frightful would be the legends surrounding it, that the valley would never be inhabited again. Even when forests towered there and hawks soared, no roads would lead to Nockmaar, no hunters would venture close. In time the fortress would be overgrown and crumble to ruin. The green world would claim it once again; but until then Bavmorda's tower remained—a stark warning of awful possibilities. . . .

When the last of the dead had been buried, and the sally ports and main gates of Nockmaar Castle had been sealed, Willow and Raziel, Sorsha and Madmartigan rode west, toward Tir Asleen.

That was a triumphal procession. In the vanguard fluttered the proud standard of Airk Thaughbaer. Behind, ringed by banners, rode Willow Ufgood with Elora in his arms. Then came Fin Raziel, then Sorsha and Madmartigan, and then the Galladoorns, their pennants high. All the way, at every village, people strewed flowers in their path and crowded close to see and touch Elora. All the way, her laughter joined the laughter of the brooks and streams.

Two stately eagles escorted them all the way to Tir Asleen, bearing two proud brownies.

Tir Asleen was most miraculously transformed. Bavmorda's maze had vanished, as had all traces of the battle. The broad avenue was thronged with citizens. Royal banners flew on the towers of the castle, and music and laughter drifted across its battlements. The gates stood open, and as Willow and his party approached, an equerry bearing the king's standard rode out to greet them.

Many days the festivities continued in that valley, for there was much to celebrate—the joyous reunion of Sorsha and her father, the commencement of the reign of Elora Danan, and the restoring of Madmartigan to knighthood and to honor.

Urged by his friends and by the king to stay with them, Willow lingered for three days. Then, on the evening of the third day, he confessed his great yearning for Nelwyn Valley, and for Kiaya and his children. The king smiled. "You shall have our best pony," he said.

So, next morning, Willow bade farewell to Sorsha and her father. He accepted the gift of a sacred book from Fin Raziel, and heard her tell him that he could, in the fullness of time, be a great sorcerer. He kissed Elora Danan. Madmartigan lifted him onto the white pony and he rode away down the broad avenue and through the valley toward the banks of the Freen. He was going home, toward the Lake of Fin Raziel and the Woods of Cherlindrea where he said good-bye to the brownies. He was going back to Nelwyn Valley, home to Ufgood Reach.

There is no need to dwell on his arrival—how Vohnkar was the first to greet him and question him about the child and Tir Asleen; how Meegosh welcomed him soon after, and how his two friends led the pony down the last stretch of the river road, where it came out of the forest as if from the end of a long tunnel; or how, as they passed the old burial ground in the meadow, the High Aldwin materialized, saying, "What? What?" and led the little procession to the village, holding his staff high and shouting, "Triumph! Triumph! Sound the gongs! Beat the drums! Music and revelry!"

There is no need to describe how warmly Willow was welcomed by all, even by Burglekutt; or how the Council declared a festival in his honor; or how the High Aldwin, beaming with pride, insisted that he change a stone into a white dove; or how the bird spiraled higher and higher above Ufgood Reach until it was lost to sight.

The honor, the acclaim, the gratitude—these embarrassed Willow Ufgood, for he was, after all, a modest and private person. His most important welcome came later, when he was free at last to walk with Kiaya and the children down the path to Ufgood Reach, and when, laughing wearily, he promised to look at all Mims's new paintings the very next morning, and to answer all Ranon's questions, and to tell them both the story of Elora Danan as often as they wished.

Then, when the children were settled for the night, Willow embraced his beloved Kiaya, and they walked a little distance away from the house to a spot where they could watch the moonlight on the bountiful fields of Ufgood Reach and the silver eddies of the Freen. There they stood a long time in one another's arms, content with that simple life, at peace in the Mystery of that green world.

ABOUT THE AUTHOR

Wayland Drew was born in Oshawa, Ontario, and received his early education there. He began to write seriously in high school and continued while studying English language and literature at the University of Toronto. Since graduation he has combined high school teaching and writing. He is the author of <u>The Erthring Cycle,</u> a trilogy published by Del Rey books.

Mr. Drew and his wife Gwendolyn live in Bracebridge, where he has taught English for eleven years at Bracebridge and Muskoka Lakes Secondary School. They have four children.